8

Sarasa Nagase

ILLUSTRATION BY

Mai Murasaki

New York

I'M THE VILLAINESS, SO I'M TAMING THE FINAL BOSS, Vol. 8
Sarasa Nagase

Translation by Taylor Engel
Cover art by Mai Murasaki

AKUYAKU REIJO NANODE LAST BOSS O KATTE MIMASHITA Vol. 8

First published in Japan in 2020 by KADOKAWA CORPORATION, Tokyo.
English translation rights arranged with KADOKAWA CORPORATION, Tokyo, through TUTTLE-MORI AGENCY, INC., Tokyo.

Yen On
150 West 30th Street, 19th Floor
New York, NY 10001

Visit us at yenpress.com
facebook.com/yenpress
twitter.com/yenpress
yenpress.tumblr.com
instagram.com/yenpress

First Yen On Edition: April 2024
Edited by Yen On Editorial: Ivan Liang
Designed by Yen Press Design: Andy Swist, Jane Sohn

Yen On is an imprint of Yen Press, LLC.
The Yen On name and logo are trademarks of Yen Press, LLC.

The publisher is not responsible for websites (or their content) that are not owned by the publisher.

Library of Congress Cataloging-in-Publication Data
Names: Nagase, Sarasa, author. | Murasaki, Mai, illustrator. | Engel, Taylor, translator.
Title: I'm the villainess, so I'm taming the final boss / Sarasa Nagase ; illustration by Mai Murasaki ; translation by Taylor Engel.
Other titles: Akuyaku reijou nanode last boss wo kattemimashita. English
Description: First Yen On edition. | New York, NY : Yen On, 2021
Identifiers: LCCN 2021030963 | ISBN 9781975334055 (v. 1 ; trade paperback) | ISBN 9781975334079 (v. 2 ; trade paperback) | ISBN 9781975334093 (v. 3 ; trade paperback) | ISBN 9781975334116 (v. 4 ; trade paperback) | ISBN 9781975334130 (v. 5 ; trade paperback) | ISBN 9781975334154 (v. 6 ; trade paperback) | ISBN 9781975334178 (v. 7 ; trade paperback) | ISBN 9781975334192 (v. 8 ; trade paperback)
Subjects: LCGFT: Fantasy fiction. | Light novels.
Classification: LCC PL873.5.A246 A7913 2021 | DDC 895.63/6dc23
LC record available at https://lccn.loc.gov/2021030963

ISBNs: 978-1-9753-3419-2 (paperback)
978-1-9753-3420-8 (ebook)

10 9 8 7 6 5 4 3 2 1

LSC-C

Printed in the United States of America

I'm the Villainess, So I'm Taming the Final Boss

CONTENTS

Aileen Jean Ellmeyer

A villainess who has remembered her past life. Empress of Ellmeyer.

"A husband who persists in staying young and beautiful."

"Where to retire."

Claude Jean Ellmeyer

Emperor of Ellmeyer, demon king, and Aileen's husband. The final boss of *Regalia of Saints, Demons, and Maidens 1*.

TOPIC:
Worries XX Years in the Future

I'm the Villainess, So I'm Taming the Final Boss

Character Introductions and Glossary

The Story Thus Far

When her engagement is broken, memories of Aileen's past life surface, and she realizes she's been reincarnated into the world of an *otome* game as its villainess. To escape destruction, she decides to romance Claude, the final boss! After many twists and turns, Claude becomes emperor of Imperial Ellmeyer, and Aileen becomes his empress. This is the tale of a villainess's fight to secure a happy ending that doesn't exist in the game, conquering all the final bosses that stand in her way.

Claude's Advisers

Keith Eigrid

"Taking care of milord in his retirement."

Beelzebuth

"If the king retires, does he become a high demon king?"

Almond

"Why are Demon King's wives all weird?"

Aileen's Ladies-in-Waiting

Rachel Danis

"How my son's first love will go."

Serena Gilbert

"My husband's reaction when he finds out about our daughter's first love."

Aileen's Lackeys

Jasper Varie

"Young women asking me for dates."

Isaac Lombard

"A son who's growing up just like me."

Denis

"What should I teach the kids first?"

Luc

"Figuring out who will inherit my clinic."

Quartz

"My wife's and daughter's health."

James Mirchetta

"The fact that my best friend's daughter proposed marriage to me in earnest."

Auguste Gilbert

"The fact that my daughter likes my best friend more than me."

Walt Lizanis

"I objected to my daughter dating, and now she's ignoring me."

Kyle Elford

"Finding homes for the kittens, and my son, who's been acting suspicious lately."

Elefas Levi

"The dignity of a grand duke, which I don't have either at home or at work."

Claude and Aileen's Siblings-in-Law

Lilia Reinoise

"Everything's going according to plan."

Cedric Jean Ellmeyer

"My daughter's preposterous question, 'Is Uncle your biggest fave, Father?'"

The Kingdom of Ashmael

Baal Shah Ashmael

"How to deal with my daughter's suitors once and for all."

Roxane Fusca

"Trying to get my husband to let our daughter go, and the fact that my son's being targeted."

Ares Emir Ashmael

"My daughter wants to enter the harem."

Sahra

"The fact that I don't have any worries."

The Queendom of Hausel

Amelia Dark

"Is a future I don't know on its way?"

Demon Realm

Luciel

"Will I be able to sleep properly?"

Grace Dark

"Will I be able to wake up properly?"

✦ Prologue ✦
Premonition of an *Otome* Game Sequel

On a terrace kissed by gentle sunlight, Aileen Jean Ellmeyer—now empress of Imperial Ellmeyer—drinks tea prepared by her brilliant lady-in-waiting. This is her precious time of rest.

Even if it's only for a moment, it's important to pause and refresh like this. Otherwise, she stops noticing the subtle changes from day to day, like how the wind has lost its chilly bite. She wouldn't have noticed the vivid green buds pushing their way up beneath the shade of the trees, either.

Atmosphere truly matters. Elegantly setting her cup down on its saucer, she murmurs to herself, "It's nearly spring."

"Speaking of spring, I think it's going to trigger a new *otome* game, Lady Aileen!"

This reply immediately ruins the all-important atmosphere and almost makes a vein pop out on Aileen's temple. Keeping her smile firmly in place, she glances across the table at her sister-in-law, who's munching on cookies without a care. "Lady Lilia. Haven't you realized why I, the empress, take tea with you once a week?"

The woman looks at her blankly. Her smooth, chestnut hair and lovely face give her the sort of charm small animals have. This appearance contrasts sharply with Aileen's, whose resplendent golden hair and sapphire eyes overawe others.

"Gracious, of course I do. It's an opportunity for us to brainstorm ways to handle the next game, isn't it?"

Their positions, mindsets, and everything else are polar opposites as well. A second vein throbs on Aileen's temple. "How many times must I tell you not to speak of that?! I am spending this time with you to drum into your head the bare minimum of etiquette expected of the consort to the emperor's younger brother—"

"Anyway, Lady Aileen. I do think it's standard for *otome* games to begin in the spring."

"Listen when others are speaking! You've graduated from being 'the player,' remember?!" Aileen shrieks. After all, Lilia has brought up the topic of their previous lives with no regard for who may be listening.

This world is identical to the stage of *Regalia of Saints, Demons, and Maidens*, an *otome* game series that both Aileen and Lilia played in their past lives. The countries featured in the game exist here, as do the characters. Many events from the games have played out in this world as well. No matter how ridiculous the idea may seem, it's been proven beyond a doubt.

However, this world is no game. It's reality, and the characters are living humans. That is how Aileen—a villainess who, according to the game's story, was destined to die in a haphazard way—has built a different life for herself. She's romanced the demon king and married him, making them emperor and empress of Imperial Ellmeyer.

Meanwhile, Lilia is the game's heroine. Like Aileen, she has memories of her past life. Calling herself the player, she treated Aileen and the others as her pawns, referring to them as "characters." Saying that Aileen was her "biggest favorite," of all things, she shrugged off events and tragedies as simply part of the game.

However, recently, she's begun to think of this as her own life—or so Aileen assumed...

"But, Lady Aileen, I remembered something quite clearly the other day. Game 5 really did get released."

She's referring to an entry in the *Regalia of Saints, Demons, and Maidens* series. So far, Aileen has lived through a variety of events that occurred in Games 1 through 4 and their fan discs. On every occasion, she's smashed the many death flags that menaced her husband, the final boss.

In other words, if Game 5 exists, it will mean getting dragged into yet another tiresome incident.

"I'm not positive, but I think I died on its release date. I did manage to snag an early copy, so I'd already cleared it by then."

As Lilia's story begins to sound increasingly specific, Aileen's expression tenses up. "Stop that. There is no Game 5. Y-you must have been dreaming."

"Not only that, but it also sounded like they'd begun working on Game 6. The producer publicly announced that the characters from 5 would appear in the sequel."

"Don't bring up even more troubling things. Was the series even popular enough for that?"

"I mean, probably? Lady Aileen, you really don't remember 5 or 6?"

Lilia cocks her head. Aileen's gaze wanders uncertainly.

She remembers up to Game 4. Unlike Lilia, Aileen had been a relatively casual player, so she didn't know all that much about the games. She simply romanced the characters who piqued her interest. However, she hadn't been enthusiastic enough to preorder the games, and she never proactively hunted for information about future installments. On top of that, Game 4 had been built around

Imperial Ellmeyer's legend of the Maid of the Sacred Sword and seemingly capped off the series, so she isn't sure she noticed that Game 5 had been released— No. Wait.

"Was 5 a sort of Mafia story…about secret societies?"

Lilia's face lights up. "Yes, set in Ashmael! The hero was the young boss of an underworld organization that had custody of the fiend dragon's seal, and he was also the director of the Divine Maiden Academy, a school devoted to the first Daughter of God! That meant despite being a school story, it was centered around the denizens of the underworld. The Divine Maiden Academy is built on top of an underground ruin that houses a sarcophagus containing the first Daughter of God's body, and it's a girls' school, so no boys allowed! That sounds deliciously naughty, doesn't it?!"

"If it's a girls' school, aren't all the romanceable characters older professors…?"

"Oh, there are boys of the same age there, because of course there are. The prince who infiltrates the school in drag to investigate it is the heroine's age, and I'm pretty sure the academy's director, the main hero, is twenty or so. Oh, and the homeroom teacher is actually the boss of a rival organization! And then there's the good old final boss; he's an adult character in his midtwenties."

"'The good old'…" The phrase makes Aileen's expression go taut.

Lilia leans forward. "He's actually an evil god, but he's the school doctor, and the designated fan-service provider! It's a pretty good scenario, no? There's no route where you can romance the final boss this time, though. It may be foreshadowing for Game 6, but not being able to romance him is just…" Lilia gives a regretful sigh, pressing one hand to her cheek.

"The heroine is a survivor of the Levi tribe who fled to

Ashmael. She hides the fact that her magic is strong to avoid persecution. However, in Ashmael, her powerful magic makes her valuable, so before she knows it, she gets pulled into this underworld war. She's the redhead right in the middle of the cover."

"Oh, right... The red hair is proof of her magic, after all...," Aileen responds without thinking, and she catches herself with a start. Lilia doesn't slow down, though.

"At the Divine Maiden Academy, there's a sketchy religion known as the World Unity sect. It's all the rage, and the villainess—one of the students—is exalted as its divine maiden. Even though she's a villainess, she has strong sacred power. She claims she's the true holy king of Ashmael and declares Divine King Ares a usurper. She's plotting to overthrow the government, but as it turns out, the founder of the religion is the school doctor, our final boss, and she's just being used. The final boss only wants to eat the fiend dragon and regain his power as an evil god, you see."

"Quit dropping spoilers as if there's some sort of competition! It feels like you're going to make me remember the cover... Besides, there is no fiend dragon now; she's become the Holy Dragon Consort! The final boss won't get his power back. The end!"

"Oh, and for some reason, he speaks with a Kansai accent. He uses the body of the first Daughter of God in an attempt to break the fiend dragon's seal, but then he gets attached to the corpse, because he says she looks just like the oracle-princess from the Queendom of Hausel who sealed him away eons ago. What a pervert. Still, he's a hot evil god with glasses!"

"Nobody needs an evil god who smashes up worldviews like that. Master Luciel is quite enough!"

As she recalls her father-in-law—the hero and final boss

of Game 4, a god who ruled the demons in the demon realm and attempted to reclaim his wife, Game 4's villainess—Aileen clutches her head. For some reason, this makes the memory of the game packaging grow much clearer, and she whips her head back and forth.

"As I said earlier, though, you really can't romance the final boss of 5. Maybe that means his partner is supposed to be the reincarnation of the first Daughter of God or something. That final boss is definitely a prince of the Queendom— Mmph!"

"Enough. I'm through listening." Aileen has covered Lilia's mouth with both hands.

Based on her previous experience, Aileen knows the moment she remembers, she'll realize the game has begun.

That's right. I always remember these things at the worst possible time!

...And so she's decided to forget that cover immediately. As long as she does that, this peace will last. Even so, shaking off Aileen's hands, Lilia shouts at her, "Come on, Lady Aileen, listen! This might be useful information!"

"I don't want it! Why can't you understand that?!"

"If you keep talking like that, I won't help you no matter what! I'll be your enemy instead!"

"Nothing is going to happen, so I don't need your help. And when have you ever been my ally?!"

"Hullo, Aileen. Got a minute?"

With brilliant timing, a voice addresses her from the sky.

Looking up, Aileen sees a spectral beauty in men's clothing. It's the villainess of Game 4, Grace Dark, a woman who left the stage of history dishonored as the Maid of the Cursed Sword. At this point, she calls herself Claude's mother and refers to Aileen as her daughter-in-law.

In a seemingly weightless motion, Grace descends to stand beside Aileen's chair.

"Mother. Where's Father—Master Luciel?"

"Oh, I left him at the old castle."

Grace has managed to continue persisting as nothing but a soul, while Luciel has apparently ascended to virtual godhood. Neither of them fits the description of "human," and they currently live in the demon realm. However, these two originally founded Imperial Ellmeyer with the goal of creating a land where demons and humans could live together. They boldly built the old castle directly above the entrance to the demon realm, and they often drop in for visits.

"I have something I'd like to discuss with you regarding my future self. Do you have a moment?"

Eyes widening at the unexpected remark, Aileen nods. "Of course. Should we go elsewhere, perhaps?"

"Yes, I'd prefer that. I'll be waiting at the old castle. I'd like to speak with you alone, if possible."

Grace gives her a cool smile, leaning in just a little too close, then flits away. She and Claude have a similar air about them, and between that and Grace's polished, knightly bearing, Aileen catches herself staring. She clears her throat, regaining her composure. "Very well. Rachel, escort Lady Lilia all the way back to her rooms, if you would."

"All right. But, Lady Aileen, that will leave you by yourself..."

"No matter. The demon king's army waits in my shadow."

Aileen's husband cast a spell on the shadow at her feet,

transforming it into a portal for the demons. If Aileen says the word, demons will pour out of it.

"What's more, my wedding ring is charged with Master Claude's magic. It's as if he's always at my side. Don't worry."

Rachel nods. Lilia pouts, kicking her feet in an ill-mannered way. "Oh, come on! The villainess of Game 4 is asking for your advice! I want to hear this, tooooo!"

"That obviously isn't going to happen. You don't even try to understand your position, do you?"

"Even though a new game might already have started?!"

"Refrain from linking every little thing to the game!"

"Booooring! Serena's all busy now that she's a bureaucrat; she never comes over, and Sahra's gone back to Ashmael..." Lilia puffs her cheeks out, sulking.

The names she's just mentioned belong to the heroines of Games 2 and 3 respectively. In addition, Aileen's lady-in-waiting, Rachel—who's been pointedly ignoring her bizarre conversation with Lilia—is the villainess of Game 2.

"The hero and final boss of Game 2 are in the duchy of Mirchetta. The final boss of the Game 1 fan disc has become Grand Duke Levi and shuttles back and forth between here and his homeland. The characters from Game 3 live in Ashmael. The final boss and hero of Game 4 is in the demon realm, living happily with the villainess. Heh! In the end, the only loser in Game 4 was the heroine." Lilia summarizes the current situations of the game characters, counting on her fingers as she goes. When she reaches the last one, she flashes an ironic smile, and Aileen's expression sobers slightly. Amelia, the losing heroine of Game 4, is Lilia's biological mother.

"They're living their lives, that's all. Lady Amelia didn't simply end as a loser, either."

"True. Ohhh, you know, I bet that woman knew about the developments of Games 5 and 6, too."

Ignoring that idea…

With an exaggerated sigh, Lilia slumps back in her chair. "I'm worried, Lady Aileen. The villainess of Game 4 back there…"

"Lady Grace. Refer to her properly, by name."

"…Lady Grace, then. I wonder if what she wants to talk about is damage caused by the story not developing as the game intended. About her 'future self,' she said. Even if she is in the demon realm, sticking around as just a soul is the same as whittling that soul away. At some point, she'll hit her limit and be destroyed, just like Amelia was." Aileen frowns, and Lilia's shoulders droop. "And yet here you are, Lady Aileen, with no sacred sword."

"A world with no need for sacred swords is best, isn't it?"

Lilia blinks at her, and then her eyes grow moist. "That's you all over, Lady Aileen! My biggest favorite!"

"As I keep telling you, would you please grow out of that already?!"

"I knew it! If there's no sequel, I'll just have to make one! Leave it to me, Lady Aileen!"

"…Enough. I'm going."

Tiring of this conversation, in which no actual communication is happening, Aileen quickly excuses herself.

She has mountains of work to get through. Claude is attempting to build the foundation for a country where demons and humans can live together in peace even after he's gone. His ultimate goal isn't merely being emperor.

They're building a future. A future for Aileen and the others, one that has nothing to do with the game.

Currently, as empress, Aileen's most important task is producing an heir. Thinking about it makes her cheeks flame. Before she's managed to shake off the memory of those sultry nights, a voice calls to her.

"Aileen."

"Yesh?!" She's flubbed her response, and the man who's come up behind her looks perplexed. He tilts his head, his jet-black hair streaming to the side, and blinks those ruby-red eyes.

Claude Jean Ellmeyer is both the emperor of Ellmeyer and the demon king.

He's also Aileen's husband, the most magnificent in the world.

"I-is something the matter, Master Claude? Where are your guards?"

"I teleported and gave them the slip."

"Gracious, you're doing that again?" Aileen frowns.

Her mischievous husband cocks his head again. "By the way, could you explain that extreme reaction of yours a moment ago? I'm curious."

"It was nothing! You spoke to me suddenly, and it startled me, that's all!"

It certainly wasn't because she was thinking of something indecent in broad daylight. The only indecent thing here is Claude's face; her stray thoughts aren't to blame.

However, her beautiful husband's gaze doesn't miss her flaming cheeks. "Was that really all?"

"Yes, it was. What else could there possibly be?!" Aileen bluffs.

Claude watches her steadily, then breaks into a smile. Aileen's brings her hands to her cheeks. It feels as if he's seen right through her.

"Well, never mind. I have a little free time. Would you like to get some tea?"

"Oh, I'm told your mother and father are visiting the old castle. Let's invite them, as well."

Claude leans to the side, peeking at Aileen's face in a coaxing way. "Can't it be just the two of us?"

Ngh! For a moment, words desert her. Her cheeks, which she finally managed to cool, flame up again. "N-no, it can't. I mean, um, Mother wants to speak with me, and I've already promised her."

"Mother does? I hope it's not something tiresome again."

"I can't guarantee that it won't be, but I did promise her first, so today isn't...," she mutters, making excuses.

Claude backs down without a fuss. "I see. I suppose we'll leave it at that, then."

"Oh, b-but some other time— Um, the two of us could..."

The fact he's given up so easily makes her want to keep him from leaving. As the emperor, Claude rarely has free time to begin with. Aileen peers up with a look that says she wants to monopolize his scant time in spite of herself, and her husband gives her a gentle smile. He lowers his voice slightly and whispers softly in her ears. "I'll see you again tonight, then. Just the two of us."

"I—I didn't mean one of those times!" Aileen blushes bright red.

Claude chuckles. "One of which times?"

"—Y-you're teasing me, aren't you, Master Claude?!"

"Perish the thought. I'll have to take my time and get my adorable wife to tell me exactly what she was thinking once night falls, though. Including that part just a minute ago."

"As I said! I wasn't thinking anything shameful—"

"Master Claude, Lady Aileen," calls a quiet voice.

Looking puzzled, Claude turns away from Aileen. Interrupted midcomplaint, Aileen's gaze shifts, too.

"I thought they got here awfully fast. It's you, hmm, Keith? What happened to Walt and Kyle?"

"I sent them to gather everyone. I suspected Lady Aileen would probably be with you, so I came here."

"...Has something tiresome happened?" Claude asks.

Slowly, Keith nods. "His Majesty the holy king, Baal Shah Ashmael, just sent word that the Queendom of Hausel's floating palace has vanished."

✦ First Act ✦
The Villainess Begins Anew

Half a year ago, the Holy Queendom of Hausel—a leading world power—declared war on Imperial Ellmeyer for making the demon king its crown prince. No doubt the subsequent incident will be recorded in the history books as an actual war.

However, in reality, it had been a terribly personal, lonely fight. Learning that the great Queendom was controlled by just one woman, Amelia Dark, only made it seem even more so.

In any case, Imperial Ellmeyer emerged victorious. During the conflict, the Queendom's floating palace split in two; one half sank into the ocean, while the other fell into the borderlands between Ellmeyer and the Kingdom of Ashmael, a section of desert crisscrossed by canals.

The Queendom of Hausel had been an island nation. Losing both the palace that had been its core and a queen who could see past and future plunged the land into chaos. Apparently, an oracle from somewhere or other declared herself queen, and fighting broke out not long after. After Imperial Ellmeyer fended off the Queendom's incursions, Claude felt little inclination to look after their interests. The floating palace, however, was a treasure trove of information regarding the Queendom's divine-stone technology, which had been created by combining sacred and demon stones. Claude had been planning on working with Ashmael to dismantle the palace and analyze the technology, and that should have been the end of it.

Then without warning, the floating palace awakened—there's really no other way to put it—and ejected the entire team of investigators. After pale light enveloped the entire structure, it vanished without a trace.

"So it disappeared this morning? Who confirmed this?" Claude asks as soon as he's seated himself at the desk in his office.

His guards Walt and Kyle are on duty at the door. Keith, who came to deliver the report, has insisted on making tea as usual. Aileen is seated on the long reception sofa, while Cyril Lauren d'Autriche, her older brother, sits opposite her. He took over the management of the d'Autriche dukedom for their father, Rudolph, this spring, and he's recently been appointed prime minister.

"His Majesty the holy king of Ashmael did so in person, then immediately sent a report via sacred stone," Cyril answers. The hues of his blond hair and blue eyes are more muted than Aileen's, and both his tone and demeanor are gentle as well. "The first thing he said was 'Don't tell us you stole it,' so I laughed and asked if he was sure they hadn't hidden it themselves."

"...I don't think this is a laughing matter."

"I'd imagine he didn't genuinely suspect us, either. However, if they do find it first, I can't deny there's a possibility that he might hide it. Conversely, if we find it first, there's really no need for us to mention it to them."

Ever since she was small, Aileen knows all too well that underestimating her brother because of that mild demeanor can be the worst mistake someone can make. As politicians go, Rudolph had been the type who'd laid the groundwork for things in a roundabout way, while Cyril settles everything before anyone realizes what's even happening.

"We won't hide it for no reason." Claude, who's probably seen Cyril at work several times now, gives him a clear warning.

Cyril nods. He's smiling, but he definitely finds this all supremely annoying. "We will need to confirm this ourselves. Since this is a matter involving magic, I've asked the Levi tribe to dispatch a search party. Please review the final decision."

"Very well. I'd like to get Elefas's opinion. Summon him."

"Of course. Grand Duke Levi and his wife were part of the team investigating the floating palace for a time, so I've already requested their help. I've also heard that Serena Gilbert, the newly appointed official, has knowledge of the floating palace, so we'll use her as a liaison. Aside from those individuals, I've kept this incident secret. Making a fuss would benefit no one. Once we know the details, we can decide whether or not to release the information."

Claude nods, agreeing with Cyril's decision. "Still, if even Baal can't tell where it's gone, this is going to be rough."

"We plan to put together a second search party of holy knights to look for the half that sank into the sea. As the twin of the part that's mysteriously vanished, it may have something to tell us."

Did the other half also vanish or move away? Regardless, they'll need to interview the people who live in the area.

"All right. I'll try to get the demons to help with the interviews as well."

"Very good. I've also mentioned this to His Majesty the king of Ashmael, but such a large structure won't be easy to hide. Whether it was moved by a person or some mechanism in the palace itself, we're bound to find it eventually. For now, please take care to avoid anything that may cause a stir and conduct yourselves as usual." Cyril probably means there's no need to make the citizens uneasy…or so Aileen assumes, until he abruptly turns to face her. "I do mean 'take care.' You understand, don't you, Aileen?"

"I—I haven't said a word, Brother!"

"You're the type who doesn't understand even when you claim to, so when you don't even say that, it's bound to be worse." Although his eyes are very affectionate, Cyril lectures her quite rudely before he turns to leave.

Aileen stares after him, stunned. Then she realizes her husband is laughing behind his hand. When she scans the room, Keith quickly averts his eyes, and Walt and Kyle turn away.

"…Exactly what is so amusing, Master Claude?"

"N-no, it's nothing. Your brother just dominated that entire conversation."

"There's no point in talking back to him! My brother's an incomparable genius!"

Naturally, Cyril is perfectly aware of this and thinks it's only natural for him to worry about his less capable sister and support her. Aileen went through a rebellious phase once, but Cyril forcibly put a stop to it by asking, in a genuinely mystified way, *"Have I ever been wrong before?"* Unlike their father, who enjoys watching his loved ones fail, her brother has given her different trials, but at the end of the day, he's taught her how to live with strength and confidence.

"If you can't beat them, join them…or at least, that is what I decided to do."

"I never thought I'd hear you say anything so commendable."

"How rude. Even I am aware that what we need now is information." Turning away in a huff, Aileen rises to her feet.

Claude smiles wryly. "Where are you off to?"

"I've kept Mother waiting."

"Oh, come to think of it, you did mention that… I'll go with you."

"Oh really, Master Claude?"

Grace may be one thing, but Claude is always annoyed by Luciel, who insists on acting like his father. It isn't that he hates the man, but it's certainly rare for Claude to voluntarily pay him a visit.

"Those two know the floating palace very well. They're living witnesses."

At that, Aileen looks up. "Speaking of living witnesses, Jasper and Denis have seen the palace's interior as well. So has Rachel."

"We'll probably have to let the Oberon Trading Firm in on it… Walt and Kyle, tell them to assemble at the old castle."

When Aileen became empress, she officially made Isaac Lombard head of the Oberon Trading Firm to take her place. They still have a conference room in the old castle, designated the demon branch office, but the firm is headquartered in a new building on the third layer.

The demon king's guards grimace at the idea of leaving him alone, but they know he'll probably ignore their complaints. Besides, the members of the Oberon Trading Firm are at work. Since there's no guarantee they'll all be in the same place, they can assemble everyone faster by splitting up.

"We'll come to the old castle to get you, so wait for us, all right?!"

"The demons are there, so it should be fine, but absolutely do not leave the castle in disguise. Don't go to Ashmael, either."

With those parting words, the two guards race off down the hall.

Claude mutters, "Why don't they trust me?"

"Because you aren't trustworthy. Once I tidy up here, I'll head straight for the old castle, too, milord."

"......"

"You as well, Lady Aileen."

Aileen has been caught in the cross fire. Keith sees them off with a smile, and Aileen and Claude go to the old castle on their own.

She expected Claude to teleport them, but he sets off on foot at a leisurely pace instead. The distance from the imperial castle's residential quarters to the old castle is the perfect length for a stroll. Thinking Claude is busy and probably needs a change of pace, Aileen doesn't hurry him.

"They're all so mean."

"Yes, they are. You're one thing, Master Claude, but treating me as if I'm in the habit of absconding is quite rude."

"That's right, you're not like me. You're in the habit of rampaging."

When Aileen makes sarcastic comments, her husband quickly responds in kind. Irked, Aileen frowns. "Master Claude. I do believe you've been growing increasingly spiteful lately."

"Oh, absolutely. If I just let myself be swept along, I'd never last as your husband."

"...I really don't think men who change once they're married can be called decent."

"You'd quickly tire of a man who always stayed the same. You also grow dearer to me with each passing day, you know."

He gives her a charming smile, and by the time she's realized she's at a disadvantage, it's too late. Picking up a lock of Aileen's hair with a practiced gesture, Claude kisses it as they reach the corridor. "Even if we have a child, I wager you'll still be the most precious one to me. Shall we put that theory to the test?"

"As I've said many times before, stop doing that sort of thing in broad daylight..." Aileen starts to yell at him, then goes quiet.

Claude blinks at her. "What's the matter?"

"I...don't have the sacred sword now."

A little while ago, a horde of uninvited brides descended on them from the Queendom of Hausel. It was during that commotion that Aileen heard only a woman with strong sacred power could conceive the demon king's child.

"Lady Grace was the Maid of the Sacred Sword, and I am of her bloodline, but that's all... Lately, I've begun to wonder if I'm capable of giving you a child."

"It's a bit early to be concerned about that, isn't it?"

"Yes, but I've already become empress, you see."

By rights, since Aileen hasn't borne an heir, her title should be imperial consort. In a break with precedent, she received the empress's crown when Claude ascended the throne. It was a demonstration of his resolution to have no other consorts.

To keep people from criticizing Claude's decision, Aileen must bear and raise his child—specifically, a crown prince. One who will be the next ruler of this nation, home to both demons and humans.

"I didn't do that to burden you. I merely thought the results would be the same either way."

"I know. I don't consider it a burden. 'Bring it on,' as they say."

"In that case, can we enjoy our alone time for a—?"

"In other words, I must conceive as swiftly as possible." Aileen's expression is dead serious, and Claude doesn't seem to know where to look. "This is no time to be embarrassed about making attempts in broad daylight… As a matter of fact, I've just realized that daylight may be a more effective time for these things."

"That's the first I've ever heard of it…"

"We can't know for sure unless we try! Besides, if the floating palace incident proves to be something tiresome again…!" Her own words send a shudder through her. Abruptly closing in on Claude, she hauls him up by his shirtfront. "Let us try, Master Claude! Perhaps it will be more effective during the day!"

"Talking about it as if it's work sort of spoils the mood."

"We mustn't neglect work due to something as capricious as the mood! This is my most important duty—"

A footfall echoes loudly from the depths of the corridor.

Both Aileen and Claude gasp, but it isn't because they're concerned about having been seen.

The corridor leads to the living quarters of the imperial family. As a rule, it is deserted, and no one is allowed to set foot there without the imperial family's permission. The only prying eyes here should have belonged to the long rows of portraits of previous emperors lining the walls.

And yet that footfall came from the corridor's depths—from the living quarters.

A figure appears, confirming what their ears heard.

It's a boy. He's standing there alone, in the blank space where Claude's portrait will someday hang.

The light that streams through the corridor window behind him casts his face in deep shadow, making it almost impossible to make out his features. What they can see is that he's dressed in black, with black hair. Both seem to melt into the gloom. The oddest thing about him is the black eye patch over his left eye.

The most important thing to note is that none of the people who have permission to enter this place are young boys.

Aileen is as tense as a bowstring, but Claude seems rather laid-back. "Who might you be?" he asks.

There's no answer.

Instead, the boy with the eye patch takes another step forward, his heels clicking audibly on the floor. His black cloak flares out, and he runs straight toward them. Only after the sunlight glances off the blade does she realize that his black-gloved right hand holds a drawn sword.

"Master Claude!"

The boy sprints toward him. Frowning, Claude casts a barrier, and the sword's blade crashes into it.

Sadly, the battle ends almost as soon as it's begun. In an instant, the boy's sword shatters the barrier. Glittering remnants of magic rain down like fragments of glass.

He's broken through Claude's barrier—the demon king's barrier—with a single attack.

Aileen is dumbfounded. Clicking his tongue in irritation, Claude puts an arm around her waist in preparation to pull her close, but the boy mocks him. "Planning to run, *Father*?"

Who could blame Claude or Aileen for being distracted by that word?

As far as the boy is concerned, that's a splendid opening.

Magic circles appear all around them. Claude shoves Aileen

away, and for just a moment, she sees him trapped by the neck. Then, as if to blot out the sight, the geometric patterns on the layered magic circles flash.

Magic explodes. The resulting blast tears through the corridor. Thick smoke surrounds her, and Aileen squeezes her eyes shut. "Master Claude?!"

When she looks again, the magic circles have vanished, but the corridor is still filled with billowing smoke.

Straining her eyes, she manages to make out a figure. Just one. Turning pale, Aileen is about to run when a black cloak appears out of the curtain of smoke. She follows it with her eyes. It's the cloak Claude always wears.

"It can't be… Master Claude!"

"Skwee!"

With a cute little screech, something else flies straight out of the smoke.

It's a young dragon with black scales and red eyes. It spreads its wings, floating in front of Aileen at chest level, and spits flame at the cloud of smoke.

As the smoke dissipates, Aileen's vision clears.

The boy with the eye patch is standing on the scorched patch of floor, smiling. There isn't a burn or a scratch on him.

"Serves you right." The boy is looking at the young dragon. The young dragon glares right back at him, and Aileen puts her arms around it, pulling it to her. It's about the size of a human one-year-old, and it's surprisingly light.

The dragon swivels its red eyes to focus on Aileen.

Claude is human, but he's also the demon king, and his demon form is a black dragon. He's transformed several times before. Therefore, Aileen has an inkling of what may have happened.

Slowly, doing her best to hide her consternation, she asks, "You aren't going to tell me this dragon is Master Claude, are you?"

"Yes, that's right." The boy gives her an artless smile.

Now that he's standing in the sunlight, she can see he's almost frighteningly handsome.

A body as lithe as a young sapling. The sharpness of his face and eyebrows, his straight nose, skin as smooth as porcelain, even his thin lips—no doubt many would call them a gift from the gods.

Then there's his black hair, which is glossy even though it's been cut carelessly, and that right eye, as red as a ruby.

Put simply…he looks just like Claude. Claude made young again.

"…You called Master Claude 'Father,' didn't you?" Aileen lowers her tone to keep from sounding overawed.

Raising one neat eyebrow slightly, the boy shrugs his delicate shoulders. "Not that I'm happy about it, but yes."

He's a little shorter than Aileen, probably around thirteen or fourteen years old. Claude will be twenty-eight this year—it isn't totally impossible.

Aileen draws a deep breath. "In other words, you're his love child?"

Startled, the dragon looks up at her. The boy looks stunned, too, and then he bursts out laughing. It's a boyish laugh and rather high-pitched, but there's also something in it that reminds her of Claude. "Hey, I like it. Yes, that."

"Skwee?!"

"Even if you don't remember me, it's a fact that we're bound by blood. It's a nuisance for me, too." The look the boy turns on Claude suddenly goes cold. Apparently, they can communicate just fine when Claude is in this form as well. In Aileen's mind, the suspicion that he's Claude's illegitimate child has cemented into fact.

"There's no way you could know, so I'll introduce myself. My name is Charles." The boy takes another step forward, smiling with eyes that are more wistful than cold now. "I'm the son of that damnable demon king. And apparently, I'm the next one."

The memories from her previous life always come back to her at the most inopportune times, but this child isn't in them.

As the wife of a fiendishly beautiful demon king, Aileen has made a certain resolution. Claude has shouldered the heavy responsibility of protecting both the humans and the demons, and she intends to let him find human happiness, as well as happiness as the demon king.

In addition, his valet did mention that he went a bit wild after being disinherited and exiled to the old castle, before she met him. Aileen has no qualms about accepting that past in its entirety.

"I want you and Father to get out of the public eye for a while… Sorry, but Father's new form is insurance. Just think of it as a minor curse and bear with it."

In the hushed corridor, Charles speaks as if this whole thing is a pain.

Holding Claude's young dragon form in her arms, Aileen breathes deeply. She's never publicly declared her resolution before, but now, finally, it's truly being put to the test.

"Or, Father, are you not yet emper—?"

"Call me Mother!" Aileen demands firmly.

The boy looks stunned.

The young dragon's mouth also falls open in astonishment. It flaps its wings, kicking and struggling. "Skwee, skwee!"

"I know, Master Claude, don't worry. You said your name was Charles, correct? If your birth mother is here, I will ensure that she is treated well."

"...Skwee, skirr...?!"

"Just leave this to me, Master Claude. You would like to live with Charles as family, would you not?"

"Skwee!"

"Yes, Master Claude, that's right. There's no need to stand on ceremony. I always knew this day would come, and I have been preparing for it since long ago!"

"Sk...skwee..."

"......"

Claude's head is drooping, and he's gone quiet. Aileen, on the other hand, throws her shoulders back. Dubiously, Charles looks from one to the other. "So you don't doubt that Father has an illegitimate kid."

"Of course not. As a matter of fact, I'd always thought it strange that he had none! In addition, Master Claude is the type who takes responsibility for his actions."

Claude doesn't say a word; no doubt he's relieved.

Determined to live up to the trust he's placing in her, Aileen steps forward. "Therefore, don't do this. I know there's ever so much you'd like to say. However, you may very well become Imperial Ellmeyer's crown prince."

"—Who'd want to be a thing like that?" Charles mutters, glaring at Aileen with his red eye. The hostility in it makes her take a step back, while Claude unfurls his wings and hisses. "Don't fight this. You know you're no match for me. Look what's happened to Father."

"What did you do to Master Claude?"

"I had him take on a little of my burden, that's all. I don't want you two getting in my way. It's fine; he won't die. Just be quiet and behave."

"That depends on what you intend to do."

"I don't have to tell you anything," Charles says coldly. Then, very slightly, his tone softens. "Don't bother trying to resist... You don't have the sacred sword anymore, do you?"

"That doesn't mean we can't fight. I really wish you'd quit underestimating us!"

"Even if you are Master Claude's child!"

Walt and Kyle charge Charles from behind.

Scowling, Charles beautifully evades Walt's kick without wasting any motion. Kyle slides in front of Aileen and Claude, firing a shot that makes the boy back up a step.

"Walt, Kyle...! Master Claude is—"

"—That dragon, right? I don't know what happened, but I can see what we're dealing with. We're used to this." With his gun still trained on Charles, Kyle glances at the young dragon, briefly indicating that he understands.

"Sweet Ailey, Kyle and I will take over here. You run for it," Walt whispers in her ear after he comes over to stand beside her and Kyle.

Aileen's eyes widen. "How could I possibly do a thing like that?!"

"Everyone in the castle—no, in the entire capital—suddenly fell asleep. That includes the whole Oberon Trading Firm."

This news makes Aileen go quiet. Kyle picks up where Walt has left off. "It's as if they've all gone into hibernation. They're alive, but none of them are waking up. Even Sir Keith, Prime Minister Cyril, and the demons."

"By the way, the sky's crazy red for some reason. That's gotta be a barrier."

"I think we've been able to stay awake because Master Claude's magic is protecting us."

In Aileen's case, since she doesn't have the sacred sword, she's probably unaffected thanks to the magic-infused wedding ring and the spell on her shadow.

Why? What for? Questions circle in her mind, but the cause is clear.

It's the boy who's standing there, very still, watching her.

"Frankly, I dunno how much longer we'll be able to stay awake, either." Walt sounds like he's joking, but Kyle doesn't deny it.

Aileen presses her lips into a thin line as she realizes this abnormal situation is far more than the simple appearance of a love child. "All right." Whatever Charles is after, if he's willing to go this far, they need to run.

If he gets control of both the capital city and Claude, the Ellmeyer Empire will truly have fallen into his hands.

An illegitimate son unleashes years of resentment on his father—I suppose this isn't anything half so endearing as that makes it sound.

This is a national crisis.

"Have you decided what you're going to do? Whatever it is, I think it'll probably end the same way." Charles tilts his head in a gesture identical to Claude's.

"Go!" Walt bellows.

Aileen makes an about-face and runs. In the same moment, Kyle and Walt lunge at Charles.

She hears magic explode behind her, but she knows she mustn't look back. Claude stirs in her arms but doesn't struggle.

In front of Aileen, a beautiful god with silver hair appears. "Aileen, and—that's Claude, isn't it?! This way!"

"Father!"

Luciel, whom she thought was in the old castle, holds his hand out to Aileen. As soon as she takes it, the world around them changes. When she opens her eyes, they're in a plaza with a fountain where broad flagstone roads merge.

"Damn! So he won't let us leave the capital, hmm?" Luciel spits out. Apparently, his teleportation has failed, and they've only managed to escape the grounds of the imperial castle.

As surprising as that is, a much more shocking sight elicits a gasp from Aileen.

People are asleep all around them, some lying on top of one another in the streets. It isn't just people, either; dogs, birds, draft horses—everything.

Most of all, the sky overhead is a vivid red.

The intense color makes it look like the heavens could start dripping blood any second now on this abnormal space. The sunlight shines through the waves of magic, which seem to pulse like veins.

"Father… Is this all that child's magic?"

"I don't know. I think it's some kind of spell, but this is strange. Even my magic can't break it. It's much more comparable to a god's power."

"What…? Then—"

Could the real sacred sword—? Aileen almost says it, but there's no sense in asking about something she no longer has. She falls silent.

A voice calls down from above them. *"Luciel! Aileen and Claude! You're all right?!"*

"Grace. Any luck?" Luciel always manages to disgrace himself in front of his wife, but this time, there's dignity in his voice.

Grace shakes her head, her expression grave. *"I couldn't slip through that barrier, either. Time throughout the capital seems to have stopped. Not only that, but the barrier is also expanding. It may cover all of Ellmeyer."*

"It doesn't seem to have any effect on the demon realm, but this space has been completely cut off from the outside world. Making a spell like this in the first place is… And even if he did manage to make it, casting this would require an enormous amount of magic… What in the world is that boy?"

"The analysis can wait. Luciel, isn't there any way to get out of here?"

"Oh, there you are."

Pulling Aileen by the hand, Luciel leaps into the bright-red sky. Claude spreads his wings, launches himself out of Aileen's arms, and spits flame behind them, but all it can do is slow their pursuer down.

Slashing through the flames with one stroke of his longsword, Charles gazes up at the group as if they're being a major annoyance. "Look, there's no point in running."

Jumping up from the stone-paved street, he closes the distance between them in the blink of an eye.

Even if they keep climbing, they'll quickly run into that red barrier. From beside Aileen, Grace says, *"Aileen, let me borrow your body. I may be able to use the sacred sword through you."*

"No, Grace! If you become the sacred sword now, you may not be able to go back—"

"He's right, *Grandmother.* Just sleep and behave yourself. I'll settle everything in the meantime."

Charles's sword bears down on them. Luciel turns back, trying to block it—and then the red sky shatters.

Something darts in like a comet, cutting between Charles and Aileen's group.

"That's enough, Master Charles."

A shaft of pure sunlight lances through the red sky, illuminating rather short golden hair.

A smooth face. Sharp eyebrows. Her skin is fair, and her pressed lips are pink. The girl probably isn't much younger than Aileen, but she's still young enough that it makes sense to call her a girl—and she's lovely.

There's nothing immature about her expression, however, and there's a touch of elegance in her gestures.

Her eyes are violet—proof she possesses sacred power.

More importantly, Aileen has seen her on a game package.

The villainess of Game 5?!

"What are you doing here, Estella?!"

Charles's blast of magic feels like a manifestation of his wrath, but the girl deftly turns it aside with a barrier, then glances back at Aileen and the others. "Lady Aileen, right? I'll take over here. Hurry and run, please."

"Y-you're..."

The villainess of Game 5 has come to their rescue? What sort of twist is this? Not only that, but she's also acquainted with Claude's love child? None of this makes any sense.

Don't tell me—was Charles a secret character in that game?!

Aileen is understandably confused. However, Estella doesn't seem at all flustered, and her voice is quite composed. "You should be able to get out through the rift in the barrier. I'll cover you."

She's heard those lines somewhere before. Estella continues, her dignified gaze fixed on Charles, "If Master Charles fights in earnest, even I won't be able to stop him. Hurry, before he patches that hole."

"Let's go, Aileen!" Luciel pulls Aileen along by the hand while Grace flies ahead of them.

"Wait!"

Charles hastily raises his sword, but another barrier blocks his way. That must be Estella's. Even though Charles managed to break through Claude's barrier, he can't get through this one, and he *tsk*s in irritation. "Stay out of my way, Estella! What if you get hurt?!"

"If you don't want me in your way, then explain yourself."

"Shut up! How did you get here anyway?!"

"You won't tell me anything, so I'm under no obligation to answer that."

The odd argument unfolding behind Aileen piques her curiosity, and she glances back. In the meantime, Luciel stops abruptly. He shouts as if he's spotted something, "Why are you alive again?!"

Even as he yells, a ray of heat blasts out of the blue sky from beyond the clouds, piercing his shoulder, and he falls.

Charles is still inside the red barrier. This attack came from a new enemy.

Grace screams, *"Luciel!"*

"Ghk… No, Grace, stay back… Aileen!" With his uninjured arm, Luciel flings Aileen—who's holding Claude—out into the blue sky.

"Father!"

"It's fine, just run! I'll keep that Charles kid pinned down here— You too!"

Abruptly, even though she'd been blocking Charles's way, Estella appears beside Aileen. Just as Aileen realizes Luciel must have teleported her there after that yell, the hole in the red barrier closes up. Or rather, Luciel has cast a fresh barrier, sealing the crack.

Pale-faced, Grace shouts angrily, *"That idiot! Is he planning to make himself the core and seal himself in with him?!"*

Charles, who's been shut inside Luciel's barrier, seems to yell back, but they can't hear him now. The red of the double-layered barrier grows even deeper, hiding the imperial capital from view.

"Father, please wait!"

"Look out!"

Estella yanks on Aileen's arm, and Claude breathes fire, intercepting the light ray that's targeted them.

"Th-thank you. You're—"

However, before she can express her gratitude properly, another attack comes their way.

Estella thrusts both arms out, casting a barrier that surrounds Aileen and the others like a sacred shield. More attacks rain down like a meteor shower, but the enemy is nowhere to be seen.

One of those landed a solid blow on Luciel even though he's essentially a god. Naturally, the barrier can't block them entirely; little by little, it's coming undone. Crimson streaks appear on Estella's palms, her arms, her cheek. Even so, she keeps her gaze fixed forward as she shouts, "If this goes on, they'll win by brute force! I'm teleporting us!"

"But Master Luciel and the others..."

"—It's fine. Let's go, Aileen. If they're inside a barrier Luciel cast, then he's protecting them. Things won't get worse in there. Everyone will simply sleep."

Looking at the situation below them, Grace gives her consent. The attacks are also hitting the red barrier, but it shows no sign of breaking. On the contrary, it seems to be rippling from the inside—Charles may be doing his best to break out of Luciel's barrier.

It's clear that if they get caught between Charles and this unseen foe, they won't be able to deal with either.

Holding Claude with one arm, Aileen taps Estella on the shoulder. She doesn't yet know whether the girl is friend or foe, but she's the only one they can rely on. And since the villainess of Game 5 has appeared, their destination is bound to be the Kingdom of Ashmael, the setting of that game. Once they go there, they can get help from Baal as well.

"Teleport us to Ashmael!"

"Right!" Just as Estella nods, the barrier shatters. In the moment before the attacks can reach them, space warps. The sensation of falling from a great height sweeps over Aileen, and her consciousness fades.

Even then, she keeps her arms locked around Claude, holding him to her chest, determined not to be separated from him.

Baal Shah Ashmael, Ashmael's holy king, is enjoying a leisurely afternoon nap. The sun shines year-round in the Kingdom of

Ashmael, but the sunlight is relatively merciful in this season, and the days are pleasant. Mana's pool has cool water and shady trees, and it makes a perfect spot to rest. Additionally, no one can come near it without Mana's permission. Mana seems comfortable, too. Like Baal, she's lying on the grass, drifting off to sleep.

"Terrific weather, isn't it, Mana?"

"Skwee..."

"We don't want to go back to work. Frankly, we don't care what's become of the floating palace. Don't you agree?"

"Skwee..."

"Roxane has entered her second trimester, and she's settled down. We'd like things to stay peaceful."

And right then, with no warning, several people fall out of the sky into the pool.

Water splashes Baal in the face, and he sits there blinking in abject shock. Mana, who's also been soaked, gives a pathetic cry.

"Wh-wha...? What in the...?! What happened?"

"Baal."

Just as Baal hears his name, something black surfaces in the pond. He scoots back involuntarily, then exhales in relief. "Claude, hmm? We thought you were seaweed."

"Who are you calling seaweed? Never mind that, help them." Claude first drags Aileen then a girl Baal doesn't know up onto the shore.

They don't seem wounded, but Baal has a nasty feeling about this.

The demon king climbs out of the pool, giving no indication whether he is aware of Baal's feelings. "We're going to impose on you for a bit."

"...What's that supposed to mean?"

"Exactly what it sounds like."

"Go home."

"We can't. The thing is—"

"Don't say a word. We don't want to hear it. Don't drag us into your problems. Deal with it yourselves."

"—a boy who says he's my son has occupied the empire."

For a moment, Baal stops breathing. Then he sucks in a lungful of air. "It serves you right, you idiot! Go fall with your nation!"

"I can't do that. I genuinely don't remember him. I'm begging you, believe me. Please."

"No one would be fool enough to believe a man with your face. Try it with a mirror!"

"Also, give me clothes. I was a dragon until a minute ago."

Falling silent, Baal takes another look at Claude. Now that he's paying attention, both the arms the man used to pull Aileen and the other girl out of the water, and his neck—which is usually buttoned up so severely that it looks uncomfortable—are decidedly bare.

"You… You're…"

"…It couldn't be helped."

Claude looks away awkwardly. Suddenly feeling very tired, Baal covers his face with a hand and heaves a long, long sigh.

This is the moment he realizes what a fragile thing peace really is.

When Aileen opens her eyes, her husband is there with a smile, so she hopes she's just been having a nightmare.

Oh, thank goodness. I thought a game might have started again… I needn't have worried, though. We've been through all of the events connected to Ellmeyer and this timeline already…

Still, Claude always has trouble waking in the mornings, and it's unusual for him to rise before her. She nuzzles her cheek into his cool palm, asking for attention. The difference in temperature is nice. She hears a door open, and when he takes his hand away, she actually feels lonely.

"Is Aileen awake?"

"She still seems out of it. How about the other one?"

"The girl's still asleep. We're having Ares watch her, just in case. Who is she?"

"Your guess is as good as mine. All I know is that her name is Estella."

"Estella…"

"She seems to be an acquaintance of Charles, the boy who attacked us. I don't think she's an enemy, but it might be best to stay wary."

"You're certain you don't have a second illegitimate child?"

"I never even had a first one."

Aileen bolts up in bed. Claude is sitting on the edge, and she grabs his shirtfront. "You mustn't speak like that, Master Claude! Imagine how the child would feel, having his own father deny him!"

"That's the first thing you say?! Wait, Aileen, calm down and listen to me."

"No. As his mother, I object to the term *illegitimate* as well."

"I think you've adopted him a little too quickly!"

"Well, his face! It was the spitting image of yours, Master Claude."

Claude falls silent, his expression stiffening.

Baal steps into the room, chuckling. "Ah, is that so? They look that alike, do they? He'll never talk his way out of this one."

"Master Baal? Why…? Oh, of course, I asked her to teleport us to Ashmael… Wait—Master Claude?!" She pats her husband's chest and arms to make sure what she's seeing is real. He's human. Didn't Charles's curse transform him into a young dragon?

"I reverted the moment we reached Ashmael. It's a bit better inside the holy king's barrier."

"You'd better be grateful to us."

Baal—who's arrogantly drawn himself up to his full height—possesses enough sacred power to suppress the demon king's magic. Sacred power is meant to protect people, so it isn't good for offense. However, by neutralizing magic, breaking seals, and lifting curses, it purifies the demonic.

"It's the same as when your magic was unstable. Wearing that earring should slow its progress."

"Progress…? Master Claude?!"

Claude has abruptly begun removing his shirt—a black garment in the style of Ashmael, which Baal must have loaned him—and Aileen is aghast. The moment she lays eyes on his exposed skin, though, she falls silent.

From his collarbone to the vicinity of his heart, the skin on the left side of his chest has turned dark and dull. When she gingerly touches it with her fingertips, it's rather hard for skin. More like soft scales.

"…If this covers you entirely, will you become a dragon again?"

"Probably. I'm sorry." Claude lowers his eyes.

Giving him an intentionally self-assured smile, Aileen points to the area around his heart. "Oh, what a pity. I was hoping to keep your adorable young dragon version as a pet."

"Don't even joke about that." Claude grimaces. Then his expression softens, and he puts an arm around Aileen's shoulder, pulling her close.

To keep the symptoms at bay, he'll need to avoid using magic. For Aileen, just having him by her side is enough.

"Conversely, that does mean the curse isn't very strong... Why do you think he did something so negligent?" Baal murmurs.

"Claude is the demon king," Aileen reminds him. "Perhaps he simply wasn't able to cast the curse fully?"

"We sent scouts to the national border. They tell us Ellmeyer is surrounded by a red barrier and they can't see anything. As you probably suspected, they can't get in. We can't imagine someone with the power to cast a barrier that strong over the whole of Ellmeyer failing to cast a curse. It was all even that demon god could do to cover the barrier and hold him in, and we doubt he could have broken through it."

The image of her father-in-law, who sent them outside the barrier, rises in Aileen's mind. "Master Luciel... That's right, where is Mother?"

"Watching for any changes to the barrier. As long as Father's barrier holds, that boy Charles won't be able to move, and the situation shouldn't deteriorate. I think we can be sure of that."

Grace encouraged them to retreat. She probably won't make any reckless attempts to rescue Luciel. After all, Luciel bought them this time so they could come up with countermeasures.

"Speaking as Ashmael, we're concerned that the red barrier might extend to us. However, as of now, it doesn't appear to be expanding. We intend to stand by and treat this as Imperial

Ellmeyer's internal conflict, but… Claude. Are you really innocent?"

"What are you talking about?"

"The love child."

"Completely innocent." Claude's voice is low, practically a groan.

Aileen frowns. "Master Claude, try thinking back carefully."

"I'm telling you, there's nothing. Why doesn't anyone believe me? I really wish someone would. At least one person."

"Master Claude, in this world, there are things that can be done and things that can't. Come, think hard."

"No matter how many times you say that, if there isn't anything, then there just isn't! In any case, even if he did catch me off guard, he had enough magic to fight me on equal terms. If he's really my child, why haven't the demons stirred or noticed him before? It makes no sense."

He has a point. Aileen falls silent. This seems to relieve Claude; some of the tension drains out of his shoulders. "And so let's set the love child theory aside."

"If you don't remember, Master Claude, there's no help for it… If Sir Keith were here, I believe he could have given us a list of potential mothers, but…"

The demon king's adviser must know all of Claude's movements like the back of his hand. As Aileen falls deep into thought, Claude slumps over. "So you're still going to doubt me."

"If he were a total stranger, there would be no explaining this. It would make more sense if being your love child has made his life pointlessly hard, and he's come to repay that grudge by destroying the empire."

Claude can't argue with that. He broods. "If we take everything at face value, this appears to have been an attempt to get rid of me and take over Imperial Ellmeyer. But strangely, his heart didn't seem to be in it… He probably has some other goal."

"It's likely. That is precisely why we need information about that child now, including the identity of his mother. Without that, we can't even negotiate, much less deal with him."

"Look for information on his father, too, please. I want to clear my name."

"If you're going to insist that you don't know, Master Claude, we'll just have to ask that girl Estella. Where is she?"

When she ignores Claude's protests, Baal gives him a rather pitying look. "She's still asleep, or so we're told. By the way, that girl—"

"King Baal." There's a light knock at the door. The voice outside belongs to Ares, Ashmael's general. "The girl is awake now. Sahra is with her."

Baal tells him he'll be right there, and Aileen slips out of bed to go with him.

"Can you see? Yes? Good. Do you think you can sit up? It's all right; your wounds have been healed."

In Ashmael's royal harem, which is slated to be dismantled, the Daughter of God's kind voice echoes. The palace is well-maintained but noticeably shabby and generally gloomy.

Sahra, the Daughter of God, is the heroine of *Regalia of Saints, Demons, and Maidens 3*. As such, she has the power to heal wounds. While her abilities aren't quite what they were in the game, her power is undeniable.

When Aileen and the others enter, Estella is sitting up in bed with Sahra's help, drinking water from a pitcher.

"Drink slowly. Talking can wait."

"I... Where...?"

Surrounding her with unfamiliar men at a time like this doesn't seem like a good idea, so Aileen makes Claude and Baal wait by the entrance, then approaches the bed alone.

"I've only healed her wounds," Sahra tells her. "You mustn't make her push herself."

"I know," Aileen says, and Estella looks at her with hazy eyes. Lovely violet eyes, and golden hair that reminds her of starlight. The cut of Estella's navy-blue uniform is rather curious; in Aileen's previous life, it would have been referred to as gothic. At a glance, Estella almost looks like a nun.

Now that she's taken a good look at her, Aileen is even more certain.

This girl really is the villainess of Game 5.

If memory serves her right, the girl in the center of the jacket had flaming red hair. She was probably the protagonist. By process of elimination, she can safely say that the girl with the dark smile in the corner was the villainess.

On top of that, Game 5 had been set here, in Ashmael.

She has a bad feeling about this, but she has to make sure. This girl is their only possible source of information regarding Charles, Ellmeyer's invader.

"Thank you. Because of you, we were able to flee to Ashmael."

"Ash...mael... Is that where I am?" Estella asks in a hoarse voice. Aileen nods. Slowly, the girl looks around her. She thinks for a while, and then her eyes come back to Aileen. "And who might you be?"

"...Pardon? But you know me."

"I've asked the wrong question. Who am I?"

Seeing Aileen's eyes widen, Estella draws her eyebrows together apologetically. "Why am I here? I'm sorry, but do you know me?"

"My dear… Don't tell me…"

"I don't remember. I can't remember… Everything's gone." The girl's long eyelashes tremble.

Aileen can't believe it. Gently, Sahra squeezes Estella's hand. "It's all right. You're a little confused, that's all. Calm down, okay?"

"But I think there was something I had to do…"

"We have a clue, so we'll find out quickly. That's the uniform of Ashmael's Divine Maiden Academy, isn't it? If we ask them—"

"The Divine Maiden Academy?!" Aileen's temples throb. She recalls what Lilia said. *Right…apparently, Game 5 was set in the Divine Maiden Academy, which was supposed to be run by the hero…*

As Aileen struggles to get all the information straight in her mind, Baal steps closer. "That's right. We were going to mention that. Is this girl not one of our citizens?"

"Well, um…" Aileen is at a loss.

Estella's gaze goes to Baal. "Who are you?"

"Hmm? Very well, let us introduce ourselves. We are Baal Shah Ashmael."

Instead of responding, Estella winces as if she's fighting a headache. Seeing this, Baal laughs. "Don't push yourself. If you have amnesia, you can't be expected to remember names, even if it belongs to the king. Once you're back in shape, why not stop in at the Divine Maiden Academy? Someone there may know you."

"I'll accompany her," Aileen volunteers.

Baal blinks. Claude, who's come up beside him, speaks tentatively. "There's no need for you to go in person, is there? If we send an inquiry—"

"Her identity is tied to Ellmeyer's continued existence, Master

Claude. After all, she is our sole source of information regarding your love child."

"How many times must I tell you I have no love children?"

"I beg your pardon. She alone may have information regarding Master Charles, your illustrious son."

Claude moans something about how she's gotten it wrong, but Aileen is confident she has the right of it.

"Now that Ellmeyer's in that state, it may be dangerous for Ashmael to attempt to uncover Estella's identity. No doubt the Divine Maiden Academy has its own secrets and will take action! That's clearly where this is going!" All eyes are on her, and every mouth hangs open, but Aileen goes on, almost defiantly. "Some may attempt to take advantage of Estella's missing memories and use her for nefarious purposes. We must investigate carefully and swiftly. There's bound to be something we can learn about Charles, and there's no doubt it will be linked to Ellmeyer's secrets. We can't simply leave this in others' hands, nor should we inquire in a careless manner."

"I understand, but if we can't ask directly, then...what do we do?"

"Why, that's obvious."

Aileen still isn't sure whether a game has begun or not. However, if Estella really is the villainess of Game 5, there's certain to be a denunciation in her future. There's no way the game developers got all the way to the fifth game and suddenly changed their policy.

Aileen doesn't know what sort of person Estella really is. However, she did save them, and she has enough sacred power to oppose Charles. She's someone extraordinary.

Aileen refuses to let the girl be condemned.

"Estella and I will infiltrate the Divine Maiden Academy, posing as ordinary students."

She may be setting up a development identical to the one in the game, but so what? That's how she's always smashed through difficulties before. Aileen smiles dauntlessly.

Even when she pinches his cheek or pushes him, Lilia's husband won't wake up. The same is true of his bodyguard, and of Aileen's brilliant lady-in-waiting, who escorted her here.

What's going on?

She's noticed the noise outside, but she wants to figure out this situation first. However, she's starting to tire of tugging on her husband's cheeks and making funny faces.

Sensing an intruder, she hastily pretends to be asleep like the others.

"You're awake, aren't you? I was told you would be."

At the sound of the brusque voice, she opens one eye. He's looking right at her. Lilia recognizes this boy. *Or…do I? I think I might, but perhaps not…* Sitting up, she puts a finger to her temple, thinking.

"…I shouldn't be the one saying it, but I'm pretty sure this counts as an emergency. What are you doing?"

"Searching my memories."

The vaguely-familiar-yet-not boy seems exasperated. He is young and a little untidy, but the beauty of his face is perfect enough to cover for all that and then some. If he grows up that way, in terms of the game, he'll be a classic hero or a final boss. With a face like that, he could be a romanceable character either way.

"Did you do all this? Aren't you surprised I'm awake?"

"...I'm here because I was told to greet you."

"Gracious, by whom?"

His only response is silence.

She has the feeling she knows who advised him, though. Should she sense respect for a previous game, or is it provocation?

"My name is Charles Jean Ellmeyer," the boy tells her. Then he turns on his heel. "That's all... I don't plan to hurt anyone, so don't get in my way."

He seems to be in a hurry, because that's all he says, and then he's gone.

Lilia blinks a bit, then starts thinking.

Charles Jean Ellmeyer—that name proves he's a member of Ellmeyer's imperial family. Charles is the false name James used, and in the game, it refers to the next demon king.

In other words, this is the next demon king, and he belongs to the imperial family. Add that face, his hair, and the color of his eyes, and there's no room for doubt.

"The sequel is heeeeeeeeeeeeeeeeeeere! That's the spirit!"

If that's the case, she has to hurry and get ready, or she'll miss seeing Aileen in action.

Will the stage be Ashmael, home to the Divine Maiden Academy with the holy sarcophagus and the Daughter of God's corpse? She has no idea how this came about, but beginning her investigation there is probably the correct approach. Humming cheerfully, she starts to pack for a journey—and then she notices it.

The sky is bright red. Is it a barrier or something? Ellmeyer has been cut off from the rest of the world. On top of that, there's the state of the people around her...

How is she supposed to get to Ashmael like this?

What? Don't tell me—am I going to have to stay home?

Inconceivable.

"......"

For a moment, the light vanishes from Lilia's eyes. Then she chuckles, her lip curling, and takes out her frustration on her husband by pinching his cheek again. "Wake up, Cedric."

"......"

"At times like this, as a rule, the heroine and hero are inexplicably the only ones left awake, and they have to solve the mystery! So why are you asleep? Wake up! Take me to Ashmael! I swear, prince characters are so useless. Wake up, waaake uuuup, I'm going to divorce you, wake up! Fine, divorce it is—"

"Look, you, this is an emergency. What do you think you're doing?"

Lilia's eyes widen. She looks between her husband, who's still stubbornly asleep, and the newcomer. "Serena, my goodness. Were you actually a hero instead of a heroine?"

"There you go, making no sense again. You're not the one behind this mess, are you? I heard something about the floating palace disappearing, too."

This woman—who's addressing the second prince's consort without even a semblance of courtesy—is Serena Gilbert. She's an outstanding individual who was appointed as a bureaucrat this spring—a fact that Lilia cannot possibly care less about.

What truly matters is that she's a character from the game.

"Anyway, come here a second. The demon king's father has collapsed. It looks like he's hurt."

She probably means Luciel, the demon king and hero of Game 4.

"You can heal him, can't you? Assuming he's alive."

Serena is the heroine of *Regalia of Saints, Demons, and Maidens 2*, the Saint of Salvation whose special ability amplifies every sort of power there is. Unlike Sahra, the heroine of Game 3, she doesn't have her own healing abilities, but she can accelerate others' inherent healing ability.

Lilia's suggestion is quite natural, but Serena frowns at her. "In this situation, I don't know whether it's okay to heal him or not. Obviously."

"You're really wary about that sort of thing, Serena. Don't you have the heart of a saint?"

"Nope. I've never been a saint. Anyway, he's tossing around and babbling about weird things. It's extremely suspicious. He said 'Evare' or something like that."

"Evare?! But that's the name of the final boss of 5…! We have to hear more. Let's help him!" Gleefully, Lilia starts rising to her feet, then pauses, thinking hard.

The evil god Evare. The final boss of Game 5… In that case, who is the boy who called himself Charles?

He can't possibly look just like Claude and not be a game character, and yet…

But the hero of 5 didn't look like him, and if he isn't the final boss, either, then… Hmm…

This is a mystery worth pondering. It may be best to start her search at the beginning.

Aileen seems to have escaped, and she'll no doubt be hard at work wherever she is. Perhaps Lilia's best move is to find out what she can here.

Someone told Charles to introduce himself to Lilia…not to

Aileen. It's as if they've challenged her to a contest: *Figure out who Charles really is. We know you know this.*

Could he be, for example, a character from Game 6, the final installment of the series, which was supposed to be linked with 5?

"Heh-heh! This is going to be so much fun. You think so, too, right, Serena?"

"In a situation like this? You're as crazy as ever."

She can say what she wants, but the heroines of 1 and 2 are both here.

How can they let the sequels underestimate the first two games in the series?

✦ Second Act ✦

Covert Maneuvers for the Villainess, Rules for the Demon King

- Game 5 is set in the Kingdom of Ashmael's Divine Maiden Academy.
- The hero is the young boss of an underworld organization that's in charge of keeping the fiend dragon sealed, and he's also the director of the academy. Name unknown.
- The heroine is a Levi tribe survivor, a redheaded girl with magic. Name unknown.
- Based on the jacket, the villainess is probably Estella.
- The villainess is lauded as the divine maiden by the World Unity sect and attempts to kill Divine King Ares. Probably condemned later.
- The final boss is the school doctor. Wears glasses, speaks with a Kansai accent. Secretly the founder of the World Unity sect. Wants to eat the fiend dragon and regain his power as an evil god, so targets the corpse of the first Daughter of God in the underground ruins. (Puppets her corpse.)
- There are three characters to romance at the school. The final boss can't be romanced.
- Charles isn't on the package of 5, but at present, he and Estella know each other.
- Game 6 was apparently in development, but the details aren't known. Features the same characters as 5?

"...At this point, I believe that's everything we have to work with."

Aileen has combined the information Lilia gave her about the games, their current situation, and her own memories, then jotted what she knows down on a piece of paper. She dips her quill into the ink again, putting check marks by the information that's inconsistent with her present reality.

"First, the fiend dragon has become the Holy Dragon Consort. However, according to Baal, there is an underground organization that was in charge of the seal on the fiend dragon; their role has shifted to conducting rituals in honor of the Holy Dragon Consort, and they still run the Divine Maiden Academy. In other words, the Divine Maiden Academy exists. As a matter of fact, Estella was wearing their uniform..."

In the true ending of Game 3, which was set in Ashmael, the fiend dragon was sealed away. However, in reality, the fiend dragon has been purified and is now the Holy Dragon Consort, so the role of the underground organization has changed significantly.

"In addition, even if the final boss of 5 wants to resurrect the fiend dragon, that's simply impossible. Since the Holy Dragon Consort has been purified, eating her wouldn't help him regain his power... However, the holy sarcophagus that holds the body of the first Daughter of God *does* exist. I suspect he could use Lady Sahra as a proxy and skip puppeting the corpse entirely, but..."

From what Lilia said, though, the final boss is obsessed with the first Daughter of God. It could be some sort of romantic fixation or simply foreshadowing a bigger development, or perhaps manipulating the corpse is just easier than using a living human.

"The biggest difference is the fact that the age of Divine King Ares never came to be."

Baal should have been taken over by the fiend dragon and become the final boss of Game 3. Instead, he's still the holy king, and while Ares has been pardoned, he's been branded a traitor who instigated a failed revolution. Even if the villainess of Game 5 is taken in by the World Unity sect, there's no divine king for her to kill.

"According to the villainess, Ares is a usurper, correct? Estella really does seem to have enough sacred power to become the holy king, but..."

Aileen abruptly realizes something, and her pen stops moving.

It's about the bloodline of the villainess, who calls the divine king a *usurper* for killing the holy king in Game 3. Following that to its logical conclusion, wouldn't that mean she comes from the bloodline of the *previous king*—in other words, a descendant of the holy king?

"...Don't tell me it isn't just Master Claude, and Estella is Master Baal's love child—"

"Did you call me, Lady Aileen?"

"N-no, it's nothing!"

Estella, who's just returned to their dorm room, seems perplexed by Aileen's cracking voice.

That golden hair against the navy blue of her Divine Maiden Academy uniform, and those cool violet eyes. Aileen has just realized that the girl looks remarkably similar to Baal.

I-it can't be. Master Baal ascended the throne quite a long time ago, and though the harem's been dismantled, it's existed for ages. Even if there was a chance before he met Lady Sahra and Lady Roxane, h-her personality is completely unlike his...

Baal is cheerful and friendly, while quiet Estella seems somehow noble and unapproachable. Unlike Claude, Charles wore an eye patch and had a very different, decadent aura about him, but— At that point, she shakes her head. *In the first place, isn't her age rather implausible? I do think she's younger than I am, but unlike Charles, our ages seem quite close. Oh, but there's no way to confirm her age if she has no memories…*

No matter how many times she thinks it through, she always reaches an impasse there.

Estella notices Aileen's furrowed brow. She tilts her head and asks, "Are you feeling unwell? Perhaps the fatigue has caught up with you."

"I'm fine. Remember, I remained in the dormitory on our first day so we could see if anyone tried to strike up a conversation when you were on your own… How did that go?"

"Unfortunately, no one seemed to know me. Neither the teachers nor the students found it strange that I could be a transfer student. Everyone was very curious about my amnesia."

On their first day at the academy, on Aileen's suggestion, Estella attended classes like a normal student.

Aileen and Estella are currently enrolled at the Divine Maiden Academy as transfer students sponsored by Roxane, Baal's principal consort. The academy has a vast campus on the western edge of Ashmael's royal capital, and all students are required to live in the dormitories. Roxane arranged for them to room together, set up dates and times for them to make regular contact, then left them to it.

"However, there was a recruitment attempt by a dubious group known as…the World Unity sect, I think it was. It seems to be popular among the students."

That term appeared in the game as well. Aileen frowns. Not only that, but Lilia also mentioned that the villainess of Game

5 was set up as the divine maiden of the World Unity sect and became the puppet of the final boss.

"You should stay far away from suspicious people…no matter what they say about your memories."

"Of course. No doubt it's an old trick."

Estella doesn't seem the least bit interested, but they'll likely need to be careful. There's a high probability that the game has already begun.

"Was there anything else that seemed odd? For example… Er, I don't suppose you happened to see a prince dressed as a girl…?" she asks, averting her eyes slightly.

Estella looks blank. "I saw no one suspicious. Is there someone here who fits that description?"

"No, it's fine, pretend I didn't ask. I don't think he's usually present… I only needed to make sure, just in case."

"If I see someone like that, I'll report him immediately."

If the love interest in drag appears, will he end up being reported to the police by the villainess? Aileen gets the feeling they may be a villainess death flag. "I understand why that's your first instinct, but please refrain; it would draw attention to you. What about your homeroom teacher?"

"He's a very kind, elderly man."

"…I see. You may not originally have been in this year, after all… I had them put you in the highest year so we would be together, but you could easily be a first-year student."

The Divine Maiden Academy is a four-year boarding school that admits girls fourteen and older. Most students graduate by the age of twenty. While there have been new students in their twenties, it's rare. Aileen is nineteen, so she prioritized not standing out and had them both placed in the highest year.

"This uniform doesn't seem brand-new, though." Estella looks down at her skirt.

Aileen nods; it really doesn't. "You may even have graduated already."

"But would I still be wearing the uniform? Perhaps I only borrowed it, and I'm not even a student here. There were no students named Estella in the student register, correct?"

"That's right. It's too soon to make that assumption, though. The uniform may be a hand-me-down from someone else."

"About that… My uniform seems to be a bit different from everyone else's."

Turning over the notes she's written so that the other girl won't see them, Aileen rises to her feet and takes a closer look at Estella's uniform.

The academy considers the first Daughter of God its ideal, and so the uniforms are navy blue and designed to resemble the garments worn by nuns. At the same time, Ashmael's culture tends to favor flamboyant outfits, and the uniforms reflect this: The sleeves are puffed, the shape of the skirts is rather adorable, and lace peeks out around the hem of the skirt and the gathered cuffs of the sleeves. In Aileen's previous life, this would have been considered a nun-themed gothic Lolita costume.

"…They aren't the same?" At a glance, Estella's uniform looks much like what Aileen is wearing. As far as she can recall, the cut and color are the same as what the protagonist of Game 5 wore on the package.

Estella shakes her head slowly, holding the cuff of her sleeve out to her. "The design of the lace is a bit different. The skirt hems are the same."

Aileen puts her cuff next to Estella's, comparing them.

It's true; the delicate lace that peeks out of their cuffs is slightly different.

Baal provided the uniform Aileen is wearing. It's most likely the same as the uniforms of the other current students. In other words, Estella is the one who's different.

"I think the skirt is a little shorter as well… Where do you suppose I really came from, and why?"

Estella has lowered her voice slightly. Her face is still expressionless, but somehow, she seems rather forlorn. It makes her seem much younger than Aileen.

Aileen is the empress of Ellmeyer. Her first priority must be saving her empire. However, exploiting a girl who's forgotten who she is would be unforgivable.

"It's all right. No matter who you may be or where you're from, you are yourself." She hugs Estella's shoulders, gently stroking her back. "You mustn't brood about this. Both Master Claude and I are counting on your memories, but if it comes down to it, we'll deal with this on our own somehow. It is our empire, after all."

"…But I have the feeling there was something important I needed to do."

"As I said, don't overly concern yourself. Master Baal fully intends to protect you as one of his citizens, and Lady Roxane will aid us to the best of her abilities. She said it was possible that you were an exchange student."

Estella blinks.

"The Kingdom of Ashmael maintained a policy of isolation for a very long time, but even during that period, they continued to conduct student exchanges. Lately, they've been very active on that front. Master Baal may not look it, but he's quite fond of diplomacy. It's possible that you are from a foreign land, and you planned to come to Ashmael on exchange."

"No, I'm a citizen of Ashmael," Estella declares, then looks rather surprised at herself. "I think...I am. No, I mean... I may be wrong, but..."

"Oh, and why not? Be confident in yourself. It means there's bound to be something here."

"You're...right. I'm afraid it will be a nuisance to the holy king and principal consort, but..."

"It's nothing to worry about. That is, in fact, the duty of a king." When she gently presses a hand to Estella's cheeks, the tension finally drains from the girl's shoulders. It's possible she's been on edge all this time. "All that's left today is evening worship and dinner, correct? Sit and relax for a while."

"Thank you— Oh no, Lady Aileen. I'm sorry, I forgot. I have a message for you from Professor Claude."

Aileen twitches, her face stiffening. Estella is perfectly serious, though. "I see. From Professor Claude..."

"Yes, Professor Claude. He says he's waiting behind the chapel."

Putting a hand to her forehead, Aileen heaves a deep, deep sigh.

As the name suggests, the Divine Maiden Academy is a school exclusively for girls. That meant Claude couldn't gain admission as a student—even if passing him off as one had been remotely possible—and so they originally planned to have him stand by in Ashmael's royal palace. Aileen was also concerned about his physical condition while under the influence of Charles's curse. It would definitely be best to have him stay near Baal.

Of course, Claude loves going around incognito, and there was no way he was going to stay behind and wait quietly.

"Has something happened, Master Claude? Why have you summoned me?"

"You mean 'Professor' Claude, don't you?"

Claude tilts his head to the side. He's tied back his black hair; the night wind makes it flow like silk, and his alluring aura makes her want to ask exactly what he's meant to be a professor of. This melancholy, attractive new professor is wildly popular, and he's banished the topic of Aileen and Estella's transfer far beyond the stars.

Estella and Aileen have entered the school to investigate Estella's origins in order to learn more about Charles's attack on Ellmeyer. And of course, Claude only agreed with this plan of action on the condition that he be allowed to join them as a member of the faculty.

Incidentally, the subject he teaches is art. Aileen thinks bitterly that he should just become a work of art himself. "...You appear to be enjoying yourself."

"I am, a bit."

He seems to be in a very good mood. That's far better than having him feel unwell, but for some reason, it irks her. "You are terribly popular, aren't you?" she says, giving him a chilly look.

Claude blinks at her, then chuckles. "Correction: I'm enjoying myself a lot. To think I'd get to see you look like that."

"I'm happy for you. And, Master Claude? What did you need?"

"You mean 'Professor.'"

"Quit playing, would you?"

"If I must." No sooner has he spoken than Claude puts his arms around Aileen's waist and pulls her close. In a practiced movement, his lips trace a path from her temple to her ear.

"Wait— Master Claude! J-just where do you think we are—?"

"In a girls' school intended to raise divine maidens—or in layman's terms, virtuous wives—where both boys and love are banned, not only are lovers barred from entry, but even fiancés chosen by their families aren't allowed to visit students. They can't even exchange letters. Married students are out of the question. It's a school with the strictest precepts, and any student who demonstrates unbecoming behavior is immediately expelled."

"In that case..."

"And you refuse to call me professor. That means, right now, you are my wife."

What sophistry is this? While she's trying to word her complaint, he very nearly stops her lips with his own.

"Honestly, Master Claude!"

"Professor."

He's determined to make her say it. Nibbling on her earlobe, Claude coaxes her. She grabs the back of his jacket and attempts to pull him off, but he won't budge. He knows exactly how hard to hold Aileen so that it doesn't hurt her while also restraining her. His hand has strayed below her hips and is beginning to behave suspiciously, so Aileen gives in.

"Very well, Professor Claude! What did you need?!"

"Nothing in particular."

There's a pause. Then Aileen stomps on Claude's foot as hard as she can. "I am about to be very angry with you!!"

"I was a little concerned. I just wanted to make sure you were all right."

"We only infiltrated two days ago. Why would you overreact like—?"

"I hope everyone else is all right, too. The demons, Keith and Walt and Kyle, Elefas, Cedric, Father…my people, everyone."

With a sigh, Claude embraces her, leaning against her. Removing the foot she used to stomp on him and uncurling the fists she raised, Aileen puts her arms around him.

The one who feels most responsible for Imperial Ellmeyer's current state is its emperor.

That's a flaw of mine. I immediately get absorbed in finding solutions, and I neglect the feelings of those around me.

Grace is keeping an eye on the red barrier. If anything happens to Ellmeyer, she'll contact them. Baal is continuing the search for the floating palace. They're doing everything they can. In the end, though, perhaps Claude has disguised himself as a teacher because he can't allow himself to simply stand by and wait.

The only one who can provide emotional support for such an emperor is his empress.

"There's no point in being anxious."

"You're strong, aren't you?"

"Of course I am. After all, Master Claude, I have you. It's like having the strength of a hundred men."

She rests her forehead against his, and Claude breaks into a smile. "Having you makes me worry more, actually. There's no telling what you may do."

"Don't be rude— No, you mustn't!"

Claude has tilted Aileen's chin up and is on the verge of kissing her when she claps both hands over his mouth. She can't let her guard down for a moment.

"What if someone sees?"

"Isn't that the best part?" He licks her palm, but she endures it. An unfortunate shudder runs down her spine, but she really can't afford to take her hands away now.

"If you want me to call you professor, follow the rules properly."

"You expect the demon king to follow the rules? My adorable wife is so virtuous."

He chuckles, and his throat moves in a terribly alluring way. Still, she does get the sense that this is another display of Claude's anxiety. As proof, he lowers his eyes. "I'll settle for just once. I want to feel safe."

Asking in a husky voice isn't fair. The strength drains out of Aileen's hands. Catching both of her wrists, Claude pushes her against the brick wall behind the chapel and leans in for a kiss.

She's very nearly swept up in the moment, her eyelids falling, when she realizes something with a start.

Wait. Master Claude said nothing about only *taking a kiss—*

"Whatcha doin' over there, Professor Claude?"

The light of a lamp emerges from the bushes, along with a human silhouette. Aileen stomps on Claude's foot with her heel. Claude staggers, and Aileen pushes him away, then dons the best smile she can manage. "I-I've just transferred in, and I got lost. He was helping me, so—" She's trying to cover for them, but then she breaks off, catching her breath.

The person who's held up the lantern, illuminating her, smiles gently behind his spectacles. "Oh, I see. It's almost time for evenin' worship, but it ain't in this buildin'. It's in the cafeteria, so you got the wrong place—we'll leave it at that for now, yeah?" He gives her a significant smile. He definitely suspects something.

However, that isn't the reason behind Aileen's strained smile.

In the light of the lamp, she sees blackberry-colored hair with a single tuft of red in it, and a pair of equally red eyes. His lopsided smile seems open and glib, but also like he's sneering at the world.

"I'm Professor Evare. It's good to meetcha."

His cheerful smile makes Aileen recall the jacket of Game 5.

The silver-haired youth who was trying to take the redheaded heroine's hand was probably the main hero. The man she's looking at now is the character who was also right in the center of the package, wearing a knowing look on his villainous face.

"I'm the school doctor, so if you get hurt, I can fix you up."

On top of that, he's a bespectacled fellow with a Kansai accent—everything about him matches what Lilia said.

In other words, he's...

The evil god and final boss of Game 5, who plans to eat the fiend dragon and restore his original form?!

So the game really has begun? Aileen tenses, and the young man who's introduced himself as Evare takes a step forward. His movements couldn't be more human. "Aw, no need to be so nervous, Miss Aileen. Let's get along, okay?"

"Oh, y-yes... Wait, you know my name?"

"Sure I do. The principal consort recommended you herself. 'Sides, I had a li'l somethin' I wanted to ask..." He reaches out to touch her cheek.

She blinks, and then there's a sharp *thwack* as something knocks Evare's hand away.

Claude, who's stepped between the two of them, speaks coldly. "No teacher worthy of his title would conduct himself in ways that blatantly violate the rules," he says brazenly. Aileen can't believe the words coming out of his mouth.

Evare flashes a wry smile. "In that case, Professor Claude,

why don't we escort this student back together? Just to make sure nobody breaks the rules." He claps Claude on the shoulder without a trace of discontent.

Claude frowns. "I can do that on my own."

"Well, you're new here. 'Sides, maybe I don't look like it, but I'm a responsible guy. Just because a teacher's sponsored by the holy king himself don't mean I can ignore his violatin' the rules."

"And what about you?" Claude glances at the bushes behind Evare. Evare looks blank. As he turns back, the lamp moves, and its light abruptly reveals a figure.

"Aaaaaaaaaaaaaaaah!"

"Eeeeeeeeeeeeeeek!"

Evare's scream makes Aileen shriek. She clings to Claude, then catches herself. Evare doesn't seem to notice. He's genuinely startled by what's appeared behind him, and he's busy getting his breathing under control.

"Wha—? You followed me, huh?"

"......"

A girl with short hair is standing in the bushes, a vacant look on her face. She doesn't answer. The light from Evare's lantern hazily illuminates her silhouette.

"Agh, don't scare me like that. You ain't got no presence to begin with... Sorry 'bout that, Professor Claude. This girl's my assistant."

"Assistant...? She's not a student?"

"Nope. This's Machina. She can't do a thing, but treat her right, okay? Now, let's get on over to the cafeteria."

Nonchalantly, Evare sets off with the lantern. Machina silently follows him. At that point, Aileen finally gets a good look at the girl's face, and her eyes widen.

Instead of the student uniform, the girl is dressed a bit like a maid, and she looks dead. Her short hair is as white as snow, and her violet eyes seem lifeless. Her lips are purple as well. The girl trails after Evare in a way that's more like "moving" than "walking." She doesn't spare so much as a glance at Aileen and Claude.

However, Aileen recognizes that face. She could never forget it.

The girl's head had been severed, she'd used up her soul and everything else, and yet she wore a satisfied smile in her final moments. She'd struggled against fate all alone without fulfilling any of her wishes and made her exit without giving anyone a chance to recoup their losses.

The person who tried to prove she was the one and only true queen of Hausel.

The first Maid of the Sacred Sword—Amelia Dark.

Why...?

The only ones who saw the girl's true form were Aileen, Lilia, and Luciel and Grace, who knew her personally from the past. Aileen fought her hand to hand just once, but she could swear that this girl's face is absolutely identical, and there's no mistaking it. She can declare with certainty that the only difference is the color of her hair.

"Let's go, Aileen."

Claude has never seen Amelia. She hesitates, wondering how she should tell him, but Claude's gaze is already scarily severe. Whispering softly, he gives her back a gentle push. "Steer clear of that girl. She's no ordinary human."

She gives him a questioning look, but Claude shakes his head. Does he mean he doesn't know any more than that?

At the same time, the fact that Evare has someone like that with him means he's not ordinary, either.

"That Evare fellow is dangerous as well. His magic doesn't feel human or demon… He's probably the one who shot down Father."

"What?"

"If you keep whisperin' like that, you'll make everyone suspect you two're lovers or married." Evare turns back, raising his lantern again with yet another smile. A step away, Machina turns around, mirroring his movements.

Evare's lantern is bright, and it makes the shadows sharper and deeper.

"Let's all get along. For now anyway."

Hair and eye color are tied to the laws of this world. Since the color of Machina's hair is different, she can't be Amelia.

However, the fact that she's with the final boss of Game 5 can't be dismissed as mere coincidence. She wasn't on the jacket of 5, but this girl, who looks almost identical to Amelia, is most definitely someone to watch.

Claude offers to investigate the faculty, Evare included. Aileen wants to object but can't. Without his help, she'll be spread too thin to keep an eye on Estella's surroundings.

During their first lecture of the morning, Aileen sits in a seat diagonally behind Estella, resting her chin on her hand. *The others simply treat us both as transfer students. One would think they might recognize Claude and myself, but… Perhaps it's because this is a boarding school, isolated from the outside world.*

Some of the professors must have caught on, but Baal probably told them not to pry, because no one's actively approached them yet. The one who's been the most blatant about acting as if he knows everything is Evare… Although, that man would have been deeply suspicious even if they hadn't spoken with him.

Now then, how should she begin? Should she steal into the underground ruin to see the corpse of the first Daughter of God? If she goes in without a plan, though, she'll merely be sightseeing. That said, she does have one lead…

It's something Baal told her when she casually asked about the underground ruin.

He said the door to the underground ruin could not be opened by anyone other than those who'd inherited the blood of the first Daughter of God: direct descendants of Ashmael's royal family, and only the women at that…

She looks at Estella's back. The girl is listening attentively to the lecture. If she really is Baal's illegitimate child—in other words, a direct descendant of Ashmael's royal family—she'll be able to open that door.

However, what good will it do to confirm that? Even if they ask Baal's permission, he'll wonder why they're going to a place even he couldn't open. She heard that even Sahra, the second Daughter of God, wasn't able to open the underground ruin because she wasn't a blood descendant.

In the first place, according to Lilia, the final boss of 5 wants the corpse of the first Daughter of God so he can break the seal on the fiend dragon. Wouldn't opening the door end up helping him?

Since the fiend dragon no longer exists, I doubt there's any point in puppeting the first Daughter of God's body, but…Lilia didn't seem to think Estella's story would end as Evare's marionette. Saving the world is always the heroine's role; what if she says that purifying a defiled world means destroying both the evil god and humans? In a game, that could definitely happen…

She wonders what Lilia's doing. It doesn't seem likely she's simply sleeping inside that red barrier. Aileen gazes out the window. On the edge of the horizon, if she looks closely, she can just make out the top of the barrier.

"Distracted, hmm? We can't have that."

Something thumps the corner of her desk lightly, and Aileen looks back, startled. Claude smiles at her. He's teaching an art history class—or rather, he's only reading the textbook, but it's annoying how good he looks while doing it.

"Is my class making you drowsy?"

"N-no. I'm sorry, sir."

With a small, amused smile on his lips, Claude bends down slightly and whispers to Aileen. "Come to the art room later. You've earned yourself a lecture."

If she doesn't get this shameless professor fired and returned to the imperial throne as soon as possible, he'll ruin the students' morals. He's just oozing sex appeal, and the students around them are blushing bright red.

Even Aileen, who's used to him, can't hide her flushed cheeks. It's all she can do to glare back at him. "Yes, I understand," she says, hoping her intention to completely fail to show up will get through to him.

"Very good."

The dangerous art teacher nods mildly. As he passes her desk, a paper flutters out of the textbook he's holding. Aileen isn't dense enough to instinctively say, *Professor, you've dropped something.*

The sheet is folded in two. When she opens it, the missive—which begins with *My dearest Aileen*—is a veritable wall of words. It's one of his usual long letters.

What does he intend to do if someone else sees this...?

He may have been trying to cheer himself up, but surely, he's gotten carried away.

Every day, the sight of you without your wedding ring depresses me more and more. I'm wearing mine, you know...

In order to disguise herself as a student, Aileen has temporarily removed her wedding ring. She skips several lines about how sad this makes him.

Evare hasn't made any suspicious moves, but make sure to stay away from him. The very idea that man is a school doctor—he's definitely doing something shameless.

She's fairly sure the art teacher is winning the shamelessness contest by a mile.

At noon today, I'll be meeting with the academy's director. I'll contact you again soon.

Finally, at the very end, he's written something pertinent.

Aileen suspects that the director is the hero of Game 5. She'd thought she might be able to greet him when she transferred in, but as in Mirchetta, it was the student council president who appeared. When she casually inquired, she was told, *"The director is almost never seen. Even at the school, only a handful of people are granted audiences."* It was a very gamelike explanation.

If the director is the boss of an underground organization, it's only natural that he'd be like this in reality as well, but...

Technically, Claude shouldn't be doing this. Emperors don't do their own sleuthing. They have others do it for them. Their role is to take responsibility and make the final decisions. Under the current circumstances, he can't do that, and Aileen finds it utterly humiliating—but this is a critical moment. Their empire has practically been stolen from them.

That means Claude has no choice but to be on the front line in person.

I must do what I can as well. Master Baal's regular contact should come at noon.

Praying there will be some new development or clue, she refolds Claude's letter.

Claude has been walking around the classroom, and as he passes her desk again, he deliberately runs his fingertips along its edge. On his finger, his wedding ring gleams. It's the mate of the one that's currently on a chain around Aileen's neck, hidden beneath her clothes.

Aileen reaches out, pretending it isn't intentional. Just for a moment, she touches Claude's wedding band. Their eyes don't meet, but she sees his lips soften into a smile.

Now he won't get mad when she doesn't appear for her lecture...probably.

At noon, when she sees the pair who've come to the academy's front court to facilitate the contact, Aileen blinks.

"Lady Aileen."

One of them is Sahra, who's carrying a large basket of some sort. She and Aileen are acquainted, and in terms of servants who can travel back and forth between the girls-only school and the palace, she isn't an unexpected choice.

"How are things progressing?"

However, the one who's appeared from behind her is Roxane, and her visit is most definitely unexpected. Instead of the gossamer veil that hides half her face and the red robes that mark her as the principal consort, she's dressed like an ordinary noblewoman.

However, she carries herself with such grace that it's clear at a glance she's someone extraordinary. Not only that, but she's also pregnant.

"Lady Sahra is one thing, but even you're here, Lady Roxane? I'm surprised Master Baal let you leave the harem."

"My pregnancy is advanced enough to be stable, and it's best if I move around a bit. Besides, the palace is rather hectic at the moment. Also, I had business here."

"Has something happened?" Aileen asks.

Sahra looks in the direction of the palace a bit uneasily. "Thieves entered the treasure house and set fire to it last night. No one was badly hurt, but there's a lot that we don't understand. Ares has his hands full with that at the moment."

"In other words, the thieves weren't caught?"

Roxane nods, gazing right back at Aileen. "That's right. In addition, they only wreaked havoc in the treasure house; nothing was taken. However, when Master Baal ordered an investigation of the whole palace, we discovered that materials related to the underground ruin were missing."

Aileen's expression tenses. "Th-then the thieves were after the Daughter of God's holy sarcophagus…? Is that what this is about?"

"If the ruin is involved, then yes, probably. Since the academy's director is here today, I've forced—or rather, *persuaded* Master Baal to let me come as his representative."

She's coerced him into letting her leave. Aileen is rather amazed, but since it wouldn't do for them to stand around talking, Roxane boldly enters the academy.

"As it happens, it was time for our scheduled contact with you, and no men are allowed here. Of course, as the holy king,

Master Baal may enter, but we didn't want to cause more of an uproar than necessary. The body of the Daughter of God is our kingdom's sacred relic, but it isn't as if she has the holy sword."

The holy sword is a weapon the Queendom of Hausel made, based on the sacred sword. While it isn't as powerful as the sacred sword, it can be mass-produced and used by anyone, which makes it very practical. However, mass production is only possible due to the Queendom's technology. Both that technology and the majority of their holy swords were lost in recent battle, and if one breaks, the current Daughter of God is the sole person who can repair it. Now that the sacred sword no longer exists, since the holy sword can use sacred power to attack, it's a rare weapon. To the Kingdom of Ashmael, it's a national treasure that slayed the fiend dragon.

"...Come to think of it, why was the Daughter of God's body preserved in the first place?"

"Probably because she was somebody important, right?" Sahra sounds mystified.

Aileen shakes her head. "If the body had been kept with the holy sword, that would make sense. However, because the holy sword was in the consecrated area where the fiend dragon was sealed, they couldn't do that. In which case, I assume burying her would be the normal thing to do...and they even went out of their way to build an underground tomb instead of keeping her in a place she had a connection to in life. The harem, for example, or the royal palace."

In Game 3, the Daughter of God's ghost appears in the harem. It's probably because Sahra, her successor, is there. Since everything related to the Daughter of God is in the harem, it seems odd that her body is kept elsewhere.

Roxane clears up that question easily. "From what I'm told, preserving her body was the Queendom of Hausel's idea."

Aileen is taken aback by this revelation, and Roxane continues, sounding like a historian, "The holy sword was bestowed on us by the Queendom, and there is a theory that the Daughter of God was also originally from Hausel. Considering the fact that, without her, the holy sword becomes something to be used and cast aside, it's a persuasive theory."

"Then both the holy sword and the Daughter of God were gifts from the Queendom...?"

"I believe that's correct. At the time, this land was poisoned, and it's hard to believe that any humans lived here earlier. The idea that the Queendom sent the Daughter of God and the holy sword in an attempt to reclaim this land, which had been polluted by the fiend dragon, seems more plausible."

The Kingdom of Ashmael, born from the myth of the Daughter of God, was founded after Ellmeyer. At the time of Ashmael's foundation, Amelia Dark was already ruling as Hausel's one and only queen.

In other words, it's very likely that the holy sword, the Daughter of God, and the underground ruin were all prepared by Amelia.

"The ruin under the Divine Maiden Academy was built under the Queendom's guidance, to celebrate the Daughter of God's achievements. The same is true of the holy sarcophagus that holds her remains."

"In other words, both the ruin and the sarcophagus were made with the Queendom's technology?" Aileen asks.

"Yes. I'm told the same is true of the mechanism that will only respond to women directly descended from Ashmael's royal family. There is a record stating it was made that way because Hausel insisted," explains Roxane.

"...Wait just a moment. If it's being preserved by the Queendom of Hausel's technology, then the body of the Daughter of God..."

"It's apparently in extremely good condition. Granted, that's based on testimony from a princess who went to look at it several generations ago, so that report is perhaps two centuries old."

Amelia's real body had been asleep on the Queendom's altar, and if the same principles are at work here, this body may actually be in nearly the same condition as it was in life.

Does that mean it could move, provided it had a soul?

"The world must be purified!"

They've passed through the school building, and just as they step into the central courtyard, they hear a shout. "Our era's Daughter of God was an impostor. Our neighbor Ellmeyer has been corrupted by the power of the demon king and cursed. There could be no greater proof than that red barrier. In addition, the queen of Hausel has passed away, and her queendom has collapsed."

"Just as the land of Ashmael was once steeped in poison, the world is being defiled. We must come together and resurrect the true Daughter of God, and it must be done now—!"

A group is giving an impassioned speech on the lawn in the courtyard. Someone thrusts a flyer at Sahra, who's walking a little ahead. "The World Unity sect," Roxane says indifferently.

"I've never seen them before... Are they popular here?"

"What, the World Unity sect? They're basically playing, and it's largely limited to the school. This is the Divine Maiden Academy, after all, and worship of the Daughter of God is particularly fervent here. However, Master Baal has been concerned that the events in Ellmeyer have made them bolder." The unsettling appearance of that red barrier over Imperial Ellmeyer has accelerated the development of a new religion. When Aileen's gaze falls to the ground, Roxane frowns. "It isn't Ellmeyer's fault, Lady Aileen."

"Even so, we genuinely are causing trouble for Ashmael. Besides, the idea that the first Daughter of God was from the Queendom gives me a very bad feeling..."

"Since they worship the Daughter of God, this involves our country as well. It's nothing any one person should have to take responsibility for. That goes for you as well, Sahra."

Roxane's remark makes Aileen glance over at Sahra, who's still holding the flyer.

She is this era's Daughter of God, but no one looks to her for help. After the way she disgraced herself, that's only natural, but being treated as a fake can't be pleasant for her, either.

...And yet she smiles. "I know, Miss Roxane. I'll just do my best at what I can. I won't say I can do what I can't."

She hadn't been able to risk her life to repair the holy sword and save her kingdom, and yet she did so to repair the sacred sword and save Lilia's life. Still, she probably can't call herself the Daughter of God anymore.

Roxane nods, acknowledging her resolve. "I'm counting on you."

"Huh...? R-really? Do you really mean it?! Even though I got water and disinfectant confused the other day?!"

"...Provided you calm down just a little," Roxane adds wryly.

Aileen thumps Sahra on the shoulder. "Pull yourself together. Luc tells me you intend to study medicine. The kingdom's first female doctor will bear much greater responsibility toward future generations than the Daughter of God would."

Sahra squeezes her hands into fists. "Yes, I'll do my best!"

"Refrain from overdoing it. When you get too excited, the results are never good."

"Oh, you know, I can see that," Aileen says.

"What?! That's mean!"

The flyer exhorting the Daughter of God's resurrection slips from Sahra's hand. As Aileen and Roxane make their way deeper into the school building, Sahra runs after them. When she catches up, she sails right past them before turning around. "By the way, what is Estella doing?"

"Oh, she's probably..." Aileen takes a look around. "Yes, there she is."

The cafeteria is bustling with people. Estella is in the exact opposite direction, in an old gazebo in the middle of the rather cluttered courtyard, eating a roll purchased from the school's shop.

Naturally, she's all alone.

"So she doesn't eat lunch with her friends... Maybe she's just not the type. In that sense, Estella's rather like you, Miss Roxane."

"...Sahra, what is that supposed to mean?"

"That's perfect, though! Let's all have lunch together!"

Apparently, lunch is what's in Sahra's basket. Before they can stop her, she runs off. She's as guileless as always. Or maybe *thoughtless* would be more accurate.

Aileen is rather shocked. Beside her, Roxane sighs. "Surely, there are times when the girl would prefer to eat alone... Although, I suppose I needn't worry about anyone thinking she's the Daughter of God if she does things like that."

"I noticed you haven't tried to use Lady Sahra as a check on the World Unity sect."

"Of course not. After all, *she's no longer the Daughter of God.*"

She's speaking in the political sense, but it's clear she also wants Sahra to be free to live her own life.

"Does Master Baal suspect the World Unity sect? In the palace robbery, I mean."

"Yes, actually. One of the reasons I've come in person is to speak with the director about it. They may have begun looking for a way to enter the underground ruin in earnest, in search of the Daughter of God's sarcophagus. I'm told the royal family's genealogical chart has disappeared as well."

"Would they have taken that in the hope of finding a living female descendant of the Ashmael bloodline?"

"I would imagine so. However, I believe the attempt will end as a fool's errand. Master Baal is an only child, and the previous holy king had no sisters. The king before that had an older sister, but she passed away years ago... If this child is a girl, she will fit the requirements, but..." Roxane strokes her belly, which is still barely noticeable.

Aileen presses her lips together tightly. "Lady Roxane. As a purely hypothetical question..."

"Yes? What is it?"

Roxane is an intelligent woman, more than suited to being the principal consort. Trusting in this, Aileen begins. "...if Estella happened to be Master Baal's illegitimate child, what would you do?"

"I would adopt her and raise her as the first princess, of course."

She answered immediately, with no hesitation or consternation.

That's a relief. "I'm not certain yet. Please don't mention any of this to Estella."

Roxane blinks, understanding that this conversation is not, in fact, purely hypothetical. "Very well. In that case, I will investigate her origins with that in mind. I doubt Master Baal will confess honestly…and something about this does ring a bell."

"Gracious, really?"

"One of the names Master Baal is considering for the child I'm carrying is Estella."

"That's…difficult for both of you, isn't it?"

"It certainly is."

Nodding once, Roxane goes over to Estella, who's bewildered by the lunch Sahra has begun to unpack. Roxane chides Sahra, then speaks gently to Estella. There's a very tranquil tenderness in her profile.

Even if Estella does turn out to be Baal's love child, things will probably work out. The fact that he's considering naming Roxane's child Estella is worth strangling him over, but if Baal himself isn't aware, then there isn't much to fuss about.

"That's the principal consort, and the Daughter of God—Nah, maybe that should be former Daughter of God? Either way, it's quite a sight."

A shadow falls over her, and she turns with a start. Lanky Evare grins, shading his eyes with a hand. "Afternoon, Miss Aileen. The sun in this country sure is intense. Be careful you don't get heatstroke."

A little behind Evare, Machina stands like a statue, immobile and unblinking. Her eyes are as lightless as ever.

"There was somethin' I wanted to check on. See, Professor Claude got in the way earlier."

Aileen is flustered, but Evare ignores it. He points to Estella. "That girl, the one who transferred in with you. Is Estella her real name?"

His question isn't what Aileen was expecting at all, and her eyes widen. Putting a hand to his chin, Evare broods. "I hear she's got amnesia. Which means there's no point in askin' her 'bout it."

"...Why would you ask me?"

"Well, you transferred in together. On the principal consort's recommendation. You're *close*. Right?"

What he says is completely innocuous, but the exaggerated way he's said it makes it sound as if he's implying something.

"Is the question of whether her name is really Estella that important?"

"Well, sure. Names matter a whole bunch. For example, there's stuff people wouldn't pick up on if your name wasn't *Aileen* and Professor Claude's name wasn't *Claude*."

"......"

There's no telling where he's gotten his information, but this man is clearly convinced that she and Claude are the empress and emperor of Ellmeyer. Of course, it also isn't something that's impossible to piece together given all the information.

Evare is nonchalant, as if he doesn't feel the need to hide anything.

"Those names, black hair and red eyes, a gorgeous blond, the fact that you've got an in with some big shots, and the stuff that's been happenin' recently... None of that info's a huge deal by itself. Put it all together, though, and what you've got is certainty."

"So the name Estella is part of that certainty for you?" Aileen asks. She's dropped all pretense of speaking to him as a teacher.

Evare gives her an easygoing smile. "Yup. Between this and that, I think that's probably it. Still, names can trick you real easy. It happens all the time: You hear that so-and-so who shouldn't be here is here, and then you meet 'em, and they're somebody completely different. So I'm bein' cautious, see. It's secondhand intel, and it's not like I know what she looks like."

"...You know who she is?"

"Nah, nah, other way around: I *want* to know who she is. Heck, maybe she got nothin' to do with anythin'." Evare laughs, waving his hand in denial.

He has information about Estella that Aileen doesn't have. All he knows is her name and some hearsay, though, and he doesn't know what the real one looks like. As a result, he can't figure out whether this is the same Estella he's heard about—is that what this is?

...Lady Lilia said that Evare, the final boss of Game 5, was the founder of the World Unity sect. It's dangerous to assume that events in reality will match the game, but...

Documents detailing the underground ruin and the royal family's genealogical chart have been stolen from Ashmael's palace. It seems sensible to assume that the World Unity sect was behind it. That meant either Evare did it himself or it was done on his orders. If that's the case, he can't ignore Estella's identity—or more specifically, her origins.

What Aileen doesn't understand is how he's tied this matter to Estella's bloodline. Roxane said the genealogical chart wouldn't help. Even if the chart holds some sort of hidden information that only Evare will recognize, the thieves struck the palace just yesterday. Could he have discovered Estella's origins in such a brief span of time?

Isn't that the sort of conclusion he could only have arrived at by working backward, as Aileen had done, based on knowledge he already had? For example, the fact that Estella is the villainess and that she may be part of Ashmael's royal family?

...He can't possibly know about the game, can he? No, not possible. If he did, he'd know he was the final boss and destined to be defeated, and he'd avoid following the script... Mentioning hearsay means he learned these things from someone else. Could Charles have told him?

Either way, this man definitely knows something Aileen does not. In particular, she recognizes the unsettling way he has of throwing up a smoke screen in his conversations. She saw the same thing during her fight with Amelia, the woman who knew both past and future. Unbidden, her gaze goes to the girl who wears that woman's face. "...Who is she?"

"Huh? Where'd that come from? Don't go changin' the subject. I told you, she's my assistant."

"Have you known her long?"

"Uh, lessee, how long's it been...? Maybe three years or so?"

"Dr. Evare! Would you attend tonight's séance in the chapel with us? The divine maiden says she'll channel the voice of the Daughter of God who sleeps in the holy sarcophagus!" calls a student from behind them.

Evare shrugs, turning around. "What're you tryin' to do, breakin' the rules right out in public? You ain't allowed to leave the dorms after dinner. You've got a curfew. Get goin' now!"

"But we'll be able to hear the founder speak directly!"

"If you really do believe in the Daughter of God, then you gotta follow the rules. C'mon."

"But how could a séance where we hear the Daughter of God speak be against the rules?! That can't be right!"

A group of girls chimes in, agreeing with her. While Evare's trying to wrangle them, Aileen slips away to the gazebo. Roxane and the others have heard the girls' shrill voices; they're looking in her direction, seeming worried. Aileen smiles and brings it up before they can: "It looks as if things may get a bit noisy. Shall we go elsewhere?"

"Yes, that sounds wise… I never dreamed they were holding actual séances. I must report this to Master Baal."

"I was invited to that, too." Estella takes a piece of paper from her pocket. It's a handbill, neatly folded into quarters, with a time and place written on it.

When Aileen sees the sheet, she grimaces. "I didn't receive anything of the sort."

"The girl who tried to recruit me on my first day here gave it to me just now. Apparently, this séance will be held on an unprecedented scale. She said the founder is going to bring a divine maiden."

In the game, the divine maiden was Estella. However, Estella's memories are still missing.

…Someone must have taken her place, Aileen thinks.

Sahra peeks in at Estella's hand, reading the flyer. "'The noble divine maiden will hear the voice of the first Daughter of God and open the door to the underground ruin…' What? Is this real? Aren't princesses of Ashmael the only ones who can open that door?"

"—I think I'll attend this séance," Estella says.

Aileen stares at her, startled. She doesn't know whether the divine maiden can hear the voice of the Daughter of God or not, but if Estella actually is Baal's love child, she'll be able to open the door to the ruin.

"Why would you do that? Is it something to do with your memories? Have you recalled something about the World Unity sect…or its founder, or the divine maiden?" Roxane asks calmly. She seems to have picked up on the same possibility as Aileen.

Estella hesitates for a moment, then looks up at Roxane. She seems unusually unsure of herself.

"...Is the Daughter of God's body really *still* there?"

It's an entirely unexpected question. Blinking, Roxane responds with a careful question of her own. "What do you mean?"

"I, um... I'm sorry. I don't know. I seem to remember telling someone that the Daughter of God's body was *no longer there*... I saw them leave for the underground ruin...and then I..." Estella winces, as if her head has begun to ache.

Beside her, Sahra gets flustered. "You mustn't push yourself."

"I-I'm all right. Only...unless I remember what it is I need to do quickly, I feel as if I won't make it in time..."

"I understand your concern. I'll speak with Master Baal, and we shall check at the proper time. Since this involves your memories, I will arrange for you to come along when we do. In the meanwhile, you mustn't participate in suspicious gatherings like this one."

Roxane has made the right decision. Aileen has no objections, and Estella gives a small nod. "...All right. I won't get involved with the World Unity sect."

"Let's have lunch, then! Okay?" Sahra's voice is intentionally buoyant, and it resets the mood as intended.

However, from the look in Estella's eyes, she's come to some sort of decision. Neither Aileen nor Roxane miss the fact that she's put the flyer back into her pocket.

On Aileen's invitation, the outrageous professor has boldly stolen into the female students' dormitory room at night. "I'd hoped you'd called me here to apologize for ignoring my summons earlier today," he says.

Aileen has been pretending to sleep on the lowest bunk bed, waiting for Claude's visit, and he's pushed her down onto it. She looks disgusted. "Master Claude. I believe you may be enjoying life as a professor far too much."

"*Professor* Claude."

Ignoring her husband's incorrigible demand, Aileen asks, "Has Estella gone to the chapel?"

"Yes. Apparently, there are adherents on the faculty as well. Tonight's assembly is an open secret. Everyone's there."

"I see… In that case, let us go after her."

"We have a little time."

"No, we do not."

"Can't you listen to your professor?"

"I am about to get very cross with you."

"Even though I borrowed the clothing we'll need to attend the séance?" Claude shows her two supremely suspicious-looking hooded cloaks made of dark-purple fabric. Hooded cloaks are quite common, but that color would be very hard to mimic. Do all participants wear these?

"Don't you think I deserve a bit of a reward?"

Claude is looking down at her, seeming entertained, so Aileen smiles back at him. He can't possibly think his wife hasn't caught on, can he? "I'd expect no less of you, Master Claude. And? Where did you find these? Don't tell me you asked one of the students. Or was one of your female colleagues kind to you?"

"…We should probably hurry."

Dropping a light kiss on Aileen's chilly forehead, Claude gets up and hands her a cloak, as he should have done in the first place.

Aileen gets up as well, pulling the cloak around herself. "If it is an open secret, I assume we may leave through the door," she murmurs as she puts Claude's cloak on him. He waited for her to do it, as if that's only natural.

Putting an arm around her waist, Claude opens the window. "This way is shorter."

"Wait— Master Claude, this is the third floor! You can't use magic now…!" But by the time she says that, Claude has already gone out the window, grabbed the branch of a nearby tree, found footholds on its trunk, and made a skillful landing on the ground, all while holding Aileen close.

"The chapel's that way."

"……"

Aileen looks stunned. Claude's eyes return to her, and he smiles mischievously. "Have you fallen for me all over again?"

"…No! I was aware that you were skilled in the martial arts!"

"Why are you being stubborn about this?" Claude chuckles deep in his throat. Escaping from his arm, Aileen smacks her red cheeks, trying to cover the fact that she's blushing as she hurries down the path.

It's nearly time for lights out, and yet girls with lanterns are standing here and there, marking the way. Evidently, it's true that there are believers among the professors. Even Claude, who's clearly male, joins the crowd that's moving toward the chapel without drawing any complaints.

The ancient flagstone road is buried under the throng. There's no way all these people can be students at the Divine Maiden Academy.

"…Are there are outsiders here as well?"

"Apparently. I heard the principal consort and the director talking today. They said that several students are recruiting outsiders."

So Claude has been diligent about gathering information as well. With a start, Aileen looks back at him. "By the way, Master Claude, how was the director? You did meet, didn't you?"

"Yes. She was a cheerful woman with beautiful white hair," Claude says briefly.

Aileen stares at him. "...Pardon? A woman? Th-the director wasn't a young man...?"

"I'm pretty sure that wasn't a man. At the very least, you couldn't call her young. Even standing seemed to hurt her. She was complaining to the principal consort that she wanted to step down in favor of her successor already."

If the woman spoke with Roxane as well, it isn't likely that Claude saw wrong or that he was taken in somehow.

The hero was the director because he was the boss of the organization that ran the school... Has that changed? Or perhaps the era's slightly different?

Realizing that the hero may be the successor the woman mentioned, she tries again. "Who is this successor? Were they there with her?"

"Yes, I did greet him. She says he's still only three, though, so there's no telling whether he'll actually remember me."

"Three?!" Aghast, Aileen hastily claps a hand over her mouth. *Wait, hang on. That's the hero of Game 5...? It can't be, can it?*

There's simply no way a three-year-old could be the hero of an *otome* game. If Estella is part of that generation, he should be either her age or a little older. He'd have to be about Charles's age, at the very least. More than anything, the game's package showed a rather intellectual-looking young man and most certainly not a toddler.

What can it mean?

Something's not right. Between Estella asking if the Daughter of God's body is *still* there and Evare knowing about Estella, something isn't…

"She really is here," Claude murmurs as soon as they enter the chapel. Pulled back to the present, Aileen looks around.

She finds her almost immediately. Estella is sitting toward the front.

If they're going to split hairs, Estella said she didn't intend to get involved with the World Unity sect, but she never said she wouldn't attend the séance. Turns out she's rather stubborn and once she's made up her mind, there's no stopping her.

"Lady Roxane promised she'd investigate on her behalf. How could she ignore all that?" Aileen asks.

"When it comes to this sort of behavior, I really don't think you can talk."

"Did you say something, Master Claude?"

"No, nothing. Since we have the chance, let's watch for a little. I've cleared it with Baal already."

While her attention was elsewhere, Claude has circled around behind her. When she looks up at him, he smiles, puts his arms low around her waist, and rests his chin on her shoulder.

"And here are the noble founder and the divine maiden, right off the bat."

From the entrance to the restless venue, Aileen hears the clear peal of small bells.

A man in a hooded white cloak steps into the throng of purple-cloaked adherents, walking straight down the central aisle to the altar at the back. A smaller figure in a similar white cloak follows him, holding a staff with bells hanging from it. They ring in time with the figure's steps, and silence spreads like widening ripples.

The founder takes up his position in front of an enormous pipe organ, on a platform surrounded by a semicircular railing.

There's a brief pause.

"—Friends, thanks for comin'."

Aileen has been a little nervous since this whole event started, but at the sound of that voice, her face goes impossibly tense. *The founder's identity is blindingly obvious! And the divine maiden—that's Machina, isn't it?!*

Perhaps this is part of the open secret, too. Flashing his usual smile from beneath that hood, Evare begins his speech. He clearly has no intention of hiding anything.

"I'm real glad to see all y'all together like this. I still have a hard time believin' I've got a big ol' crowd here listenin' to me. Just six months back, I was totally alone in the world, and all I could do was watch as the world crumbled. I tell ya, this is a real shock. Even if I did rig the game a bit."

Six months back. Rig. Although her tension almost disappeared for a moment, those words brought it right back. When Aileen looks around, the whole assembly is listening intently to Evare. No one stirs.

"...Master Claude. Was Professor Evare staffed here recently as well?"

"Not that I've heard. I was told he'd been on the faculty for ages."

"I'm not pullin' the wool over your eyes, though. I mean, you're just gonna forget me and everythin' I say anyhow, but this is the real deal. The world has been defiled—or rather, it's gonna be."

A shadow seems to fall over Evare's bright eyes.

"It all started with the Kingdom of Ashmael. An evil god who'd been sealed by the Queendom of Hausel long, long ago was reborn as a human and awakened. Evil gods eat the darkness in humans. Once the water dragon was soiled with human malice, it made for a fine feast. If he opened the underground ruin, used the Daughter of God's body to break the seal on the fiend dragon by pullin' out the holy sword, and ate that dragon when it resurrected, he'd get his powers as an evil god back. As y'all know, though, the fiend dragon's gone and become the Holy Dragon Consort. The evil god doesn't have enough food to revive. He never even woke up."

Slowly, Aileen draws a breath, then exhales. *Wait. He's talking about Game 5...isn't he?*

However, it sounds as if Evare is describing events that should occur in the game beyond this point, and a present in which they've already failed to happen.

"The world has a proper shape, a form it should take. That'd be destiny. Human darkness defiles the world, and by takin' on that darkness, the evil god would end up savin' the world. That right there was foreshadowin' that was gonna save the future."

Evare pushes his glasses up on his nose, then spreads his arms wide, reaching toward the ceiling.

"And yet that never happened! Each of the separate causes were tiny li'l things. Like the Holy Dragon Consort. That happened 'cause the demon king became emperor of Ellmeyer."

Claude's arms tighten around Aileen, pulling her closer.

"The demon king got to be emperor because the Maid of the Cursed Sword stole the sacred sword from the proper Maid."

Aileen squeezes Claude's arms in response.

"*Conquerin' destiny.* That's a wonderful phrase. As a result, the world's chargin' toward the future, mistakes and all. The Daughter of God, who purifies the world; the Saint of Salvation, who fosters it; the Maid of the Sacred Sword, who opens it up—they're all gone. Even the enemies that need defeatin' are gone. The future's full of nothin', buried in white ash. If you're born into a future like that, what do you do? Should you just give up? Even though you did nothin' wrong?"

Evare raises his head. There's a twisted smile on his lips. "There's somebody here who should take responsibility, but it ain't me. Ain't that right?"

Everyone in the chapel turns to look at them. Eyes glittering with purpose, they reach out to grab Claude and Aileen. Claude swings his sword without removing it from its sheath, knocking several of their assailants unconscious, but there are too many of them.

"I-is Professor Evare controlling all these people?"

"Probably. I should have caught on sooner."

Tossing Aileen over his shoulder, Claude kicks the chairs over, retreating into the cleared space. "The school was already under his control. —Baal. Just inside the academy is fine, but take down the barrier!"

In response, Claude's earring shines. An instant later, his magic knocks away the people who've been trying to mob them, along with their chairs. At the same time, soldiers flood into the chapel. They're Ashmael's troops.

A shadow falls over Aileen's vision. Baal is floating in midair, arms crossed, looking down at them.

"Don't summon the king of a country as if he's your personal servant, you fool. —Arrest everyone here and take them outside!"

"Nah, we can't have that. Don't you care what happens to this girl?"

The voice is quiet, but it carries well, and everyone freezes.

Since most of the crowd has been blown out of the way, they now have a clear view of the pipe organ, and Evare in front of it. Next to him, Machina stands with her white hood removed. Although she's as expressionless as ever, she's twisted Estella's arm up behind her back and is covering her mouth.

"It's a real cliché, but I've got a hostage. Nobody move. Let's have you clear those soldiers out, too."

Aileen and the others glare at him, but Evare shrugs. "Aw, don't look so scary. What else am I s'posed to do, huh? I'm up against the demon king and the holy king here."

"Oh-ho. So you do understand that much. For all that, you don't seem worried."

"Well, I mean, it ain't like I'm up against Luciel in his prime. Now *that* was ugly."

Claude's eyebrows twitch.

Evare gives a thin smile. "Old stories like that don't matter. Let's get this job done, eh? Machina."

Machina tries to drag Estella with her, but the girl digs her feet in, refusing to budge.

Evare shrugs. "They tell me your memories took off without you. You must wanna know who you are by now."

"Wh-what I want to know…is…"

"There's a *real* easy way to find out. *Lessee if you can open the door to the underground ruin.*"

For a moment, Estella freezes.

Baal sounds disgusted. "It won't open. Starting a dubious religion won't help you. Only direct female descendants of Ashmael's royal family can open that. If there's another way to do it, we'd like to know it ourselves."

"I guess seein's believin', then."

Evare grabs Estella's arm. The girl winces, and Aileen shouts at him, "Don't hurt her!"

"Hey, it's fine. If it don't work, it don't. It'll be my fault, too, for just followin' the stories and not checkin' her face properly. I had no idea you'd end up bein' such a key person, though."

Evare's claim that the villainess is not a key person shows he really has no knowledge of the game.

In that case, why does he have his suspicions about Estella's bloodline? Ignoring Aileen's glare, Evare goes on in a laid-back way. "There wasn't time, and most of all, that prince kept his guard up tight. You're so loved."

"What…are you talking about? What prince…?" Estella asks faintly, glaring at Evare.

Evare just keeps talking. For some reason, he turns to the pipe organ and begins removing the keyboard. "It looks like this era is where it all starts. I can't go back any further. The Queendom of Hausel's only just broken up, so I figured it'd work out somehow, but even Mother's spare didn't stick around. I misread that one bad. On top of that, although Lilia Reinoise would've been a sure thing, she got locked up in Ellmeyer."

"Was that barrier over Ellmeyer your doing?" Claude asks in a low, irritated voice.

Evare smiles brightly. "What're you talkin' 'bout? Your son did that."

He isn't even trying to hide the fact that he knows Charles.

"It's always possible that you made him do it."

"Egged him on, you mean? C'mon, don't talk like that; what

will people think? That boy's still a kid, but he's smart. Now then…"

Evare steps back. The pipe organ begins to play on its own, swinging open from the center to reveal a smooth, jet-black door that reaches all the way to the ceiling.

"Master Baal, is that the door to the underground ruin?"

"That's right. The door to the holy sarcophagus. It won't open, though. It's impossible." There's a stern look on Baal's face.

Grabbing Estella's wrist, Evare pulls her over to stand in front of the door, which has no handle. "Lessee if this thing opens or not."

"Estella, don't! You mustn't open it!" Aileen screams, although even she doesn't know why. She shouts the warning because she suspects the door will open.

"You wanna know who you are, don'cha? Open that, and we'll know one thing for sure: your bloodline."

"Why did you come here?! To open that door?! You know that isn't it!!"

Estella turns back. Her eyes are wavering. Evare grabs her shoulders, makes her open her hand, then presses it to the door. "If you open this up, you'll save your prince."

As if to show that Estella's heart has tilted in a certain direction, a heavy *clunk* echoes through the room.

A fissure of light runs across the surface of the black door, tracing the outline of a square. That section recedes, as if the door is being reconfigured.

"It's…opening? Impossible… Wait. Then is that girl…?" Baal murmurs.

Estella sits down on the floor with a *thump*. "What…did I…?"

"Thanks. To show my gratitude, lemme tell you somethin'. Your name."

Evare grabs the front of Estella's cloak and hauls her up off the floor. She hangs in midair; he's practically strangling her.

"You're Estella Shah Ashmael."

Baal gasps. Evare shoots him a mocking glance. "That's your dad over there."

"What are you doing to Estella, Evare?!"

The ceiling of the chapel explodes, and a black shadow flies in. *Tsk*ing in irritation, Evare shoves Estella away. Catching the girl in midair, the boy with the eye patch descends to stand in front of Aileen and the others.

His black hair streams in the wind, showing just one red eye. Then he shouts at Estella, "And you! Why are you with Evare?! What happened while I was shut up in there?!"

"Wh-who...are...you...?" As she looks at the boy—this screaming child who's come out of nowhere and is holding her like a newlywed bride—Estella winces as if she's fighting a headache.

"Charles! Estella has lost her memories!" Aileen shouts.

Charles blinks at her, but a blast of magic is already bearing down on him from behind.

"You're a prince, all right. Very cool. Who woulda figured you'd break through Luciel's barrier that fast?!"

"Charles!"

Pushing Estella into Baal's arms, Charles turns back. A complicated geometric pattern appears in front of him, expanding vertically and horizontally. It's a barrier. Evare's magic bested even Luciel, but Charles blocks it all as if it's nothing. When he speaks, his voice is quiet. "What are you trying to do, Evare? You can't possibly believe you can kill me."

"'Course not. I just wanna get rid of the lot behind you."

"That wasn't the deal. You said you wouldn't touch my family."

Evare laughs a little. "But those folks won't just let me go, will they?"

The man hurls another, more powerful blast of magic at him. Clicking his tongue, Charles expands his barrier even further to block it, then glances back at them. "What are you doing? Get out of here, now!"

"We can't. We still don't have any idea what's going on. Besides, Baal is stunned. Abruptly finding out you have an illegitimate child can do that."

"Huh? Who's illegitimate…? Oh, right. She's got amnesia, huh? For the love of—! Okay, listen up. That girl's a genuine princess of Ashmael, the daughter of Holy King Baal and his principal consort, Roxane!"

Baal, who's caught Estella but hasn't managed to say anything, twitches.

Claude tilts his head in a rather laid-back way. "It's true that Consort Roxane is pregnant, but she hasn't given birth yet. What is her daughter doing here?"

"That's what I want to know! I don't care if you don't believe me—just get out of here!"

"Are you telling us she's from the future? And if she is, who are you?"

Although Charles has been screeching at them, that makes him shut up. Claude keeps going. "You wouldn't be my child with Aileen, would you?"

Aileen does a startled double take. Refusing to look at her, Charles shouts, "Who cares about that?!"

"...I see. I think I understand." Claude draws his sword.

Wordlessly, Baal pushes Estella onto Aileen. "...We don't understand this one bit, but very well."

The two men have begun to radiate something ominous, and Aileen's expression tenses.

""Whatever's going on, it's that man's fault!""

The demon king and the holy king can harmonize at the oddest of times, and their voices synchronize perfectly. Leaping out from Charles's barrier, they head straight for Evare.

Evare laughs, putting some distance between himself and the two of them. "That's one heck of a false charge."

"What false charge?! You've been openly attacking us for the past several minutes!"

"To begin with, no acquaintance of that annoying imitation god of a father could be anyone decent."

"Well dang, I can't argue with that." A mysterious light glows in Evare's eyes, and he intercepts Claude and Baal's attacks, forming a wall of magic with his right hand and a wall of sacred power with his left. "There are opponents even you two can't beat, though."

Above Evare's head, a girl in a white hood leaps into view. It's Machina. The bells on her long staff ring, and it transforms into a grim reaper's huge sickle.

"! Claude, get back!" Baal steps out in front, knocking the sickle back with a barrier. Expressionless, Machina spins once, then caroms off the wall of the chapel, heading straight for them again. That sickle is clearly aimed at Estella.

"Estella!" Charles is the first to react. Darting in between the two of them, he grabs Machina's wrist. Magic and sacred power crackle, both scattering sparks and repelling the other. "Machina, she's got nothing to do with this! Evare, call her off!"

"What, bossin' me around? You're born royalty, all right; you really dunno how to ask people for favors. Or are you tryin' to look good in front of your fiancée?"

Estella has been watching the flying sparks with a dazed look on her face, but that remark makes her eyes widen.

Charles winces, then shouts back angrily, "There's no way! Our parents decided we were engaged, that's all!"

"Oh yeah, that's right. You said you broke off the engagement. Whoops." Dodging Claude's sword, Evare sits down on the head of the goddess statue that is beside the platform, then smiles. "So what's Princess Estella doin' here then, hmm?"

"How should I know?! We're strangers now! She's nothing to do with this— Never has been and never will be!!"

A sharp noise rings out. Estella slapped Charles across the face.

The sound is loud enough to drown out the scattering magic and the noise of the fight.

In the hushed chapel, Charles slowly puts a hand to his struck cheek and turns around.

"What do you mean, 'nothing to do with this'? How dare you say that to your fiancée?!" Fists clenched, Estella looks Charles right in the eye and shouts, "This isn't what I want, either, but it's a diplomatic issue! And yet you keep whining about it like a spoiled child— How can you call yourself the crown prince of Ellmeyer?!"

"...W-woman..." Charles sounds stunned.

Estella's eyebrows come down. "Don't call me 'woman.'"

"S-so those lost memories were a lie?! You tricked me!" Charles yells back.

However, Estella stands her ground. "I haven't tricked you. My memories returned just now. The disgustingly irresponsible things you're saying made me very, very angry."

"Oh, they did, huh?! Then go home right this minute! It's not like you know how I feel…!"

"I'd like to send those words right back to you. I can't leave like this. I don't even know how."

"Huh?! How did you get here, then?!"

"What about you? How did you reach the past?"

"I asked first! Nobody put you up to this, did they?!"

"Let me change my question, then: What are you trying to achieve by doing something this selfish?"

"Don't just push the conversation along! I told you, answer my question first! How did you even get here?!"

"Is that girl the reason you broke off our engagement?"

Charles abruptly falls silent. He's still holding Machina's wrist. Just a moment ago, he seemed to be protecting Estella from Machina, but now it's beginning to look as if he's protecting Machina from Estella.

"I-it's…nothing to do with you… I, um, broke off…our engagement anyway…," he retorts weakly.

Estella's gaze cools rapidly. Charles seems to pick up on the danger in the air; he lets go of Machina's wrist but looks at a spot on the floor off to the side, pressing his lips together tightly. For some reason, Machina doesn't move; she just stands there, her face blank.

It's obvious what sort of situation this is, though. Watching the three stand there at an impasse, Baal mutters to Claude. "In other words, should we consider this…one of those matters?"

"...And to think he's my son. Pathetic."

"Hey, why not? It's charmin'. Besides, bein' able to get that worked up in a situation like this... The beauty of youth, huh?"

Just as everyone's eyes snap back to Evare, there's a new development.

Behind him, light floods from the door to the underground ruin. It's fully open. Reflexively, Aileen crosses her arms in front of her face, shielding her eyes.

"She's finally awake."

Particles of light erupt from the ruin, making the night sky shine as if it were broad daylight.

There, in the midst of light that seems to herald the dawn, is a girl. She's dressed in the style of Ashmael, asleep inside a vast wall of ice.

As the light dissolves the ice, her jet-black hair gleams. Her slim, athletic body seems rather androgynous, like a knight.

Aileen knows that figure and face all too well. So does Claude.

"Mother...?!"

The ice evaporates. Those long eyelashes tremble, then rise. Her hazy eyes are violet: the sign of one who possesses sacred power.

The twin sister of Amelia Dark. The second Maid of the Sacred Sword, who has been despised in history as the Maid of the Cursed Sword—Grace Dark.

This girl's face is identical to hers.

Abruptly, Luciel presses a hand to his chest. Someone's just broken through his barrier and escaped.

Instead of staying inside the barrier and acting as the barrier's core, he was currently outside it. He knew the weakened barrier wouldn't hold forever, but this is a lot sooner than he was expecting.

Seriously, who is that boy?

The youth calls himself Charles, and he's just like Claude—and Luciel. Based on the magic's movement, he seems to be flying to Ashmael. It's probably because that's where Aileen and the others are. Grace should be there as well.

However, Luciel keeps flying in a different direction. He glances down. "The floating palace is really in the Queendom of Hausel? ...You're sure?"

"But of course! If the game's started, that's where it should be!" the girl in his right arm says brightly.

"And how would you know a thing like that?"

"There's no point in asking. The woman's not normal," says the girl in his left arm before the other one can answer. This girl is the one who saved Luciel, though, and as far as he's concerned, she's plenty abnormal herself.

On second thought, the god of demons is currently headed for the Queendom of Hausel with the Maid of the Sacred Sword and the Saint of Salvation—former or otherwise—in tow. This situation is plenty abnormal to begin with.

Luciel has been pulled along for the ride by these two ever since Serena's power roused him. Lilia in particular has managed to make him share lots of stories, such as the fact that he and Evare are old acquaintances who were cast down by the creator god, and that the mischief-loving Evare got himself sealed by the

Queendom when he tried to mess with them in the distant past. Lilia even picked up on the fact that Luciel's been worried about his future with Grace, and he asked her for advice.

They, in turn, explained that the humans inside the barrier were only sleeping and waking them up could wait until they knew what had happened, so he did as they told him and borrowed Serena's power to get the three of them through Charles's barrier.

"In Game 5's story, Evare was reborn into the Queendom's bloodline as a prince of Hausel to slip out of his seal. The Queendom was also going strong in the game. That means if the floating palace disappeared when the game started, it's a safe bet that it's in the Queendom! The only thing is, Evare can't use the fiend dragon to regain his power as an evil god at this point, since it doesn't exist, so I don't know what he's actually going to do."

"All that is news to me… You're right that Evare's not the type to just let the Queendom be after they trounced him like that, but how would you know—?"

"Don't worry about it!"

That doesn't seem like a reasonable demand. While Luciel is trying to figure out how to respond, Serena snorts. "Never mind that—he's a prince of Hausel? Meaning he's your brother? The Queendom doesn't really have a royal family, but you're technically their princess."

"If it's like the game, then yes. Only Amelia Dark wasn't decent, so there's no telling how she procured that boy."

Amelia. The name makes Luciel's heart twinge. Still, he's aware that he probably shouldn't think that way. Especially because Grace will laugh and tell him he's been beaten hollow.

He hasn't pulled that thorn out of his heart yet, though, and he hasn't managed to really consider his future with Grace, either.

"It's fine," Lilia says, and Luciel realizes he's been hanging his head. "Both Grace and Amelia will be fine."

"...How can you be so sure? If Grace stays like this, she may disappear..."

Human souls are reincarnated. Ordinarily, Grace should have been reborn as someone else long ago. However, Amelia kept her prisoner, while Luciel—an imitation god—had poured everything into a desperate wish. Between those two things, her soul has stuck around for too long.

As a result, Grace is on the cusp of vanishing. Just like Amelia, who was destroyed, soul and all.

Things would be different if her body was around, but Grace's head was lost after Amelia cut it off. They might find a different body that's compatible with her soul, but that will effectively be the same as reincarnating: She'll be a different person. She may not even remember Luciel.

All the options are hard for Luciel to swallow, so he's been unable to make a move in any direction. Even though Grace has probably steeled herself already for what's to come.

All I wanted was to see her one more time.

Luciel gives a wistful smile. "In the end, Amelia's getting what she wanted. She's taking Grace from me."

"Isn't that because you're pathetic?" Serena says.

That's the last thing he was expecting to hear, and Lilia gives an innocent shriek of laughter. "That's true! You're always complaining about that side character, Serena, but the reason you don't steal Rachel away from him is because even if he's a side character, he's really got it together."

"I have no idea why Rachel just came up there."

"That's how it is, though, isn't it? That means there's still a chance."

"A chance?" Luciel asks.

Lilia looks back at him mischievously. "A chance to improve her opinion of you. Hint: Why don't you try granting Amelia's wish for once?"

"Amelia's wish?"

"I bet that's what Grace wants, too. —Say, is that the Queendom?"

When he faces forward, through the clouds, he catches glimpses of the small island that was once known as paradise.

The Queendom of Hausel is made up of islands of varying sizes scattered across the ocean like water lilies. The only thing on the small central island is the site where the palace once stood: an expanse of bare white earth in the vivid blue sea.

Luciel is very nearly a god, and even for him, teleporting here is difficult. That's why he had to fly.

I had quite a time sneaking in here, long ago.

Descending, he alights on the white sandy beach. Setting the two girls on their feet, Luciel tries to step into the gouged-out site of the palace, only to be repelled by something that crackles audibly.

"Wha—?"

Backing away a bit, he strains his eyes, but he can't see anything. Serena braces herself, clearly wary; she's noticed the sound and the impact. Lilia's violet eyes are shining. "A seal of sacred power. I knew it. The floating palace really is here."

"It's an illusion spell, then. Breaking it is going to take quite a lot of pow— Wait, huh?!"

Lilia's stuck her hand in as if it's nothing. A blast wind rages right in front of them.

Serena screams, "What are you doing?! You don't even have the sacred sword!"

"It's fine, just let me handle this. After all, that woman was planning to make me the next queen." Smiling wryly, Lilia intones the words with a deep sense of irony.

"'Hear, O past. Open, O future. I am the maiden who inherits the regalia of saints and demons.' Right?"

Suddenly, the wind stops. Then transparent membranes fall away, one by one, like the petals of an opening flower, revealing the palace of the queen who once controlled the world.

"The floating...palace..."

It doesn't look as it once did, though. The palace is split in two, and its time in the desert and the ocean has left the halves caked with salt and sand. Tendrils of magic and sacred power are writhing noisily in the rift down its middle, attempting to stick the two parts together again.

The palace is trying to repair itself.

Shuddering, Luciel takes an involuntary step back. *Amelia. What in the world have you made? You did all that to...*

...I wonder what she actually wanted.

The earth abruptly rumbles. Startled, Serena yells, "Hold on! Is this thing trying to float again?!"

"Then let's hurry and get inside!"

"Huh?! Oh, for the love of—!"

Lilia has started for the double doors at a run, and Serena follows her. Luciel hastily goes after them.

Rocking unsteadily, the palace rises into the air. The movement is precarious, without a trace of its former majesty, but even so, the palace is moving. For some reason, this makes him sad.

"I wonder where this is headed. Toward Ashmael?"

"Probably, if Evare's calling it. Never mind that, let's hurry!"

"Hurry where?"

"To the altar where the ritual to appoint the queen is held. That woman may have left something there."

Lilia smiles, and her spirited eyes look very much like Amelia's—ready to take on the future. The thought pierces Luciel's heart.

For some reason, he remembers the way Amelia smiled when she stole out of the palace with him and Grace, before she became queen, and how they stuffed their faces with food they bought at the night stalls. He just can't believe that smile was an illusion or a lie.

Amelia's wish…

What was she planning to do, after she defeated destiny?

If he'd reverted to the god she'd wished for, would he have known? But Luciel only loves Grace. He can't be the sort of god who could save both Grace and Amelia. Not yet.

✦ Third Act ✦
The Villainess Warps Others' Destinies

If this world were a game, then Grace Dark was probably the first person to escape its framework. She should have been the villainess: born frail, resenting the fact that she couldn't become queen, resenting her younger twin for becoming the Maid of the Sacred Sword, and then dying.

Except she hadn't resented her sister. Not only that, but she also whipped her body into shape, said being queen didn't suit her, and bowed out voluntarily. Then she lived as she wished, won her beloved—the demon king—and produced the sacred sword before being beheaded by her sister. On top of that, her sister used her corpse for further plots. And in the end, Lilia destroyed it with the sacred sword.

What does this mean? Grace Dark was the first Daughter of God? That can't be right…

Aileen can see Machina out of the corner of her eye, standing still and expressionless. A girl who looks just like Amelia Dark—and now a girl who looks just like Grace has turned up. It really doesn't seem as if that could be a coincidence.

"I've been lookin' for you. You're Lucia, ain't you?"

Is that the girl's name? Evare leaps toward the core of the light. "I searched and searched, and it took me all the way back to the past." With a terribly gentle whisper, he reaches out to the girl.

The light that envelops her recedes. Evare's eyes and those violet eyes meet.

"—No." Evare's hand freezes. Flustered, he backs away, gazing at the Daughter of God's unseeing eyes. "She's got no soul. She's just like Machina. Why...? Why? Where'd she go?"

"Aileen! Claude!"

"Mother?!"

A voice abruptly speaks above them, and Aileen turns, looking up. Evare's head also snaps that way, as if he's been struck. Grace doesn't notice.

"Something's broken out of Luciel's barrier! Is he here?!"

Almost none of what Grace is saying gets through to Aileen. All she sees is the body of the girl who looks just like her, and Grace herself as nothing but a soul.

Claude seems to have picked up on the same thing. "Mother, run!" he shouts.

Startled, Grace blinks. In that moment, a shadow falls over her back.

"What are you—?"

Grim-faced, Grace turns around, squaring up to fight—but then she freezes. It's Machina. In an instant, she's moved from Charles's side to Grace's.

"Ame...lia...?!"

That delay proves fatal. Chains tangle around Grace, and she vanishes. As soon as she's gone, the sacred sword rises from Machina's palm.

The essence of the sacred sword is the soul of a maiden. It's clear that the sword in Machina's hand is a barrier that's trapped Grace's soul. As further evidence, Evare's laugh rings out. "I see, her soul— So her sacred sword was split off, huh? Yeah, that's right, *that's how she explained it.*"

"What do you intend to do?! Your goal is regaining the evil god's power, isn't it?!" Aileen shrieks.

Evare shrugs. "What's the point of resurrectin' as an evil god this late in the game? That's just a step in the process." Taking the sacred sword from Machina, he smiles happily. "What I want is to bring back the Maid of the Sacred Sword."

His heartfelt smile sends a shudder through her.

"It's fine, I've got all the materials. With this body and the real sacred sword, *I can make her.* —That's what the Queendom of Hausel's knowledge is for."

Evare is gazing into the distance, toward the far edge of the sky. In the darkness, Aileen didn't notice it before, but now her eyes widen.

Creeeak, creeeak. With a sound that seems oddly warped, the Queendom's palace is floating in the blackness.

Baal has seen it, too. "Was it you who stole the floating palace, you scoundrel?!"

"Aw, don't put it like that. You'll ruin my reputation. I had you give it back, that's all. Okay, I'm off."

"No one here is fool enough to just let you get away," Claude says coldly. He lunges at Evare's back, but for some reason, Charles gets between them. Crackling with magic, Claude's and Charles's swords repel each other.

"What do you think you're doing?"

Shoving Claude's sword back, Charles answers coldly, "Not having a Maid of the Sacred Sword is a problem."

"No one mentioned anything about that to me."

"Estella...! You idiot, what are you doing?!" Charles yells.

Estella has positioned herself in front of Evare, blocking his way. Sacred power rushes from her hands as she attempts to restrain him. "You know I'd never let you go like this."

"Machina, blow yourself up." Evare turns to Machina, who's following him, and issues a cold order. Estella goes very still.

As everyone around him freezes, Evare gives a smile so gentle, it seems awfully out of place on his face. "I'm sorry. Thanks for everythin'. I can get by without you now, though."

Machina, who's been standing perfectly still, raises her head. She might not even have been breathing before, but now her lips move. "Under...stood."

A pillar of light rises from Machina's core. Claude pulls Aileen into his arms without giving her time to object. She sees Baal grab Estella and yank her away, as if getting her out of Evare's sight.

Charles— Where is Charles?!

Before she can find him, light explodes. As Aileen clings to Claude, the ferocious wind of the blast buffets her. She can't open her eyes.

That's all, though. There's no heat. It's as if someone's suppressing it—and then abruptly, silence falls.

Timidly opening her eyes, Aileen raises her head in Claude's arms. Her vision has opened up substantially. Her surroundings are just a little brighter than they were before; it's a sign of the coming dawn.

When she looks at the sky, both Evare and the floating palace are gone.

Instead, she sees two overlapping shadows.

At the center of the power that's blasted everything away, Charles's body tilts. He's holding Machina, and they're plummeting out of the sky together.

"Charles!"

Claude catches them both, then sets them down in the chapel, whose floor is now bare earth.

Hastily running to them, Aileen puts her ear to Charles's chest, trying to listen to his heart, and is relieved to hear a heartbeat. Although both Charles and Machina are covered in cuts and bruises, they're only unconscious.

"That Evare lout escaped, hmm?" Baal descends to the ground, holding Estella.

Claude sighs. "For now, let's get everyone treated. Then we'll restrain them so we can get the story out of—"

Before he finishes his sentence, there's a *boomf*, and Claude transforms into a young dragon. Silence falls.

Baal presses an index finger to the spot between his eyebrows. "Look, you… No doubt this is because we lifted our barrier, but at least try to consider the time and place."

"Skree!"

Aileen picks up the disgruntled young dragon and turns to Estella.

Estella is looking steadily at Charles, who's still lying there with Machina in his arms. The emotion in her eyes is too complicated for Aileen to read. However—

"You will talk to us, won't you?"

"Yes… Although, I know almost nothing about this."

Estella lowers her eyes, then looks up again. Aileen smiles at her.

In the early morning sun, the color of her hair and eyes are just like Baal's, while her dignified bearing and firm gaze are nearly identical to Roxane's.

★ ★ ★

"In losing my memories, I'm afraid I've caused you a lot of trouble. I'm not certain, but I believe getting too close to the past version of me confused my sense of self."

In Principal Consort Roxane's palace in the harem of Ashmael, Estella begins her story. The table in front of her holds tea for three, provided by Roxane.

Aileen, Estella, and Roxane are the only ones present. Apparently, this is not an ideal place for Claude to turn back into a human, so Baal and Claude are in another room. Rather than waste time waiting for everyone to reassemble, they've decided to hear Estella's story first.

"Confused your sense of self...?"

"Yes. I haven't been born yet, but I'm alive inside you, Mother."

Roxane looks down at her own belly. Estella is perfectly impassive. "It's all right if you don't believe me. Since I'm interfering with the past, the future may be different. The child you bear might not grow up to be like me. After all, neither you nor Father has ever mentioned meeting me."

"Do you mean...this version of you will die?" Roxane's eyebrows come together.

Estella nods. "That's always a risk. I made my peace with it before I came."

"And what compelled you to do something so dangerous?"

Estella is intelligent, and Roxane can't imagine she's acting purely by choice.

The girl looks down at her hands. "...I came because I wanted to know that myself, actually."

Roxane and Aileen exchange looks. Estella's delicate eyebrows come down slightly; then seeming to make up her mind, she raises her head. "I'll tell you what I know, from the very beginning. Or the bare minimum of it anyway, so that it won't affect the future too much. —Less than twenty years from now, an engagement will be proposed between myself and Master Charles, who has been tentatively named crown prince of Ellmeyer."

"What do you mean, 'tentatively named'? Was it someone else before?"

"Master Claude."

Her husband has returned with Baal, in human form again.

"Master Charles is the youngest child," Estella tells him. "He has an older brother and sister."

Estella won't give them any more details about their family. She wants to interfere with the past as little as possible, and they should respect her wishes. Aileen doesn't interrupt again.

"Prince Charles himself is against it, so it's still only tentative. He's holed up in the old castle in the forest, ignored the ceremony for the appointment of the crown prince and everything else, and is prepared to fight an all-out war with His Majesty the emperor..."

"So he defied the demon king, did he? That's some spine." With a rather astounded smile, Baal sits down beside Roxane.

Claude takes a seat next to Aileen, crossing his long legs. From what they've been told so far, Charles is Claude's son. Just as she's feeling impressed that he decided to defy him, Claude puts in a quiet remark. "He probably takes after his mother."

"Did you say something, Master Claude?"

"You aren't going to tell us he loathed the idea of becoming crown prince so much that he fled to the past, are you?" Ignoring Aileen's critical eyes, Claude prompts Estella to continue.

The girl shakes her head. "I don't know... I've only spoken with Master Charles a handful of times."

"Even though you're engaged?"

"The engagement was decided only recently. It was a little before his tentative appointment as crown prince was made public... As a student at the Divine Maiden Academy, I didn't have much contact with the outside world in the first place."

It seems like no boys are allowed at the future academy, either. However, Roxane interrupts. "Still, it seems a little unnatural for you to have spoken so little. Imperial Ellmeyer and the Kingdom of Ashmael are friendly nations. If we have children, Lady Aileen, don't you think we should let them get to know each other from infancy?"

"Yes, in terms of national interest, I think that would be my choice as well."

Estella seems unsure whether she should respond to Aileen and Roxane, but in the end, she does. "As you say, our families met several times before our engagement. However, Master Charles always avoided those occasions entirely or slipped out in the middle, and I didn't have the chance to speak to him."

"Could he be unexpectedly shy...?" murmurs Claude, who is unexpectedly shy. He sounds as if he has mixed feelings about it.

"His older siblings are brilliant, so until now, everyone has been lenient with him. However, if he is to be crown prince, he must refrain from such behavior. As his fiancée, I've cautioned him about it several times, but he must have found it annoying. One day, out of nowhere, he sent me a notice that our engagement had been dissolved."

Estella's voice is growing chillier, and Aileen and Claude exchange a look.

"The marriage of an imperial prince and a royal princess is a contract between their nations. It isn't the sort of thing anyone may break for self-centered reasons, and certainly not with a single piece of paper. Growing angry, I marched into Imperial Ellmeyer. I am the daughter of the holy king, after all. For me, destroying the barrier around the old castle was simple."

Estella speaks impassively, her eyes set. For no particular reason, Aileen sits up straighter. It doesn't seem real to her, but this is an offense perpetrated by her son. She must hear her out in good faith.

"Master Charles wasn't there, so with no other recourse, I tried to intimidate the nearby demons into telling me where he was. However, Master Charles had given them strict orders not to say, so they refused to tell me."

Claude also uncrosses his legs and sits up straighter. He's picked up on Estella's anger.

"Then unable to stand by and watch, Master Charles's attendant told me he'd headed for the underground ruin at the Divine Maiden Academy. At that point, I remembered: A little while earlier, for some reason, Master Charles had stolen into the dormitory of the Divine Maiden Academy at night to visit me."

"He *what*?! He'd better not have done anything inappropriate."

Anxiously, Baal leans forward on the couch. Roxane frowns slightly. "Master Baal, let us listen to what she's saying for now. In addition, I think it's a little hasty of you to worry like that."

"W-well, yes, but… We mean, now that we've been told she's our daughter, no matter what we do, it—"

"He doesn't have the spirit for that sort of thing," Estella responds coldly.

Baal silently takes his seat again while Claude's gaze goes distant.

"He only asked me a question. 'Is the Daughter of God's body really not in the underground ruin?' I told him it wasn't. There was no need to hide it. Everyone knows her body isn't in the ruin. I'd heard from Father and the others that it had been moved to a safe location before I was born."

"Moved…? You're sure you don't mean 'stolen'?" Aileen asks, trying to match the situation to their current one.

Estella nods. "I don't know the details, either. However, in my era, it's true that the body isn't in the ruin. I thought it was odd that he'd ask about a thing like that, but he only said, 'That's good,' and left…"

She pauses for a moment, as if getting her thoughts in order. "Due to that incident, his attendant's statement seemed plausible, so I went after Master Charles. In my time, although the underground ruin is on the grounds of the Divine Maiden Academy, anyone may tour it. I saw that man—Evare—and Master Charles enter it together."

It had already been very late at night. In the darkness, Estella had stolen into the chapel after the pair, and that was when she overheard them talking.

"The man said, 'Change the past. That's the only way there is.'"

Findin' you here was a stroke of luck. Still, it looks like the Daughter of God's body ain't in this era, neither. And the World Unity sect's nowhere to be found. In the first place, since you've been born here, maybe it's already too late.

"I had no idea what they were talking about. Still, Master Charles seemed to understand…"

I have to go back further into the past and do stuff over. Yeah, I know:

If you help me, I won't erase your family or your brother and sister or your country. That's a promise.

"While what he was saying mystified me, I knew better than to expect a suspicious stranger to keep his promise. I thought, *Danger is bearing down on Ellmeyer's imperial family.*"

As a matter of fact, as Estella feared, Evare has just broken his promise to Charles.

"No doubt Master Charles didn't believe him, either. He told the man he was going with him."

You go on and look for the Daughter of God's body and the sacred sword. I'll seal Ellmeyer with a barrier, so you can't touch it.

Claude covers his face with a hand. "...So he did that to protect Ellmeyer from Evare?"

"I believe so. However, I didn't think that would be the end of it. Particularly when I heard the Queendom of Hausel's floating palace come up in conversation."

All eyes turn to her, and Estella looks down.

"My parents told me of the war with the Queendom of Hausel. The floating palace is a structure—no, a weapon that we don't yet understand. That's what I was taught. They said it was located in territory that we absolutely must not enter. I don't know where the palace is, either, but that was what the man said they had to obtain. He also said he was going to leap to the past. That, as long as a girl called Machina was with him, he could travel through time."

"Only the gods may do that," Baal mutters.

Estella nods. "Yes. However, both of them—Master Charles included—disappeared along with Machina. Or rather, it felt as though they had been wiped out of existence. I was sure it wasn't merely teleportation. Since I was supposed to become the holy king, I don't think there's any mistake."

"You *were supposed to*?" Aileen asks.

Estella looks startled, then promptly bows her head. "I've said something uncalled for. Please ignore it… At any rate, I was very anxious, and I rushed back to the old castle. If Ellmeyer's crown prince vanished, there would be an uproar. Because Master Charles had holed up in the old castle, his absence wouldn't be discovered immediately, but it wouldn't be long. First, I asked his attendant and his master—his teacher—for advice."

"His teacher… The boy's emotions seem to have no effect on the weather or nature. Should the credit for that go to his teacher?"

That's all Claude asks; he doesn't really seem to be expecting an answer. Estella is probably hoping they won't ask more pointed questions. It's dangerous to know more than they need to about the future.

"His teacher told me the demon realm presented a way to go after Master Charles. An individual with strong sacred power would probably be able to enter the demon realm and make it out safely, but there was no guarantee. When he asked if I still wanted to follow him, I said I did."

As Estella speaks, her gaze is clear and firm.

The teacher and attendant had shown Estella to the basement of the old castle. Aileen had already heard that there was an entrance to the demon realm there from Luciel and Grace.

When she fell into that pit, the world seemed to turn over. The very first thing she saw was a palace that looked like a reflection of the old castle, with the sky as the boundary between them. The horde of demons that surrounded her told her to go to it.

"The demons are Master Charles's allies, but they didn't try to stop me. They must want me to bring him back as well… I entered the castle that floated in the sky of the demon realm."

The next thing she knew, she was in a space that was pitch-black both overhead and underfoot. All that was there was a large door that only someone with sacred power could see. Even the way back had vanished. She had no choice but to go forward. However, neither pushing, pulling, nor hitting the door with sacred power was enough to open it. Deciding it must have some sort of spell on it, Estella abruptly remembered a saying.

"I won't reveal who it was, but someone once taught me a spell that would open sealed doors, so I chanted it."

"—'Hear, O past. Open, O future. I am the maiden who inherits the regalia of saints and demons'?" Aileen recites from memory.

Estella's eyes widen, but she smiles without responding directly.

"After the door opened, you know what happened. For just a moment, I thought I saw a pure-white room. Then light enveloped me. The next thing I knew, I was in Ellmeyer, which was covered by a red barrier..."

"Thank goodness for that. The story alone is rough on our heart." Baal, who'd been listening in silence, covers his face with his hands as if he's exhausted.

Frowning slightly, Estella apologizes, "I really know almost nothing, and you're all very busy, and yet I've talked for so long. I'm sorry."

"No, that's not it... Good grief, did you get that denseness from your mother? We mean we're glad you're safe. What a dangerous thing you've done... Do you have a way to get back?"

Estella looks troubled. "I don't even know how I got here to begin with."

"We hope the future holy king isn't having a breakdown over this. Will he come to pick you up?" asks Baal.

"I really don't know. I felt I needed to settle the matter before it was discovered, so I came without even reporting it to the emperor… Um, I'm very sorry." Estella conscientiously apologizes to Claude. She's earnest to a fault, and as Baal has pointed out, she tends to get things just a little wrong.

Claude shakes his head. "I remember none of this, but don't worry about it. That teacher is probably handling things. More importantly, when Baal finds out you've vanished, too, he's going to be a pain… We'll have to cover it up somehow."

"Yes, Master Claude, you're right. Our son has done something foolish, and he's dragged someone else's daughter into the mess. How can we gloss it over?"

"Hey, Demon King and spouse, we can hear you! Is hiding the truth all you can think of?!"

"It's nothing to concern yourselves over. As I am Master Charles's fiancée, it is my duty to stop him," Estella declares.

Everyone else falls silent.

The odd hush seems to puzzle Estella. She tilts her head. "Have I said something strange?"

"No… We, er, think that's fine as well, but… Your duty, hmm? Yes, we see."

"We understand what you've told us, Estella. However, even if that red barrier isn't harmful, we don't know why he was capable of cursing Emperor Claude. That will be a problem. He is the demon king, you know. Even if they are blood relatives, I think it must have been something rather peculiar," Roxane points out.

Pulling himself together, Baal nods. "Come to think of it, he did repel both sacred power and magic as if it were nothing."

"Yes," Estella says. She seems satisfied with the direction the conversation is taking. "I've never seen it, since it's hidden by that eye patch, but I'm told Prince Charles's eyes are different colors. One is red, the other purple."

"...The same as my father, hmm? No wonder he's strong." Claude sighs. Aileen heard that when Luciel was a god, he had one red eye and one purple one as well.

If his eyes are the same color as a god's, that would explain why he's stronger than both Claude and Luciel. That, and how he managed to shoulder the full force of Machina's self-destruction and get by with mere injuries.

"Nn..."

Sensing that someone is waking up, everyone's gazes go to the corner of the room.

Charles's eyelids flutter, opening slowly—and then with a jolt, he registers the fact that he's wrapped in chains. "What is this?!"

"Good morning, Master Charles." Rising to her feet, Estella crosses to Charles, who's lying on the floor.

His hands are bound behind him, but he manages to sit up. There's a deeply unhappy look on his face. "Estella..."

"How are you feeling?"

"Rotten, obviously. What happened to Machina?"

Estella frowns. In her place, Aileen answers from her chair. "Lady Sahra—do you know who that is? At any rate, the Daughter of God is tending to her in another room, so don't worry."

"All right, then. I'm glad she's safe." Charles looks relieved.

Quietly, Estella asks, "What is your relation to that girl?"

Charles averts his eyes rather obviously. "It's none of your business."

Estella's aura grows colder than it's ever been. "You've caused an uproar this serious, and you're still saying irresponsible things like that?"

"Irresponsible? You're more irresponsible than I am. I don't exist, but you do, even if you're not born yet. You could have ended up with a whole lot worse than amnesia."

"It could all have been avoided if you hadn't done this."

"How did you get here, woman? Even you don't have the power to go back in time."

"Answer my question first, please."

"No, woman. You don't know how to get home. What are you planning to do?"

"...I've told you time and again not to refer to me that way."

"We should probably stop them, don't you think? This isn't much of a conversation," Claude murmurs, looking a little appalled.

Aileen rises to her feet. "Stop that, both of you."

Estella's eyes are wide, and her expression is menacing. Roxane puts an arm around her shoulders, gently leading her away. Aileen crouches down in front of Charles.

The boy's lips are pressed together tightly, and he's looking at Aileen defiantly. Aileen gazes back at him, then sighs. "Well done, future me... He's a really lovely child."

"Huh?"

"Charles. Who gave you that name? Was it myself? Or your father?"

Keeping his guard up, Charles thinks for a while. "…Father. I heard he got the name from Uncle James."

"I see. Yes, when I first met him, he was calling himself James Charles."

There must have been some meaning in it. Aileen nods in satisfaction.

Charles narrows his eyes. "Does that matter right now?"

"Yes, it matters. After all, it's related to you. Sahra has healed your wounds; does anything still hurt?"

"If you're being kind to me so I'll get careless, it's pointless, *Mother.*" Charles snorts, as if he's mocking her. "I know how you work. I haven't been your son for years for nothing."

Aileen chuckles right back. "You're my son, all right. I don't suppose you'd care to remove the curse on Master Claude?"

"No."

"Not even if I pat you on the head and tell you you're a good boy?"

"How old do you think I am? Gross."

He's a formidable opponent. Just as she's thinking, *He's definitely our son*, Claude joins them.

"Aileen. Would you leave this to me and Baal?"

At the sound of his calm voice, Aileen and Charles both look up.

"Of course, but… What will you do if you turn into a young dragon again, Master Claude?"

"That's why Baal is here."

"What are we, your babysitter?"

"There are questions you want to ask, too, right? We'll have a man-to-man talk."

Baal scowls, then glances to the side and nods. "Very well.

Roxane, let us borrow this room for a little while. In the meantime, prepare a place for Estella and Aileen and the others to rest."

"Very well."

Prompted by Roxane, Estella gets to her feet. She's being quiet, but dissatisfaction is written all over her face.

Aileen thumps her shoulders lightly. "Let us leave this to Master Claude and your father."

"We don't need to talk."

As Estella finally managed to start moving, Charles spoke behind her, as if to prove her concern is right on the mark.

Claude is calm. "You're saying there's no room to negotiate? I'm fairly sure this situation already falls outside your plans."

"There's no point in talking like you know and trying to pry information out of me. I won't say a thing, and I'm not taking that curse off you, Father. The barrier over Ellmeyer stays, too."

He's young, but his expression is dignified, and his words hold strong conviction. She doesn't know what he's struggling with privately, but they've raised a fine, strong-willed child.

Claude seems to have thought the same thing. Calmly, he looks down at Charles, who's completely shutting him out. "So you won't explain the situation, no matter what… Then you leave me no choice. First, I'll guess the name of the girl you like."

He isn't mature about it, though.

"Wh-what…?!"

"I'd really prefer not to. If I were in your position, I wouldn't be able to take it. The moment she hears it, the shame will probably make you die an agonizing death. I don't want to put my son through a thing like that, but…"

"Well, if he's going to be recalcitrant with us, there's no way around it."

Baal and Claude both nod. When it comes to this sort of thing, they're weirdly on the same page.

Poor Charles turns pale. He tries to speak several times, but nothing comes out, and finally, he turns bright red. "Wh-what the hell are you talking about! Does this look like the time for that?!"

"We can hardly tell whether it's the time for this or not if you won't talk."

"Just so you know, this doesn't mean we've accepted you for our daughter. However, you're free to love whoever you wish."

"D-don't talk nonsense! I—I don't even have anybody I l-like!!"

"So this is puberty. Well now, Baal, who do you think it is?"

"You're going to make us say it? Maybe we don't look it, but our feelings about this are complicated. Very well. The girl this fellow loves is—"

"St-stop it, don't say it! Fine, I'll talk, just don't you dare say it!!" Charles screams. Estella tries to look back, but Aileen pushes her along, and they both leave the room with Roxane.

"You mustn't listen. It's a conversation between gentlemen," Roxane warns her.

Aileen nods firmly in agreement. Her son is probably about to get his pride shredded by his father, and as his mother, she'd like to protect him as much as she can.

Even so, Estella is distracted by what's happening behind her. "But, um, is it really all right to leave this to them?"

"It's fine. Let's do what we can while we have the chance."

"What we can do? But there's nothing..."

"Lady Roxane, I have a favor to ask. I would like to go to the Divine Maiden Academy once more."

Roxane blinks. "The Divine Maiden Academy… Did you forget something?"

"I want to investigate why the Daughter of God's body *wasn't* there," Aileen tells her.

Roxane and Estella exchange looks.

Aileen has seen the ghost of the Daughter of God once before, in Ashmael with Lilia. Even in the game, there wasn't a proper illustration; her features were blurred. However, at least in reality, the ghost they saw didn't look like Grace. If it did, she probably would have felt that something was off at the time, and Lilia would have read too much into it and gotten all excited.

Just in case, she goes to speak with Sahra, who's still tending Machina. After all, the girl spoke with the ghost of the first Daughter of God when she retrieved the holy sword from the sanctuary.

When she broaches the topic, Sahra's eyes widen. "No, I don't think the first Daughter of God looked like Grace. If I had to say, she looked more like Machina."

Roxane has accompanied Aileen, and Sahra's words make both of them blink.

"Do you mean she looked like Amelia Dark?"

"Umm… Not quite like that. There was a resemblance, but… Right, it's more her overall demeanor. The way she seemed rather lifeless was similar!"

"You're certain that wasn't because she was a ghost?"

"Amelia was unsettling, but she was also incredibly lively, wasn't she?"

It's a wonder that the mastermind behind that whole uproar

can be summed up with the one word *lively*. Not that it's inaccurate or anything.

"Machina looks like Amelia but doesn't give off the same impression at all, you see? That's what made me think the first Daughter of God looked more like Machina. It's as if Amelia lost all her vitality and became a doll."

"Yes, and that's because the Daughter of God was dead, isn't it?"

"No, Lady Roxane, she may actually be onto something. Amelia used her own body as the medium to seal Grace's soul. She appeared before us in Grace's body, but I can't imagine she'd been using it for several centuries."

On the contrary, she would have been very careful with Grace's body, keeping it in reserve for the moment of Luciel's oath. Even without that, she'd been completely obsessed with Grace. Aileen has heard from Auguste that Amelia said she wouldn't allow anyone else to hurt her sister.

"I think she'd created spare bodies. I don't know how advanced Hausel's technology was, but perhaps she made copies of herself... She may also have borne children besides Lady Lilia."

"That's true. I can't assume that the genealogical chart of the Queendom of Hausel was a complete fabrication."

"Still, Lady Amelia was capable of transferring her soul to different bodies. She was hardly an ordinary human anymore. Whether she made other bodies or bore children, perhaps they were soulless, like Machina."

It's very likely that Lilia, protected by her destiny as the Maid of the Sacred Sword, was the sole exception.

"In the first place, there's no way Lady Amelia would have left the holy sword to someone else. It's quite possible that she was controlling the first Daughter of God herself, just as she puppeted Lady Grace's body."

"Huh?! Then the Daughter of God was Amelia's daughter or, um...a second self?"

Sahra's question triggers a memory.

"...That's right, Evare said that Lilia Reinoise could have opened the underground ruin. That would mean the first Daughter of God, the progenitrix of Ashmael's royal family, was from Amelia Dark's bloodline. At the very least, she can't have been from Grace's..."

No one argues. There's probably no way to know the truth, but as possibilities go, it's good.

"The biggest issue is that we have yet to see the underground ruin."

"...What do you mean?"

"When the door to the ruin opened, there was a girl preserved in ice just inside it. It's as if she abruptly left the holy sarcophagus. We haven't seen anything else."

It was like the contents of holy sarcophagus had suddenly manifested above ground. There was no "underground" there.

"...Debating is futile. Let us visit the underground ruin ourselves. Fortunately, we have time before sunset. Is that all right, Estella?"

Uncharacteristically, Estella has only been listening all this time, and her attention has been elsewhere. Hastily, she nods. "Yes. I'll accompany you, Lady Aileen."

"In that case, Estella and I shall go. You must stay here and watch Machina, Lady Sahra. And you mustn't overexert yourself when you're with child, Lady Roxane."

"Huh? But shouldn't somebody at least…? What about Ares? Wouldn't it be better to have him go with you?"

"He is a general, Sahra. We mustn't use him simply because it's convenient. You'll need transportation as well… Perhaps we should discuss this with Master Baal."

"It's nothing to trouble Master Claude and Master Baal over," Aileen says firmly.

Beside her, Estella timidly raises a hand. "…Um. The Holy Dragon Consort is here, isn't she?"

After a quick flight from the harem, the Holy Dragon Consort ferries them to the chapel at the Divine Maiden Academy. It very much seems like it only took them a single step.

"Thank you very much, Lady Mana."

"Squee."

Mana, the Holy Dragon Consort, throws her chest out proudly, and Estella strokes her.

Watching them, Aileen folds her arms. "Are the two of you close in the future?"

"She's like an older sister to me. She often played with me, and so…"

"That's all? You seemed quite used to that; are you certain you didn't slip out of the palace together?" Aileen asks mischievously.

Estella's gaze wanders a bit uncomfortably. "She…hid me frequently. When unpleasant things happened. I knew even Father and Mother couldn't interfere with the Holy Dragon Consort, so… I was a devious child," she adds, and Aileen laughs.

"That's a good thing. If you're serious all the time, you'll never last. Now then, shall we go? Please entertain yourself, Holy Dragon Consort. We'll call you shortly."

Mana nods, whiskers swaying, then soars up into the blue sky.

The Divine Maiden Academy has been temporarily closed down in order to deal with the accident, but the cleanup is already finished. The chapel and its surroundings are deserted. That said, the ceiling is still blown off, and the blast wind has crumbled the walls in places. It will be dangerous if those collapse further.

And yet beyond the open pipe organ, the black wall is again smooth and featureless.

"It's closed." Pressing a hand to the cool wall, Aileen sighs. "Apparently, I really can't open it."

Grace Dark's descendants don't have the ability to gain entry. In other words, the only ones who can are Amelia's. Not only that, but in the future Amelia predicted—the one that matches the events of the game—Ares became the divine king of Ashmael, and Estella was destined to be condemned. In that case, once she made Lilia into her puppet and abdicated in her favor, wouldn't that leave Amelia as the only one who could open this door?

...I wonder what Lady Amelia intended to do from this point on.

The woman who knew the future. In other words, the events of subsequent games.

"Lady Aileen. It's open."

While she was lost in thought, Estella opened the door easily. The wall of ice that encased Grace's look-alike is gone. Instead, a flight of stairs leads down into blackness.

Aileen picks up a lamp that's lying on the floor. It's a typical Ashmael lamp that can be lit with a sacred stone. Estella seems very familiar with these, and she promptly lights it.

"Shall we go?"

"Yes."

Holding the lamp, Aileen steps onto the stairs.

Inside, it's dark and quiet. The footing is uneven. However, there are holes in the walls at regular intervals that flare with a pale light for a few moments as they approach. It must be divine stone-powered technology from Hausel.

"...This is nothing like the underground ruin I know."

"Really?"

"Yes. It's possible that the one I saw wasn't the real thing. Come to think of it, I believe the position of the door was slightly different."

"You did say that the body of the Daughter of God had been moved elsewhere, too."

"...Since I arrived here, everything has surprised me. Even when it comes to Ashmael, there may still be many things I don't know. I didn't know about Master Charles, either. I had no idea there was a girl he was fond of."

Aileen stops in her tracks. It seems to give Estella the wrong idea; she shakes her head. "It's fine. It doesn't bother me."

Aileen wishes it did bother her, but deciding to stick to listening for now, she just murmurs something neutral. Unconcerned by her reaction, Estella continues:

"I really was surprised... I also regretted my actions. When Master Charles confronted me with our dissolved engagement, I thought it was just a childish, irresponsible fit of temper, but perhaps I was mistaken. He may have done it to protect that woman, and to treat me with good faith."

Estella's eyes are downcast and troubled.

"If that was the case and he had said something, I would have secretly accepted that woman... No, I'm sure Master Charles detests that side of me. Still, it isn't as if I agreed to our engagement because I wanted it, either."

"You don't like Charles?"

Startled, Estella looks up, then hastily shakes her head. "It isn't like that. I have nothing against him… No, that isn't true. I must be jealous of him."

"Jealous?"

"…Will you promise not to tell Father or Mother? Now or ever?"

Aileen nods, and Estella smiles a bit wryly. "I was supposed to become the holy king."

"Yes, you did say that."

Estella has strong holy power. It probably rivals Baal's own.

"Father is one of the most powerful holy kings in the history of Ashmael. People said that I could be his equal, and that is how I was raised. I studied for dear life, learning everything from governance and politics and the languages of other nations to how to handle sacred power and proper etiquette for ladies. I shouldn't say so myself, but I think I was quite good. I was also on friendly terms with Lady Mana. There shouldn't have been any problems. Then when I was nearly grown, Mother gave birth to a boy."

Estella says, with a distant look in her eyes, that she'd really been looking forward to becoming a big sister.

"However…when my brother was born, his sacred power was stronger than mine. It may even have been stronger than Father's."

Estella steps down a stair, and her profile is lost in the shadows.

"That said, he was still only a child. There was no telling how things would go—or that was what I told myself. Right then, I'd shown what I was made of."

"Estella."

"My little brother was intelligent. He genuinely looked up to me. He was cute…really cute, and yet I…"

Passing Aileen, Estella descends the stairs, keeping one hand on the wall. She's headed down into pitch blackness, toward the unknown.

"…When I turned fourteen, I entered the Divine Maiden Academy. There, even princesses must live in the dormitories. I thought I'd put a little distance between us and get my feelings under control. However, in retrospect, I was only running away. Abruptly, Father summoned me back to the palace. At that point, I was told that Master Charles had been tentatively designated crown prince, and that I was being considered as his fiancée."

Aileen slowly follows Estella down the stairs.

"Father said it was fine to turn down the offer if I didn't want it. He said Ellmeyer felt I was the best match, so they were simply sounding me out; no one would force me. Mother said I should decide for myself. She told me to choose what I truly wanted to do."

Estella stops. It's as if she feels she has nowhere left to go.

"My fiancé would be a crown prince. There was no way we would have been engaged if I was intended to become king one day. To me, the very fact that the offer had been made was the final blow."

Her brother would become holy king, while she would be married off to a foreign nation.

"—I know there was no greater honor than that offer. My fiancé would be the next emperor, the next demon king. If I married him, my strong sacred power would become a symbol of security. My presence would reassure the entire world, not just Ellmeyer. It's an important role. When one is born a princess, political marriages are one's duty. I've been close to the imperial family of Ellmeyer since early childhood, and I couldn't have asked for a better match. Mother, Father, and everyone else had my happiness in mind. They had high expectations for me. They felt I could do this. I know. But...but I—"

"Estella."

"That isn't what I worked so hard to become!"

Her voice is almost a scream, and it echoes in the narrow spiral staircase. Slumping against the wall, Estella sobs.

"I wanted to become the holy king...to protect Ashmael... That was why I'd done everything... But I wasn't the right person. I know that. I thought my cute little brother was in the way. I wondered why I had to be the one to marry the demon king. The fact that I had those thoughts meant I wasn't fit to be the holy king! But even so—"

Setting the lamp down, Aileen gently strokes the girl's trembling back.

"—I wanted to be one. A splendid king, like Father. I can't, though. Master Charles carries everyone's hopes, their admiration—things I'd sacrifice my right arm for—and yet he says he doesn't want them as if it's easy to dismiss. He has everything I lost, and he treats them as if they're worthless. It irritated me and made me so jealous I could die, but marrying him is the most important thing I can do, and so..."

If Charles had been a fine example of a crown prince, the type she could respect... If he'd gladly accepted Estella... If he'd extended his hand to her and said, *Let's do our best together...* Even if it took time, she's sure Estella would have embraced their engagement. However, that hadn't been a possibility, either.

All she'd been able to do was rouse herself to act by telling herself it was her duty.

She's a clever girl. She's proud, too.

No doubt she hadn't been able to tell anyone the truth. She'd tried to set her eyes on the future and kept her feelings bottled up inside. She didn't want to worry anyone. She knew failure was a ridiculous reason for running away, and it wasn't the right thing to do.

Her pride wouldn't allow it.

"If you really do marry Charles, it will make me very happy."

Estella, who's buried her face in her hands, stops sobbing. Even though the girl's eyes are wet with tears, Aileen chooses cruel words. "Thank you for choosing to come here."

They look straight into each other's eyes in the darkness, the lamp at their feet the only source of light. Estella must have told herself over and over that she couldn't let a thing like this discourage her, that she should be grateful to have expectations pinned on her, even unwanted ones. Aileen chose to affirm those words.

There are some things that can't be changed. Whether one is suited to something or not is one of them. It isn't as if everyone can become the person they want to be.

Estella smiles through her tears. "She told me…the same thing. The future Lady Aileen."

"Did she?"

"Yes, when I went to tell her I accepted the engagement… When Master Charles heard that, he got angrier than I'd ever seen him, screaming that he refused and promptly ran off, but…"

"Charles was spoiled and irresponsible, so you couldn't forgive him, but you envied him?"

"Yes."

Estella nods, looking calmer than she had earlier. Then she laughs a little.

Retrieving the lamp, Aileen helps Estella to her feet.

"...Master Charles's older brother and sister are very brilliant, popular, and held in high regard; however, I'm told that Master Charles is the one who's truly brilliant. They say he's hiding it."

"I imagine that facet of his personality is fundamentally at odds with yours."

They're making their way down the stairs step by step, holding hands. Estella nods again. "If it's true, I have no idea why he would do that."

"The statement could be simple family bias. It's basically *He can do it when he tries*, you see? That's no different from a child who can't do it."

"That's true... But would Emperor Claude choose someone like that to be crown prince?"

"If so, Master Claude and I, and the people the boy has around him now, weren't able to make him into a capable child."

Estella looks at her blankly; she can feel it through their linked hands. Glancing at the girl mischievously, Aileen goes on, "Make him a better person. That's what you were intending to do, isn't it?"

Estella has consistently declared herself Charles's fiancée. She may be reluctant, but on some level, she must feel that is her next path.

Aileen doesn't know whether the road she's followed will end up being right or wrong. It's likely that no one does. However, following it has to be better than just standing still.

"I'm cheering for you."

"…Yes. Thank you…very much."

"Your mother was also so dashing that it makes people instinctively want to support her." Aileen smiles.

Estella blinks, as if she's just realized something. "Am I in the same situation my mother was in long ago?"

"The thought that my son is the one who's doing it pains me, but yes, it's similar."

Estella gives another little laugh. The traces of her tears are still there, but her cheeks are dry now.

"You've come this far, so see it through to the end."

"I will."

"…All right. It looks as if we've arrived."

The lantern illuminates the foot of the stairs.

The depths of the room are pitch-black. They're standing properly, but they can't even see the floor. With each step they take, ripples spread as if they've set foot in a puddle, but that's all.

"It's just like the castle in the demon realm, the place where I was before I was flung here."

"I'd imagine so. I recognize it as well."

It resembles the altar beneath the Queendom of Hausel, where Amelia sealed her body. In the game, it was the place where she gained her abilities as a queen: the power to see the past and the future.

Ah, yes, there it is.

When she puts her hand out, she finds an invisible wall.

"—Hear, O past. Open, O future. I am the maiden who inherits the regalia of saints and demons."

In response to Aileen's words, light blooms and expands, and the view changes. The darkness falls away like a veil, revealing a room—and the holy sarcophagus in it.

It's a small room with a smooth floor and walls that seem to be made of seamless marble. Long, narrow tanks of water are scattered around the room. They shine purple and red, serving as lights.

However, what floats in them are eyeballs, hands, and half-destroyed human heads.

"L-Lady Aileen... What's...?"

"Perhaps it's a laboratory. One for making humans."

Extinguishing the lamp, which has served its purpose, she enters the room. Although Estella is pale, she follows with steady steps.

"Why would the Queendom of Hausel build a place like...?"

"Lady Amelia must have been trying to make a spare body for herself. A vessel for her soul."

Her twin sister and her first love would be reborn someday. In order to ensure that they never met, Amelia had tried to persist for centuries, a truly staggering amount of time. That was what had produced this grand distortion.

"No doubt this was a spare facility, and the main one is in the floating palace. In the palace, that girl's body and Grace's soul could be fused."

"Lady Aileen, look..."

Two tanks are embedded in the slanting wall at the very back, each of them just large enough for an adult to lie down in. They were built as mirror images of each other, and a waist-high stone pillar stands between them. They're clearly different from the other structures.

First, the color of the water that fills the tanks is different. It's the color of the sea, a gentle blue. On the side of the palely glowing tank, there's a metal plate with a word engraved on it, and not a speck of dust. Aileen reads it.

In the old tongue of the Queendom of Hausel, it says—*Machina.*

Looking into the tank, Estella frowns. "Why is Machina here?"

The face of the girl sleeping in the tank is identical to Machina's. Or, no, *identical* isn't the word.

"It must be her past self. If the one we know came here with Evare from the future, that would make sense."

"...She looks just as she does now."

"Yes, she does. Unlike the others around her, she appears to have been a success. I'm not sure when she'll awaken, but..."

Aileen glances at the tank next to hers. It's empty. However, as with Machina's, there's a name on the plate.

"—'Lucia,' hmm? That's the name of the girl Evare kidnapped."

"The one who was frozen in ice? Do you suppose she was originally sleeping here?"

"Probably. It may have been put in a place where it would seem to be the Daughter of God's body so that it would act as camouflage to hide this. Machina's face resembles Lady Amelia's. She must have used the body that looked like Lady Grace, who didn't officially exist, to avoid suspicion."

"Why would she do something so elaborate?"

"Perhaps she could only make humans with faces that resembled the people they were based on. No doubt compatibility with her soul was a factor as well."

"Then couldn't the one used for camouflage have been based on another human, instead of Lady Grace? And yet she even gave it a name..."

That remark makes Aileen blink. "That's…quite true. Making one that resembles herself is understandable, but why make a body that's identical to Lady Grace? Not only that, but did Lady Amelia choose to vanish during the war rather than use Machina's body?"

Evare is trying to fuse Grace's soul with Lucia's body, turning her into a Maid of the Sacred Sword. If Amelia's soul was present, could Machina become a Maid as well?

"Lady Aileen. This central stone marker is designed to respond to sacred power. May I touch it?"

There's no telling what may happen, but they knew all along that there would be risk involved. Aileen nods. Estella draws a deep breath, then strokes the blank surface of the marker. Abruptly, it flares with light.

The light fans out, projecting something…no, *someone* familiar. It's a gently smiling woman, her face covered by a diaphanous veil.

"Lady…Amelia?"

"I'm glad you've awakened, Evare. You who first woke as an evil god and have now awakened in this world, which has been destroyed by the corrupt dragon's miasma. My one and only son."

It's an image—in Aileen's previous life, it would have been called a recording.

There's a startlingly kind smile on the woman's red lips.

"Now that I am no longer queen, I doubt I am among the living. The Queendom of Hausel and the other nations that once were will also have come to ruin. You inhabit a future even I cannot see. There is no Daughter of God to heal the world, and no Saint of Salvation to nurture it. However, it was your destiny to awaken there. It is how you will atone for once becoming a fallen god and plunging the world into chaos."

Aileen's eyes widen. Is Amelia relating what will happen after Game 5?

"In this world, nothing is pointless. In order to regain the evil god's powers, you absorbed the fiend dragon. That dragon is a demon that was once called the Time Dragon, and it has the power to control time itself. Now that you have eaten it, you will be able to travel between the past and the present."

"Wait, but he can't eat the fiend dragon!!"

"In addition, as a safeguard against unforeseen situations, I've created girls with a scale of the Time Dragon as their core. They can travel through time. You never know what may happen. Even if you were unable to eat the dragon, set your mind at ease."

Aileen's mouth falls open.

"You will have to change the past. As the evil god, you can already control people with suggestions, but that alone is likely insufficient. I've reinforced your ability to manipulate memories to a certain extent. Use it well."

"......"

"Just in case, I have implanted all I know of the future in your memories. To you, it will appear to be the past. Think carefully and change that past. I've made it possible for you to use both sacred power and magic, so you should be able to deal with whatever problems you encounter in any era with brute force."

"You know, it sounds as if you've given your son far too many cheat skills!!"

"Lady Aileen, it's only an image."

"Change the past and defeat the corrupt dragon. Then create the proper future—using the sacred sword."

Aileen, who's been struggling against the urge to strike the image, looks up, startled.

"Just in case, I have provided two of them."

"I'm noticing an awful lot of *just in cases*!! And where are you finding all these sacred swords?!"

"Also, just in case, I have several holy swords waiting in the back for you. Take care not to confuse them with the sacred swords."

"Did you need to get him so many that he risked confusing them?!"

"Lady Aileen, calm down."

"First, run a sacred sword into each of the girls I have made for you. If you do, they will awaken: two genuine Maids of the Sacred Sword who will bring you a future and salvation."

Two…genuine…Maids of the Sacred Sword.

This time, Aileen really does gulp. There's a gentle smile on Amelia's lips. *"Each of them are the real thing… This time, they both are. One would be sufficient, but just in case. You will be venturing into a future even I don't know, so it's far better to be prepared."*

You liar, Aileen thinks but doesn't say aloud.

"I will now go to win my destiny."

At that point, Aileen realizes how she knew this was Amelia. She's wearing the same clothing she wore when she forced her way into Imperial Ellmeyer as a candidate bride.

Did she make this right before coming to Ellmeyer?

"I pray for your success in battle. Please create a future I don't know, a thousand years from now."

The light retreats into the stone marker again. Even though it has nothing resembling a lid, there's a *clunk*, and the marker opens.

It's empty.

However, it's clear that something should be there.

The sacred swords.

There's a space just large enough for two blades of the shape Aileen remembers.

"They…aren't here."

"That's right. Because the sacred swords no longer exist."

However, if Amelia had won, she's sure they would have been here.

"...What a fool you are."

"Lady Aileen?"

After she abdicated as queen, once she saw that the world was proceeding as she'd predicted, she would surely have placed her own sacred sword here. Her sister's sword, which she'd kept all those centuries, would have joined it.

She would have wagered that, in a future she didn't know, they would be allowed to be together—but Aileen has destroyed that future.

She doesn't regret it. If she didn't do that, she would have lost her own future. Both sympathy and pity would be insulting at this point.

Still, just for a moment...

"You really are a fool."

Aileen lowers her gaze. Estella softly sets her hands on her shoulders.

"You've gone and done something on your own without telling me again."

By the time Claude returns to the bedroom they've been given, the sun has set. Aileen smiles back at him. "I've returned bearing holy swords. That was useful of me, wasn't it?"

"Do you think I'll forgive anything if you say that?"

"Master Claude, do sit down." Aileen pats the floor beneath the window, which is padded with fluffy carpets and cushions.

Frowning, Claude sits. Aileen slips into his arms and rests her forehead against his shoulder. "I'm tired. Would you stay like this for a little while?"

"...This is rare. Well, if you're trying to get into my good graces, it's not a bad move."

Her reliable husband pulls a tray with a pitcher of water, some wine, and pie-like snacks made of cheese and parsley wrapped in thin dough over to them. Aileen ordered it as a late-night treat.

"You've already eaten?"

"Yes, with Lady Roxane, Estella, and Lady Sahra. Have you?"

"I just snacked on whatever was in hand's reach with Baal and Charles. While we eat, let's have you tell me what happened."

Nodding, Aileen straightens up and relates what she saw and heard in the underground ruin.

When he's crunched his way through the last pie and licked his thumb clean, Claude asks, "In other words, Evare's from a thousand years in the future? However, he found no sacred swords, and he hasn't been able to awaken Machina as a Maid of the Sacred Sword."

"I believe so. I don't know if it's true of the future Lady Amelia spoke of as well, but there are significant gaps between what she said and actual history. Perhaps he came from the future to rectify that."

"Then he was searching for Lucia because he hoped she'd have a sacred sword already? He jumped to Charles's era first, but her body wasn't there; it had been hidden as the Daughter of God's corpse. That's why he came back to this era, where the Daughter of God still lies in state. Even then, Lucia was merely a body, but Mother was here."

"...I believe Lady Grace's soul will be compatible with Lucia." At the very least, Aileen is certain that Amelia took steps to make it so. "I hope she's all right... Under the circumstances, why do you suppose Charles said he needed the Maid of the Sacred Sword as well, no matter what?"

"Children develop intense assumptions at his age, so whatever he's thinking, it's probably nothing decent." Claude uncorks the bottle of wine. "Is the underground ruin unchanged, aside from the fact that you took the holy swords?"

"Yes. We can't risk affecting the future negatively by moving it, and in any case, it would be difficult to do."

"Then the Machina who self-destructed is still asleep?"

"Yes. According to Lady Sahra, she was moving by magic. She said that if her magic recovers past a certain threshold, she may awaken."

"Since she has no soul, Evare must have augmented her with his magic. She is human, though?" Claude pours wine into a glass.

Aileen nods. "Lady Sahra said she was, even if she was artificially created. She said she was no doll, and that she had a soul."

"Charles said something similar. He seems to be taking her side."

"That's right, what did you talk about with Charles? What about the barrier over Ellmeyer? What's happened to your curse?"

"The barrier is still over Ellmeyer. It's safer that way. I also decided to leave my curse as it is." Aileen frowns. Sitting with one knee bent, Claude gives her a wry smile. "He didn't do it out of malice. You don't have to worry."

"I believe that as well. But it's not as if there's no harm, is there?"

"The only harm is turning into a young dragon. As long as

I have Baal's earring, I know I can hang on for a while, so I'm letting it be. It's fine."

"But, Master Claude, if anything happens to you, it will wound both myself and Charles."

The boy may act like a cynic, but ultimately, he's trying to protect his family from Evare.

"True. I think he's a lot like me, but on the other hand, talking to him convinces me he's a child you raised. He's stubborn, and once he's decided to do something, he gets right to it."

Claude's soft smile makes Aileen fall silent, but her feelings are complicated. As if he's seen through her, Claude's fingers brush her cheek. "Don't sulk like that. In exchange, I've made him promise to stay here quietly until we find the floating palace."

"He is my son, you know. What will you do if he takes you in utterly?"

"I fully expect him to. I haven't left any openings. And I know his weaknesses."

"...What do you think I am, Master Claude?"

She meant it as a joke, and his straight-faced answer has left her indignant. Claude swirls the wine in his glass, smiling at her.

"What is this weakness?"

"Estella. And Machina."

She expected the former, but the latter comes as a surprise.

"Baal gave Charles special permission to enter the harem. He says he's going to help care for Machina."

"Isn't that...unwise?" Estella seems to suspect that Charles and Machina have a relationship.

Claude chuckles. "Yes, very. He doesn't seem to know that, though. Puberty is rough."

"This is no time to be enjoying yourself. How has he explained it to Estella?"

"With that personality, there's no way he'd explain. He's worried about her, and he only wants to return her to the future safely—but if he keeps acting the way he has been, she'll never pick up on it." Claude smiles meanly.

Aileen feels a little sorry for Charles. "You mustn't bully him, Master Claude. What is this about?"

"In order to return Estella to the future, Machina needs to wake up."

She recalls that Machina and Lucia were made with scales from the Time Dragon. Since Evare hasn't eaten the fiend dragon, he and Charles used Machina's ability to get to the past.

However, Charles won't tell Estella why he's concerned about Machina.

"It's hilarious. He's really anxious about whether Estella will be able to get back to the future. However, he insists that their parents set up the engagement and he hasn't agreed to it. Baal was definitely upset."

"He is your son, Master Claude."

Claude shrugs lightly, then drains his glass of wine. The thought doesn't seem to trouble him.

"What is Charles doing now, then?"

"He says he's worried about Machina, so he's going to sleep beside her. That misunderstanding is about to get even worse."

"You're finding all this far too amusing, Master Claude."

Claude is resting his forehead on his bent knee and laughing, but at that, his eyes turn toward her. "Yes, and? If it doesn't make you a bit of a fool, it isn't love."

He suddenly dons a sweet smile that's dripping with sensuality.

Putting his arms around Aileen's waist, he pulls her to him and tries to kiss her, but she sets her palm on his chin and pushes his jaw up.

He gives her an unhappy look, but she hasn't heard the really important thing yet. "And? What will we do next?"

"Look for the floating palace. We can't let someone we know so little about steal it from us. Charles said the palace will be a safer bet when it comes to helping Machina recover, too. Since our interests align there, he's agreed to help us."

"And regarding everything else…?"

"He's the same as ever."

She feels as if he's covering something up there. Dropping a kiss on her furrowed brow, Claude whispers in her ear, "If you're so worried, would you grant Charles's wish first?"

"But of course. What is it?"

"He says he wants you to have his big brother, or maybe it was his sister."

Instantly, Aileen's face feels as if it's on fire. Moving with deliberate care, she removes the shawl she's been wearing over her shoulders, acting miffed to cover her embarrassment. "At a time like this, in someone else's home…"

"Oh, why not? At least here, I won't do something pathetic like turn into a baby dragon in the middle of the deed."

When he says that with a straight face, it makes her laugh. Claude looks slightly dissatisfied while Aileen demurely wraps her arms around his neck.

A figure is making its way unerringly through the silent palace, and Luciel scowls.

"How does she know the way?"

"There's no point in asking."

"...That's really all you ever say."

He's gotten used to it by now, but he makes the comment anyway. Lilia doesn't seem to care a bit, though. She easily finds the door that leads underground beneath the throne, then jumps in without a second thought.

She might as well be a child exploring.

She opens the invisible door right away, too, and just like that, the three of them are in the depths of the palace. There's an altar, and water flows into the space from some unknown source very high up.

"Is this...the altar where the queen's ascension ritual takes place?"

"That's right."

Lilia climbs the stairs, her footsteps light, walks around the altar, then cocks her head. "Maybe there really isn't anything here. Sahra said this was where Amelia's body was, with Grace's soul sealed inside it, but..."

"Grace told me Amelia met destruction gallantly, soul and all."

"I see... I remembered several things suddenly, so I just assumed it was that woman's doing." Lilia clasps her hands behind her, then seats herself on the altar. Naturally, both Luciel and Serena are shocked.

"Look, you, that has to be blasphemous."

"Why? She was planning to make me queen. That means there must be some sort of final mechanism here. Something that would make me advance the game as that woman wished—"

Lilia is swinging her legs idly, but suddenly, her eyes widen. Serena, who's standing between her and Luciel, turns around, then backs away.

Although he feels like an idiot, he doesn't catch on until after he's coughed up blood.

"What've we got here? I knew I had a rat problem. It's you, huh, Luciel?"

From the darkness behind him, a young man appears, looking just as he did when he was a god. *Evare*, Luciel thinks, but the word doesn't make it past his lips.

The blade protruding from his stomach is the sacred sword, but he's even more rattled by the figure who's holding it.

"Gr-Grace...?"

Perfectly straight black hair. She said it was so smooth that it would slip through her fingers, and it was hard to tie back properly. But something isn't quite right— Of course. She's younger than she was when he last saw her. This is the age she was when they met. The way she's styled her hair is a little different, too.

She drags the sword out of his stomach, taking those memories with it.

With nothing to support him, Luciel crumples to the stone floor.

"Hey! No!"

Serena holds a hand over his wound. Feeling his power slowly begin to recover, he catches her hand. "You—mustn't."

"What's this? Are you maybe the Saint of Salvation? Just havin' you around is like havin' an army."

Serena's instincts are good; that remark of Evare's is enough to tell her why Luciel stopped her. However, defiantly, she pours power into his wound anyway. Wounds made by the sacred sword won't heal so easily, though. Evare knows this as well. He just stands there smiling, emphasizing that he could kill them whenever he feels like it.

"Y-you... What did you...do to Grace?"

"Grace? Was that soul a friend of yours? If so, sorry 'bout that. She's been reborn now, so I doubt she remembers you."

Breathing shallowly, Luciel looks up at his wife, who's reverted to girlhood. She's smiling.

"*This sword is for protecting you and the demons,*" she said, holding this very blade.

"Re...born...?"

"That's right. She's the new Maid of the Sacred Sword who Mom—Amelia—had waitin' for me."

That name makes him clench his fists. Amelia. His sister-in-law.

Why would you make a thing like...? What have you done to Grace...again...?

This floating palace, and the new Maid of the Sacred Sword who looks identical to his wife. Luciel has never understood what Amelia felt or what she wished for. He thinks he might, and then he never quite gets there.

"Forget that, why're you still human? You shoulda returned to bein' a god ages ago."

"Give...Grace...back."

He strains his eyes, looking at the girl with the sacred sword. He does sense Grace's soul in her...but something seems off. Soul and body haven't fully blended yet; she's just a patchwork human.

As proof, this girl who looks so much like Grace only smiles. There's something decidedly inhuman about that.

"I mean, you can say that, but...this future's the correct one.

Still, if that sacred sword works on you, the one Lucia has is definitely the real deal. We just proved she's a genuine Maid of the Sacred Sword."

"A genuine Maid of the Sacred Sword?" A mocking voice speaks from the altar, and Evare's eyes turn toward it. "So that's a real sacred sword, is it? Hmm."

"...Who're you?"

"Didn't Mother mention me? I think you're probably my little brother."

"Lilia Reinoise, huh?" Evare breaks into a wry smile. "Yeah, you're my big sis, all right. But see, I spent ages and ages sleepin' in some sort of tank. I feel like an only child—as a matter of fact, I *was* alone for a *real* long time."

"You may call me Sister."

Lilia hops down from the altar, landing with her feet neatly together, tilts her head, and smiles.

"...So you ain't queen, huh? I knew it. I tumbled to that the second I saw Luciel. Aside from that, the fact that Charles is in that era—I swear, it's all messed up. Mom must've lost big-time." Sighing, Evare turns to face Lilia again. "What 'bout you, Sis?"

"What do you mean, 'what'?"

"This situation. Mom told you what the future was s'posed to be like, didn't she?"

"Well, let's see. At this point, I've got several thoughts on that." Lilia descends the stairs, step by deliberate step. "Couldn't I have done better? If I'd known this or that sooner, if I'd managed to defeat Lady Aileen... I don't want to regret any of it, but I do."

"In that case, it ain't too late. Wanna help your li'l bro out now?"

Luciel's eyes widen. He tries to move, but Serena holds him down. When he looks up at her, she shakes her head slowly, her eyes calm.

"You were the real Maid of the Sacred Sword. I'd feel a lot better havin' you on my side. You could even be queen and rebuild the Queendom of Hausel. After everythin's over, I mean."

"Not Imperial Ellmeyer?"

"Now that it's tangled up this bad, we've gotta regroup. We've gotta make this place into the future."

"Do you mean the stage of Game 6?"

"Six? What's that?"

"The evil god is a god who takes on human malice. If he's defeated, then that malice won't have anywhere to go. If the demon king is born into a situation like that, he'll become a demon that puts the fiend dragon to shame and completely rot the world. That means we need to purify both the evil god and the world and start over—at least, that's what the first Daughter of God said in 5, when she snapped and went off the rails. There's no way that wasn't foreshadowing for 6."

What skims through Luciel's mind just then is Claude, and one other. The boy who's just like Claude and himself.

"I didn't get most of that, but if you're talkin' 'bout the corrupt dragon, that's right."

"That must be the final boss of 6, then. Yes, I see. Most of the pieces have come together. By the way, there's something I told myself I'd do if I ever got a little brother."

"What's that, hmm? If you're gonna be on my team from here on out, I'd like to hear it."

"Little brothers must submit to their big sisters completely."

Evare freezes up, the polite smile still on his face.

Lilia gives a thin smile of her own. “What did you expect? I refuse to be your mother figure.” She crouches low, then launches herself off the floor.

Evare grimaces. “What’s this? You ain’t got a sacred sword now. You wanna die?”

“Heh-heh. Don’t make me laugh. You call a thing like that a Maid of the Sacred Sword?”

Seeing Lucia raise her sacred sword to intercept the incoming enemy, Evare gasps as realization hits. “The Maid of the Cursed Sword… No, Lucia, get back! She’s gonna steal your sword!”

“I sense no respect for previous installments.”

As Lucia tries to retreat, Lilia grabs her hand and attempts to plunge the sword into her own stomach. Just before she can, Evare blasts her with magic.

Luciel reflexively casts a barrier, protecting Lilia, but the recoil sends him flying.

As the three of them hit the floor in the midst of the smoke, Luciel coughs, then starts to scold her. “Could you be any more reckless?! Grace is strong all on her own, and she’s got the sacred sword now!”

“Is having knotholes for eyes the default for heroes and final bosses in this game?”

“Huh?”

“Who cares about that now?! What are you going to do? I really can’t see you winning this!”

“Serena. Hand.”

Serena reflexively raises her hand, and Lilia smacks its palm with her own. “All right! The league of heroines is back!”

“Huh?”

“I’m going to go check my answers. If I came here, I thought that woman would answer some of my questions, but it looks this won't be that easy. Life's a pain like that, isn't it?"

Crouching, Lilia grins slyly, pointing at Serena's chest. "Whatever you do, you mustn't let them catch you. And don't look at Evare's eyes, all right? I'm pretty sure he has some sort of power of suggestion. Use me as a decoy and make sure you get away."

"What are you planning?"

Rising to her feet, Lilia gives a troubled shrug. "I get these thoughts sometimes. Couldn't Cedric have become emperor? The same goes for Marcus, Lester, you, Sahra—everybody. Couldn't we all have had different, better lives? If I'd done it more cleverly...I might even have been able to save Amelia."

Luciel's eyes widen, and the girl who says she's Amelia's daughter smiles at him. "Find her, all right? She should still be around."

"How can you know...?"

"There's no way she'd just leave Grace like that. Even if she has to crawl up from the depths of hell, she'll be here. After all, she's the heroine!" The girl offers Luciel that nonsensical answer as if it's hope. "I do think the hero's the only one who can call her back, though."

Right before his eyes, like Amelia, Lilia turns on her heel. He doesn't know why, but it makes him feel like crying.

"Give my regards to Lady Aileen! Tell her to go easy on me. ★"

"You—"

"It's fine. I may not have the sacred sword, but I've still got sacred power."

Evare's magic barrels straight toward Lilia, blowing the smoke away. She repels it easily, but Evare's hands close around her slim neck.

"That was a close shave. I only just realized. If you're from the Maid's bloodline, you can steal the sacred sword. Sorry, but I can't just roll over 'cause you tell me to."

"Gracious. We just met, and we're fighting like siblings already."

"I'm not lettin' you people get away, either. You're the god of demons, Luciel. You can't beat the Maid of the Sacred Sword!"

Lucia lunges at Luciel and Serena, raising her sword high. No matter what else is happening, their opponent has Grace's sacred sword. A barrier won't even buy them time. Luciel tries to squeeze his eyes shut—but then he blinks. Right in front of him, Lucia has been abruptly knocked back.

Luciel isn't the only one who's startled. Evare stares, his eyes shuttling between the fallen Lucia and Luciel. "What was that—?"

"Listen, can you teleport us if I loan you my power?!" Serena asks, grabbing his shoulder.

Bewildered, Luciel nods. "If I use up everything I've got, I can make it work somehow— But Lilia's… And we can't leave Grace and run!"

"It's fine! That woman's the real Maid of the Sacred Sword!!" Serena shouts at him, but her eyes are fixed on Lilia. The declaration seems to pierce his heart.

Biting his lip, Luciel pours every last bit of his power into teleporting. Incredible pressure bears down on him, but he doesn't care.

Grace is the Maid of the Sacred Sword. He wasn't able to forgive people for ridiculing her as the Maid of the Cursed Sword.

However, Amelia—who wanted to be the Maid of the Sacred Sword so very badly—was also definitely the real thing.

Both Grace and Amelia were Maids of the Sacred Sword.

That was what Luciel believed—and what he still believes, if he's being honest.

"...What did you just do?"

Evare's gazing at the spot where Luciel was a moment ago and at the barrier that's still there.

Lilia laughs, even though he's still throttling her. "What did I tell you? You don't have enough respect for the older games."

That's why he doesn't know what protected Luciel.

When she gives Evare a smile, the eyes behind his spectacles flare with magic. Or, no, maybe it's his unique hero powers. "Former Maid of the Sacred Sword. It's obvious that I can't leave you runnin' loose. Since that's so, though, this should get through to you. This future ain't the real deal."

If she looks him in the eye, it's very likely he'll overwrite her memories or use some kind of suggestion to control her.

Knowing that, Lilia stares straight into Evare's eyes.

Overwhelming pressure runs through her, from the depths of her eyes all the way to her brain. The pain seems to rattle her skull.

Even so, she doesn't look away.

Cedric.

Loser. Incompetent prince. The shameless one who flatters and fawns on the crown prince to survive. The man who's not worthy to be a member of the imperial family.

How long are they planning to keep him alive? It's a waste of tax money.

Oh, it's fine; he's a cheap prince they can use and dispose of whenever they like. That's why they let that waste of space live.

The wine they intentionally spilled on him has left a stain that won't come out. The lace handkerchief she made for him is submerged in muddy water.

I could have given you a different future, and yet—

His back as he faces a canvas behind the bars of the West Tower, charcoal in hand.

"What are you drawing?"

"It's a secret," he says with a laugh, and what he's drawing is…

In the game, it hadn't been a picture like that. Is that good fortune or bad?

Her eyes are so hot, they feel like they're on fire. It hurts. Everything's being sluiced away. She has to see it, though.

The future Lilia Reinoise has ruined.

When he opens his eyes, the face he often sees in dreams is right there, and it leaves him so stunned, he can't move.

"Are you awake, Master Charles?"

Her voice is impassive. This is no dream.

"Woman— Why are you he—?!"

He starts to bolt up but realizes while he's in motion that it's going to bring their faces closer together. In an attempt to avoid that, he twists his upper body and ends up rolling off the couch and onto the floor.

Estella, who's seated on the carpeted floor, tilts her head. The tips of her pale-gold shimmering hair sway at the level of her lovely chin. *It's grown out a little*, he thinks.

She chopped that hair off when she'd gotten engaged to him.

"What are you doing?"

"...Sh-shut up! Y-you were too...close... Actually, why are you even here?!"

"I heard you were caring for her, so I thought I would help you. She is a woman, you know."

Estella glances at the bed, a short distance away. It has a high, rounded canopy, the sort that's common in Ashmael, and Machina is sleeping right in the middle of it.

I bet Mother or somebody asked her to come check on me.

She's a very serious girl, and that would be just like her. Talking himself into believing that explanation to calm his jumpy heart, Charles gets up and grabs the water pitcher. Screaming right after waking has made his throat dry.

"So what were you doing?"

"Gazing at your face while you slept."

He almost spits out his water. Hastily wiping his mouth, he turns back. "Wh-wha-what...?"

"Since I had the chance, I thought I would observe you closely, Master Charles. I knew already, but you really do have a lovely face. It's like a work of art."

"—I'm so sorry I'm not tall and sturdy like my brother!"

His older twin doesn't look like him at all. He's in excellent shape, and he's growing like a weed. In contrast, Charles is delicate for fourteen, and he hasn't grown much yet. On top of that, his exquisitely modeled features resemble his father's, and they give him an androgynous look. He knows people compare him with his twin, and they mock him by calling him "the princess."

When his older sister and brother heard about that, they'd synchronized in an unfortunate direction: *"We'll show those scoundrels." "That's right! Our little brother isn't just a princess; he's a nation-toppling beauty!"* Then they'd forced the reluctant Charles to dress as a girl and marched him around, plunging the capital into chaos as everyone wondered who the beautiful princess was. His father scolded everyone, telling them to *"Do anything but that,"* but Charles didn't feel particularly grateful. His father was sympathetic only because he had the same problem.

"Master Charles, do you want to be taller?"

"Of course I do."

"Why?"

It's obviously better if I'm taller than you, the girl I like.

As if I could say that!

Canceling out a remark his father would probably have made without a blush, Charles gets to his feet. "Who cares about that? And Machina's…still asleep, huh?"

Unless Machina wakes up, he can't send Estella back to the future. He can't do anything else until that's done. He wants to settle this fast, but…

"…Um. What sort of person is Lady Machina?"

Charles is standing by the bed, looking down at Machina, and Estella's strangely hesitant question makes him blink. "What sort of…? All I know is that Evare brought her from the future. We've never said more than a word or two to each other."

"What did you talk about?"

"Huh? Um, well, I greeted her and stuff? …I also asked why she was doing what Evare said."

"And then? What sort of relationship did you build?"

It's not as if he has to tell her, but Estella comes closer, pressuring him. He gets anxious, and his mouth moves on its own. "Sh-she doesn't eat, and she mostly doesn't react to stuff, so I dunno. She'd help me sometimes, though, so I thought she probably wasn't a bad person… Evare's rotten." Remembering, Charles bites his lip. "He says she's not real. He's got his own story, and he got his hopes up for nothing. If I had to guess, he's taking it out on her, but he even says she's a doll who can't do anything but fight, right to her face. Even so, Machina just keeps following him, like a chick. It makes you wonder what she's thinking, you know?"

"…Yes, I see."

"Just once, I asked her if she wanted to fight. She shook her head, so…I think she might actually hate fighting… I mean, I don't know. Anyway, I feel bad for her. He treats her like she's disposable."

Because unlike me, it's okay if she lives.

"You like Lady Machina, don't you, Master Charles?"

Charles has been empathizing in a way that borders on self-harm, but that remark shocks him out of it. "Huh?! How did you come to that conclusion?!"

"You mean you don't? I had assumed that was why you didn't like me."

"Wh-who said I didn't like—?"

You, he's about to say, but he stops himself.

What's the point of telling her that?

The only thing he can do is send Estella safely home to the future.

"Or are you still saying you don't want to be crown prince and you don't want to be engaged, like a spoiled child?"

If she's gotten the wrong idea, she should stay wrong.

Loading his voice with cold feelings so that he'll seem as mean as possible, Charles glares at Estella. "It's nothing to do with you, woman."

"...Don't call me 'woman.' I am—"

"Don't go pushing your ambitions onto me just because you couldn't be holy king. Nobody needs that. Just go be holy king instead."

He doesn't want to see the hurt in her expression, so he looks away. Clenching his fists, Charles gazes down into Machina's apparently lifeless face. He hopes she'll wake up soon.

Having someone he's already said goodbye to turn up right in front of him is hard on the heart, and once was enough.

"That's...true. I may have been forcing it onto you—"

He feels a charged ripple of magic.

Yanking Estella toward him, Charles then pushes her behind him, protecting both her and the bed where Machina sleeps. Estella is startled by the sudden movement, but then she hears the crackling, twisting space. She gulps, gazing at it.

It takes time, but what finally emerges from the unstable, warped darkness is his grandfather—or that's how they refer to Luciel, the god of demons. The other person is Serena Gilbert, the duchy of Mirchetta's first female prime minister, whom Charles privately thinks is scary.

"Hey, where are we?! It looks sort of like Ashmael, but..."

"I—I don't... I used the recoil from getting slashed with the sacred sword to teleport, as if I was being pulled, so..."

Staggering, his grandfather sets his feet on the ground, and then he stares.

He isn't looking at Charles. His eyes are on the girl on the bed behind him.

"Amelia…?!"

"Huh? Wait— No way."

Luciel comes closer, dragging his feet. Picking up on his bitter sorrow, Charles lets him pass. Estella steps aside along with him.

"It is Amelia…isn't it? Her hair's a different color, but…"

"…Her name is Lady Machina. I'm told she's an artificial human Lady Amelia created," Estella tells him timidly.

Luciel falls to his knees beside the bed. "We saw a girl who looked just like Grace, too. Don't tell me she was also…"

"Was her name Lucia? In that case, yes. Lady Amelia made her along with Machina. They are both supposed to be new vessels for the Maid of the Sacred Sword."

"Two Maids…of the Sacred Sword." Eyes wide and stunned, Luciel repeats the words. Then his face crumples into a smile. "Amelia, you… Why?"

He touches the back of Machina's hand where it lies on the coverlet.

Feeling that he mustn't get in the way, Charles stays quiet. Everyone else has apparently picked up on it, too.

"I'm sorry. I don't know what made you so angry. Grace says it's okay not to know. That probably means it's better if I don't understand. There's something I thought it might be, actually, but I didn't want it to be that. After all, you were precious to me. That made me try even harder not to think about it. When you held Grace's head and called me a fool of a demon king and laughed, I pretended not to notice you were crying."

It's like a religious confession. Luciel holds Machina's hand as if he's clinging to it.

"That means you can ignore the wish I'm about to make. I'm a god, and yet I couldn't save my wife or my sister-in-law. You can laugh, even. But…Grace is—"

The body and soul, which Evare has taken away. It's easy to imagine what's happened.

"…I know. Grace is human. We'll have to part someday. And despite that, I can't become a god yet… Even though seeing her one more time was all I wanted. That thing is something else, though. I'm sure it has Grace's soul, and the strength is probably Grace's as well. But that's definitely not *her*."

Gripping Machina's hand in both his own, Luciel goes on, head bowed. It's as if he's praying.

"Please save her, Amelia."

His voice is thin, as if he's about to burst into tears. He may be crying already.

"I can't stop Grace… No, it's not just me." Luciel looks up, chuckling a little. "The only Maid of the Sacred Sword who's ever defeated Grace is you."

Machina's hand twitches. Slowly, her eyes open.

Estella gasps, and Serena gives a soft sigh. Luciel is startled, and then he smiles through his tears.

Charles just watches it all.

Both his grandfather and his father say the Maid of the Sacred Sword saved them, instead of killing them. She's a being who's far too familiar to be legendary.

Evare must want salvation as well. That's why he's looking for her.

I don't need my *Maid of the Sacred Sword, though.*

He doesn't need to be saved. He wants to do the saving. To keep himself from losing sight of that resolve, he touches his black-gloved hand softly, from its fingers to its wrist.

First, he'll ask Machina to return Estella to the future. No, before he does that, he has to deal with Evare and the floating palace. It isn't as if he has no sympathy for the man, but if he's going to mess with Charles's family, that's another story.

If Lucia has awakened as the Maid of the Sacred Sword, she'll attack soon.

And as soon as that premonition crosses his mind, the earth rumbles.

✦ Fourth Act ✦
Rematch: Villainess Versus Heroine

Aileen lifts fruit dressed with yogurt to her husband's lips, but the spoon slips from her fingers.

An earthquake— No, that's the sound of the holy king's barrier trembling. The vibrations are making the ground shake.

Claude has caught the spoon with his lips just before it falls, and now he glances up and off to the side. "Showing themselves this early in the day?"

"Well, it isn't the sort of situation where we'd spend ages glaring at each other. I wonder what they're after this time."

"Us, probably. Evare said the evil god didn't awaken when he should have because the fiend dragon became the Holy Dragon Consort. We made that happen. In other words, we're responsible for everything. Of course Baal and his people will get dragged into it, even though they weren't involved." Claude toys with the silver spoon.

His analysis makes Aileen give a musical laugh. "Gracious, are we the root of a great evil?"

"We're the demon king and his wife. We can't help it."

"I suppose we did become emperor and empress, didn't we? It's a shame the world is so fragile." Taking up a holy sword, Aileen rises to her feet.

Claude sighs. "I suppose telling you to stay here would be useless."

"Goodness. I mean, the Maid of the Sacred Sword always targets the evil demon king, doesn't she?" She sits down lightly in the chair in front of Claude. "The demon king's wife can hardly let the Maid steal a march on her." Softly, she traces the curve of her husband's cheek with her index finger.

Tossing the spoon into the empty glass, Claude rises to his feet. "It sounds as if Father is back, although he's badly weakened. I'd like to ask him where he's been and what he's seen, then plan accordingly...but it looks as if we won't have time."

Another shock hits. Screams and yells begin to go up.

A moment later, there's a noise like breaking glass. They've heard that sound before.

The holy king's barrier has shattered.

Now Claude's curse will progress again. If he fights, it will advance even faster.

Aileen looks up. Claude smiles at her; the earring dangles from his ear. "All right. Shall we go, my dear Aileen?"

"Yes, Master Claude."

He's extended his hand to her deferentially. Smiling, she places her own hand in it.

It's the hand of the evil, world-destroying demon king.

However, ever since Aileen recalled her previous life—those ridiculous "memories of the game"—it's a hand she's never hesitated to take.

As if to blot out the refreshing sunlight, a palace has appeared in the sky, and its shape is still fresh in everyone's memory. It's the floating palace of the Holy Queendom of Hausel—the seat of the majestic queen who looked down on the world, subjecting it to a rain of holy swords like the proverbial hammer of justice.

It was last seen moving on its way to destroy Ellmeyer. Why has it reappeared? The resulting chaos is only natural. As far as Ashmael is concerned, it's a greater threat than the fiend dragon.

"Master Baal, what is the situation?!" Aileen shouts in the harem. It's deserted; he may already have issued orders to evacuate.

Baal responds from the roof of the Sun Palace, glaring at the distant floating palace. "No different from what it was earlier. Or rather, since we are the ones being targeted, it's worse. However, that's true for Ellmeyer as well."

"What do you—?"

A forked flash, bright as lightning during the daytime, erupts from the floating palace.

Baal's eyes gleam. The blinding attack is repelled by both the barrier he's deployed and the red one in the distance, and after a little delay, they hear the sound of an explosion catch up.

Claude narrows his eyes. "So they're attacking Ellmeyer as well?"

"Right. Since they're spreading out the force of their attacks, even our barrier can still repel them. However, that may not hold true if they throw everything they've got at it. And we're not sure how long the barrier over Ellmeyer—the one cast by your extremely impudent snotty-nosed whelp—will last."

"Father, I'll help!" Estella calls; she's run up to stand beside Aileen.

Charles, who's appeared behind her, mutters, "What's the point of giving them the battle of attrition they want, dummy?"

"Du—?!"

"They'll run out of magic soon. That's the type that attacks with stored-up magic. As a matter of fact, the power must already be lower after that first strike, and they won't fire again for a while. The fact that even sacred power can't cancel it out is a pain, but it was inevitable. Those attacks are built around a core of divine stones."

"Oh—is it an Elefas gun?" Claude drops a fist into his palm, as if it all makes sense to him now.

Thinking of the hardships of the mage who was once pressed into service as a power source, Aileen interjects, "Be kind to him and refrain from giving it an odd name, Master Claude. If I recall, Denis fixed it, so let us call it the Ele-Doni gun."

"Wouldn't the Donifas gun be easier to remember?"

"Either will do."

Charles gives them a cold glare before continuing, "The floating palace can repair itself, but normally, it would take several centuries. Evare is using his magic to forcibly accelerate the repairs and move it at the same time. The attacks should pause here for a while."

"How do you know how the floating palace works?"

"My teacher is the one in charge of maintaining it. He's told me a few things about it."

"...Since it sounds like he's come up in the world substantially, I think we should call it the Elefas gun to serve as a warning," Claude murmurs.

Charles glares up at the floating palace. "If Evare supplements it with his own magic, it should take about ten minutes to accumulate enough energy for another attack. We'll have to bring it down before then. The problem is where—"

"Don't worry about that. It seems to be heading toward the desert at the border. That's where Father was shot down earlier. It should be fine to sink it over there," Claude says.

Baal frowns. "You're dropping more troublesome things on us? Why don't you consider dropping them on your own territory sometimes?"

"What a good friend I have..."

"Saying it like you mean it won't help you. Listen, if you persist in taking that attitude, we'll stop being your friend one of these days!"

Although Baal yells, he doesn't refuse. If they don't bring the palace down, Ashmael will be in just as much danger as Ellmeyer.

Charles has been listening to the exchange as if it bores him. Magic crackles beneath his feet and lifts him into the air. "If that's finally settled, then I'll be going ahead."

"Do you intend to go alone?" Estella scowls.

Even to her, Charles is brusque. "Yes, I am. Is there a problem? I'll make Evare regret making an enemy of me." Giving a smile that doesn't go past his lips, Charles flies off at tremendous speed.

Impressed, Aileen puts a hand to her cheek. "He does take after you there, Master Claude."

"No, I think it's you."

"It's both of you, obviously. We imagine he really could bring down the floating palace by himself, but...we can't just leave him to it."

"No, we can't."

Prompted by Baal, Claude rises lightly into the air. Aileen hastily shouts at him, "Master Claude! I'm going, too!"

"No."

"But just a moment ago, you said we'd go together!! That there was no point in trying to stop me!"

"I can choose not to take you with me, though," Claude retorts cheerfully. Aileen's smile cracks.

Baal joins Claude. "We'll go, too. If we're going to intercept those attacks, being closer is better. We can leave Ares in charge of the evacuation. We'll also be able to keep you from turning into a baby dragon."

"...You are a good friend, aren't you?"

"What, you didn't know that already? That's how it is, Roxane, so...er, quit giving us that terrifying look."

Roxane, with Sahra attending her, is radiating an intimidating silence from the ground. She sighs. "...If you promise to come back safely, I shall see you off with a smile."

"Of course. Please look after Estella. As for you, Estella... If it comes down to it, we want you to protect this kingdom."

Estella looks startled. Then timidly, she nods. Baal smiles, then redirects his kingly gaze. "And you, Sahra. We're counting on you."

"Y-yes! I'll do my best!"

"May fortune favor you, my holy king." Roxane is smiling. Baal waves to her, then turns away.

As Claude starts to follow him, Aileen shouts at him accusingly. "Master Claude! Do you seriously intend to leave me behind?!"

"Staying home once in a while will make for a nice change of pace, won't it? You'll finally know how I feel." Claude's smile hasn't faltered even slightly.

Smiling in spite of herself, Aileen issues a low declaration. "—If you leave me behind, I promise you'll regret it."

"Charles really does take after you."

With that parting shot, Claude winks out of sight with Baal.

Aileen immediately turns to Estella. "You can teleport from here to the floating palace, can't you?"

"What? —Well, yes. But Father and Master Claude both said to stay here..."

"No, that's no good. We have to go after them quickly. Our opponents have the sacred sword."

Turning in the direction of the voice, Aileen sees Luciel, who looks as if even walking is hard, and Serena, who's supporting him. Behind them is Machina, as expressionless as ever.

"Father. How on earth did you get here?"

"That doesn't matter. We've been in the floating palace. We ran into Grace there."

Luciel is trying to keep his agitation under control, and she can tell something unpleasant has happened. "...You don't mean the girl named Lucia, do you?" she asks quietly.

"That's right. She had the sacred sword. Evare, an acquaintance from back when I was a god, was there, too...and he may have captured that Lilia girl."

"Lady Lilia?! Why? She's in Ellmeyer—or no, of course she wouldn't be, not under the circumstances."

Aileen can just picture Lilia rampaging around to her heart's content, giddy over the arrival of the sequel. Just thinking about it is exhausting.

"Am I to assume that she saved you and slipped out through Charles's barrier with you, Master Luciel?" Aileen gives him a half-hearted glare.

Serena snorts. "Good guess. For some reason, the two of us were still awake, even though nobody else was. Then we used this good-for-nothing god and that woman's power and got through the red barrier…with my help anyway."

"…Yes. Yes, of course. It is Lady Lilia, after all. She would be awake, and she would slip out."

Lilia is the heroine of Game 1, while Serena is Game 2's heroine. If Luciel joined them and they all reinforced one another, it would have been possible for them to get through Charles's barrier. The game's rules are tenacious.

"As an aside, didn't you consider relying on Auguste?"

If the game's rules still apply, there's a good possibility he's awake as well, but Serena grimaces openly. "You know he'd be useless. Even if he was awake, he'd just get himself killed."

"You always try to keep Auguste out of danger by talking like that, don't you, Serena?"

"Did you say something, Sahra?"

"I'm not loaning you Ares anymore, all right?"

The heroines of Games 2 and 3 apparently have some sort of feud going, but now isn't the time for it.

"So you rescued Master Luciel, and then you and Lady Lilia charged the enemy camp?"

"No. She said Hausel's floating palace had to be around somewhere, and when we went to investigate, it was the enemy camp."

"In other words, you charged the enemy camp."

No doubt she used her game knowledge to guess where it would be. Just talking about it makes Aileen feel weary.

Luciel frowns, looking concerned. "Lilia acted as a decoy to let the two of us escape. Evare said he'd make her the next queen, so… If he's fiddled with her memories, she may be under his control."

"What?!" Sahra turns pale. "Th-that's awful. Lilia... No...!"

"Sahra, calm down."

"But, Roxane! Lilia doesn't have the sacred sword anymore!"

Serena seems to have a few thoughts on that as well; a shadow falls over her expression.

Luciel continues, "It may be best to consider Grace an enemy, too. She stabbed me with the sacred sword."

"Lady Grace stabbed you, Master Luciel? With her own sacred sword?" Aileen frowns.

Luciel nods, hanging his head. "Technically, it was probably Lucia's, but... She did stab me. She didn't seem to recognize me."

Folding her arms over her chest, Aileen gives a long sigh. "...I see. It looks as if I really will have to go myself. Estella, will you take me?"

"But won't Emperor Claude be angry?" Estella gives her a worried frown.

"Gracious." The corners of Aileen's lips curve up. "Master Claude isn't petty enough to hold a grudge over a little thing like this."

"You're the reason the imperial castle gets those extremely localized blizzards all the time, aren't you? It's a total nuisance."

"That's a different matter! This is something else entirely!" Refusing to even entertain Serena's complaint, she gets a better grip on the holy sword. Against the sacred sword, the demon king and the god of demons don't stand a chance. That is one of the cardinal rules of this world. "It is my duty to handle the things that he can't."

Luciel, who's standing without help from Serena now, nods. "I'll take you, then. She's restored enough of my power that I can teleport, and if it comes to that, I can turn into the divine dragon and fight Evare."

"Thank you, Father, please do. And then—"

Machina steps forward soundlessly. Aileen blinks. "Do you wish to come as well?"

The girl nods. Her eyes are as hollow as ever, but they're focused. Estella is gazing at her steadily, and Aileen speaks to her again. "What will you do, Estella?"

"I...um..."

"I won't insist, but you did come here in pursuit of Charles, didn't you?"

Unusually, Estella seems to be having trouble reaching a decision. She speaks rather evasively. "If I go, I think it will sour his mood, so..."

Aileen and Roxane exchange looks. Estella continues, gazing at the ground, "Besides, I tend to force...various things onto him for my own convenience. My ideal of who I'd like him to be, for example... Even if I am his fiancée, I don't think that's a good thing."

"That's fine if you're engaged. It's an equal exchange." While she's puzzling over what to do about this, Serena nonchalantly speaks up. "I married in exchange for success. If he doesn't like it, your fiancé can simply refuse. You should at least say it."

"Actually, I'm having Ares do his best at being a general, too! There are several things about it that seem to be hard for him, but he's so dashing that I don't want him to quit!" Sahra looks happy.

Serena pulls a face. "Women like you are the nastiest type to deal with."

"Huh?! Why?!"

"I tried to make Master Claude emperor as well, but now that you mention it, I suppose I never asked whether that was what he wanted to be," Aileen says, going with the flow in a vague sort of way.

Estella looks shocked. "I-is that true? And that's how the demon king became emperor...?!"

"I thought Master Claude would be a good ruler, of course, but I also felt as if he needed to take the throne. If he was going to win happiness both as the demon king and a human, it was a necessary means toward the end."

And so she didn't hesitate, and she has no regrets.

Shrugging, Serena looks in the direction of Ellmeyer. "I know of a woman who went along with a man whose mind and stance were already made up, too, though."

"Oh, Isaac! Yes, the way he's devoted to his work is rather dashing, isn't it?!"

"In what way? That guy's definitely no good, and he won't make her happy!" Serena yells.

"Wha—? Huh...?"

"And actually, who is this girl anyway?!"

Sahra beckons Serena over and murmurs something in her ear. She's probably explaining Estella's origins.

"I would like Master Baal to stay holy king as well."

"Mother...," Estella calls to Lady Roxane in a thin voice. Apparently, she does allow herself to be a little weak in front of her.

"I don't know what it is that Master Charles wants. However, I once failed to notice the hand Master Baal extended to me. With help from Lady Aileen, I made it in time, but... I don't want you to have those regrets."

Softly stroking Estella's cheek, Roxane continues, "If you'd like to go, then go. In the first place, you did not come here to help us. Isn't that right?"

Estella came to take Charles back home. Her eyes are still a little hesitant, but after a slight pause, she nods. "All right. In that case, Lady Aileen and Master Luciel, I'll take you to the floating palace. And, er—you as well, Lady Machina."

Abruptly, Machina pivots to face Estella.

Everyone flinches. They watch as Machina pats Estella lightly on the head, then pivots away again.

"Um…?"

Estella is bewildered, but just then, a flash of searing light dyes their surroundings pure white. Its source is the floating palace. There's no time to hesitate. "Hurry, Estella."

"I know. Over here, all of you."

"Wait, I've got a message from that woman." As Estella's sacred power builds, Serena announces brusquely, "She says, 'Go easy on me.'"

Aileen tucks her chin, smiling. "You must be joking. I'm going to flatten her."

Particles of light surround her. As her vision thins, she sees Serena shrug and Sahra give a tense smile.

They melt away, and the next thing she sees is the floating palace—from much higher up in the sky.

"I seem to end up in this situation far too frequently!!" Aileen screams as she falls.

Estella is flustered. "I-I'm sorry! The palace has something like a magnetic field around it, and it destabilized my teleportation!"

"N-now, now, Aileen. I'll get us all down there safely, so— Claude?!"

As Luciel screams, Aileen's eyes flick in that direction, and she tightens her grip on the holy sword. Her body registers what she's seen before her mind does. She doesn't hesitate. She doesn't even think, *Why?*

A girl is attempting to run a holy sword into Claude's chest, and Aileen cuts in from the side, slashing at her.

Pulling her blade away from Claude, the girl turns gracefully in midair. Then with a smile, she alights on the rubble of the floating palace. "Good day, Lady Aileen."

"Good day, Lady Lilia."

Lilia is holding a shining holy sword. Standing in front of Claude, squarely in her path, Aileen smiles back at her.

Barring her way and protecting Claude—those roles should always be hers.

"It's no use, Lady Aileen. I really do need to slay the demon king."

"Mm, yes. That's what I thought you'd say."

"Well, I mean, I am the Maid of the Sacred Sword."

This woman is the enemy. She always has been, and she always will be.

Charles glances at Claude and Baal, who've teleported after him. "Coming along is fine, but stay out of my way."

"If you brush me off coldly like that, I may accidentally shout the name of the girl you like."

"Die right this minute!" Charles snaps back instantly, flushing bright red.

Baal puts a hand next to his lips, screening them as if he's telling secrets, but his voice definitely isn't quiet. "Did you see that? The boy could just have teleported, but he flew away like he was showing off."

"It was probably because that looks more impressive."

"I see. So he's at the age when he's more concerned about appearance than anything else… We understand, mm-hmm, yes."

"That wasn't— You know that wasn't it! The floating castle is made of divine stones and tends to warp magic in weird ways. Teleporting here is dangerous!"

"As you flew away, she was gazing at you… Although, I won't say who 'she' was."

"She didn't gaze—she just glanced over briefly! Listen, boy, don't get carried away. We won't say who, but our precious daughter doesn't care for you at all!" Baal shouts.

"What is wrong with you people?! If you only came along to bully me, then leave!" Charles bellows. Then he bites his lip. "Besides, I don't need you to tell me that. I wouldn't get carried away… It's better if I'm not around."

"So this is puberty…!" Claude sounds deeply impressed.

Baal gives him an ostentatious warning. "If we were you, we wouldn't talk like that. We've been through something similar, and we know you'll want to die later. It's history you'll never live down. The suffering and regret will surge over you like waves… It hurts…"

"In your case, it's pretty recent dark history. That time when you were cold to Consort Roxane."

"Shut up, don't remind us! And anyway, there were reasons for that! Several of them!"

"Enough. Say whatever you want. It won't change what I'm here to do."

Up ahead, the floating palace seems to flash. Claude recognizes this group. "All-white soldiers, hmm?"

They've come to intercept them en masse, and Charles snorts, stopping in midair. Layer upon layer of magic circles appear in front of him. He's drawn a sword before they notice, and he swings it horizontally.

"You're in the way."

That solitary slash makes the summoned soldiers explode one after another in a chain reaction. The blasts spread out like a belt of fireworks, and the soldiers collapse into dust.

"So you use spells. Is that your teacher's influence?"

"I just don't like the inefficient, brute-force way you two use your power, that's all."

With a contemptuous snort, Charles drops onto the front courtyard of the floating palace. *He's a thoroughly impudent son*, Claude thinks. Shrugging, he and Baal follow him.

A demolished gate, broken pillars, and a building damaged beyond recognition. The only word for this scene is *ruin*. This place looked awful before, but now it's on the verge of total collapse. Not only that, but since the fissure down the middle has been forcibly stuck back together with magic, the ground is uneven. He can hear a strained creaking noise from somewhere.

"All right, if we're going to stop the Elefas cannon… Should we destroy the engine first? I'm pretty sure it was over there."

"We think it would be faster if you ripped the island in two again. We'll cover for you, so give it your best."

"When it really counts, you're always like that, aren't you?"

"Nah, c'mon, don't do that."

The voice comes from above them, on what remains of the palace balcony. From that perch, which threatens to crumble at any minute, Evare is looking down at them.

He puts one hand to his chest and gives an exaggerated bow, like a theater usher. "Welcome. Glad you could make it. Well, this is the crowd I figured I'd get. The holy king and the demon king. You'd be enough of a headache on your own, and now you've brought along a prince who's real close to Luciel in his prime."

"Evare, you've found the Maid of the Sacred Sword. That means you have no more business with this era." Charles steps forward; his voice is clear and carrying. "I won't run or hide. I'll keep my promise, so you keep yours. Surrender the floating palace and leave this age alone."

"Comin' from a boy prince, that ain't real convincin'. What do the demon king and the holy king say?"

"I've spoken with them already. We've reached an agreement."

"Huh?" Evare gives them a dim-witted look.

"I also explained about the corrupt dragon, and what's going to happen to me after this. On that understanding, if you surrender the floating palace and go home, they've promised not to pursue you any further."

"...Nah, nah, nah, nah! Even if you explained, there's no way they'd let you. That guy's obviously gonna stop his son!"

"Neither my father nor the demon king would risk their countries or the future for a stupid thing like that." Charles is dignified. Behind him, Baal sighs, and Claude shrugs. Neither of them denies it.

Evare looks appalled. "Is this for real...? Family should be hell-bent on shuttin' this down."

"I haven't told my wife. She probably wouldn't allow it," Claude admits.

Baal crosses his arms. "The same goes for us. There are some things it's best not to know. Especially for our daughter."

"Oh, I see. So you're doin' your duty as leaders of your nations, huh?" Evare sounds disgusted. Then he gives Charles a pitying look. "Well, that's a shock. The holy king, the demon king, and the demon king's son. I wasn't sure I could call any of you human, but I take it back. You're human, all right. Leavin' your son to die for the sake of a formless thing like a country is somethin' only humans would think up."

"...It's not really like that," Claude murmurs, but nobody hears him.

Instead, with perfect composure, Charles says to Evare, "Withdraw. Do it, or I'll get rid of both you and the floating palace."

"Here's the thing: I can't. See, I'm well aware I'm bein' reckless." Setting his hands on the railing of the ruined balcony, Evare gives a wry smile, but the eyes that gleam behind his spectacles aren't smiling at all. "I'm bettin' my future on this, too. I can't back down."

"Fine. I'll kill you and drop the floating palace out of the sky." Charles speaks calmly, as if he's simply stating a fact.

Evare takes his hands off the railing. "Oooh, scary. But listen." Gazing steadily at each of their faces, he smiles. "Did you people forget there's no way you can beat the Maid of the Sacred Sword?"

As he spreads his arms wide, a figure darts out from behind him. Claude frowns. *Lilia Reinoise!*

He doesn't know why, but Lilia Reinoise is attacking them with a holy sword.

Baal shouts, "Hey, isn't that the former Maid of the Sacred Sword?! Did you plan this?!"

"No, Evare's controlling her!" Charles tells them.

Evare laughs scornfully. "C'mon, don't say it like that. What'll people think? I made her come 'round, that's all."

"She no longer has the sacred sword, though."

"What're you sayin', Demon King? Even if she's a former one, that's the Maid of the Sacred Sword, and she's armed real well."

As if to back up Evare's warning, Lilia's holy sword gouges up a spray of dirt. A regular holy sword wouldn't have this much power.

"I think the match might be over before you even get out there, Lucia."

While their attention was elsewhere, a girl who looks just like Grace has come to stand at Evare's side.

Claude and the others flee into the sky, pursued by the holy sword. Repelling it with a barrier that has both sacred power and magic worked into it, Charles yells, "We'll fight her later; take the palace down first. There's no time!"

"Gracious, demon king's son, you mustn't get distracted." Lilia's holy sword stretches like a whip, tangles around Charles's ankle, and dashes the startled boy to the ground.

"Charles!"

"You too, Demon King." No sooner has he heard her voice than the holy sword attacks him from above. Turning, Claude parries her attack with a holy sword he's quietly brought with him.

A blast wind rages right in his face, but Charles is behind him. He can't retreat any farther.

She's strong. She can't have been training, and yet...

So this is the Maid of the Sacred Sword. The thought that his wife faced something like this makes a shudder run through him.

"You know, I think this may be the first time we've fought, Demon King."

Their magic clashes right in front of him, crackling. The girl seems to be enjoying herself immensely, and Claude frowns softly. "...Cedric's going to cry."

He is aware that this is technically his sister-in-law.

When Lilia hears that, she laughs. "You're pretty composed, Demon King. You're up against the Maid of the Sacred Sword, you know."

"You no longer have the sacred sword."

In fact, the weapon in Lilia's hands is a holy sword. He's wary, but since magic will work on it, it isn't a threat. The sacred sword would've erased Claude's magic instantly.

"Unless I get careless, that's no danger to me."

"You're certainly coolheaded enough. Unfortunately for you, though, there couldn't possibly be a game where the Maid of the Sacred Sword loses to the demon king. Especially not if he's a final boss."

Lilia slams Claude's blade out of the way. Immediately, the light radiating from her holy sword swells.

It's a pseudo-sacred sword. Realizing that, even Claude's eyes widen.

"Now then, let's change the future, shall we? Just like Lady Aileen did."

Lilia grins, then lunges at Claude and Charles, who's back on his feet. She intends to skewer them both.

*Tsk*ing, Claude kicks Charles out of the way. Even as he does it, the tip of Lilia's sword closes in on his chest. The barrier Baal casts in front of him is just a stopgap, but it does slow her down for the briefest of moments.

In the end, that moment is what separates victory from defeat— It's probably destiny.

"Claude?!"

He hears his father scream, but what he sees is his wife flying toward him.

The sacred sword is terrible. It exists to destroy the demons and the demon king, and it always bars his way.

However, in his wife's hands, any blade becomes a sacred sword meant to protect him.

"Now do you see your error in leaving me behind, Master Claude?" Aileen asks, half in jest.

Behind her, Claude seems to be smiling wryly. "Mm, yes. I have always made a point of not interfering in fights between women, and yet..."

"So what are we callin' this? The Maid of the Sacred Sword versus the Maid of the Cursed Sword? What a pain in the ass..."

Evare is looking down at them from the crumbling balcony. He has an index finger to his temple, and he seems to consider himself a disinterested spectator. Aileen gives a contemptuous snort. "The Maid of the Sacred Sword? Her?"

Lilia cocks her head. Her enigmatic smile is the same as ever, but her violet eyes are just a little unfocused. "I *am* the Maid of the Sacred Sword. Tell me you're not underestimating me just because this is a holy sword, Lady Aileen."

"You heard her. She may be the old model, but she can draw power that's a lot like the sacred sword out of the holy sword. I'd expect no less from her."

"The old model, hmm? I sense no respect for previous installments... Or I suspect that is what Lady Lilia would say, but—"

"I don't have a sacred sword anymore, so there isn't much that can be done."

The woman's learned to say some very admirable things indeed. With a snort, Aileen spins the holy sword one-handed, switching to a different grip. "Well, that's fine. Why tell you when I can just show you? We're both armed with holy swords, so let's see which of us is better, once and for all."

"Oh-ho, well, I'll hang out here and watch—or that's what I'd like to say, but you've brought all sorts of other folks along, and now we're outnumbered. The prince's princess, and Luciel— We just met a bit ago, didn't we? You look like standin's 'bout all you can manage right now."

"Grace..." Leaning on Estella, Luciel gazes at Lucia, who remains at Evare's side.

Evare frowns. "I keep tellin' you, this is Lucia. And also..." He shrugs, then narrows his eyes at the final figure. "Machina. I figured you'd self-destructed."

"......"

"Cat's still got your tongue, huh? Don't tell me you're mad or somethin'."

"...Poor... Ev..."

At the sound of Machina's faint voice, everyone stares. However, that's all she says. Then she lowers her eyes and falls silent.

"Whoa. That startled me. So you can say stuff besides 'yes' and 'no,' huh...?" Evare gives a dry laugh, then shakes his head. "There's no point in talkin' now, though... You'd have to be the Maid of the Sacred Sword, and you ain't. Sorry 'bout that." Averting his eyes, he apologizes lightly.

Looking at Machina, Aileen sighs. "I think you have the wrong idea about Maids of the Sacred Sword."

"What, this supposed to be a sermon or somethin'? You think you people have that kinda time?"

Evare opens his right hand, revealing a small, conical rock. It shines, sparkling— Is it a divine stone?

Abruptly, the stone begins to spin, and the floating palace moves. Slowly, as if taking aim, it changes direction. It's heading for Imperial Ellmeyer.

"No—is that the switch?!"

Punching through the barriers Baal and Claude both cast on reflex, the ray of light collides with the peak of the red barrier enveloping Ellmeyer. The barrier thins, as if it's melting. Cracks begin to run through it, and finally, it explodes.

The barrier Charles cast to protect Ellmeyer has broken.

"I guess I shouldn't have split it up like that. If this thing shoots at full power, it's unstoppable. One more attack, and both Ellmeyer and Ashmael are done for."

The conical divine stone is now blackened and dull, just like a regular rock. Closing his fingers around it, Evare laughs.

Baal shouts, "Stop him! Don't let him fire again!"

"Of course not. We're bringing this palace down."

"Goodness, we can't have that."

As Claude's red eyes flash, Lilia lunges at him, holy sword held high. Aileen immediately parries it. "Have no fear. I'll be your opponent even if you don't target Master Claude."

"Heh-heh! I'm glad. We can start over from the beginning, too, then!"

Apparently, her memories are intact. Evare probably isn't

controlling her completely. It should be possible to restore her sanity. "Master Claude, you focus on Evare and the floating palace!"

"Not gonna happen!"

Evare unleashes an explosion of magic from the crumbling balcony, forcing Claude's magic back. At the same time, Lilia's and Aileen's holy swords clash, and the flash of light paints their surroundings white.

The magic and the holy swords seem to have triggered some sort of reaction in the floating palace; it lists dramatically.

Magic shoots up from the fissure down its center, creating a pure-white wall. Claude and the others aren't that far away, but she can't see them anymore.

Aileen and Lilia are the only ones on the side from which Ellmeyer is visible. That's perfect.

"Come, Lady Aileen, let's settle this!"

Launching herself off the wall of magic, Lilia attacks.

This woman—that can't possibly count as playing fair!!

They're both fighting with holy swords, but she's up against the Maid of the Sacred Sword. Even if she no longer has the sword itself, Lilia has latent sacred power. Aileen's no match for her—or she shouldn't be.

"The idea of becoming the enemy's minion! This isn't like you."

"Gracious. It may not look like it, but I do have my reasons."

They obviously aren't anything decent. Blocking an upward slash, she locks guards with Lilia's blade, taking the opportunity to get a closer look at her opponent's eyes. They really aren't quite focused.

"...What did he do to you?"

"Oh, nothing. It's just...if I beat you here, I'll be able to make Cedric emperor."

Aileen frowns, and Lilia's smile abruptly disappears. Her eyes focus on Aileen's in earnest. "I want to protect him. Even a little. Even if I'm starting late. If I can make it in time."

"You mean you regret it? Now, this late in the game, you—"

"I'm going to make him happy. And so..."

Abruptly, the pressure she's resisting increases. Lilia's holy sword grows brighter. Forced back by that pseudo-sacred sword, Aileen's heels scrape across the ground. She grits her teeth, and Lilia leans in until their noses are nearly touching. Her expression is deadly serious. "Lose, Lady Aileen. Just as the Maid of the Cursed Sword should."

Somewhere along the way, Lilia has gotten the higher ground, and she's pushing down on her. On the verge of falling to her knees, Aileen tucks her chin and smiles back at her. "You know there's no way I could!"

As Aileen gets a better grip on the hilt of her blade, magic erupts from her wedding ring, twining around the holy sword.

Lilia's eyes widen, and Aileen shoves her holy sword aside through sheer brute force. "I have no time to waste on you. Return to your senses!"

Lilia has been thrown off-balance, and Aileen promptly strikes with the hilt of her sword. Taking a hard blow to the temple, Lilia slides across the ground. Stomping down on her holy sword, Aileen points her own blade at the girl's neck. "Regret the fact that you challenged me all you like."

"You're so mean, Lady Aileen..." Lilia's eyes open, and she sits up. A single trickle of blood runs down her face. "I said to go easy on me. Didn't Serena give you the message?"

"You know there's no way I could do that. Not against you."

Lilia inhales in a theatrical way, then breathes out. "Even so, owww. I'm injured. Where's Sahra?"

"Not here. And? What did you gain? You intentionally let Evare put you under his suggestion and became the next queen so you could see Amelia's memories, didn't you?"

"Huh? Oh my. Who would've thought you knew me so well, Lady Aileen…?" Lilia's blushing bright red, and Aileen brandishes her holy sword at her. Lilia puffs her cheeks out sulkily. "I was only jokiiiing."

"Think of the situation and speak accordingly."

"It isn't as if I learned anything all that important, though. Amelia's prediction: Evare, the final boss who's defeated in Game 5, will awaken again in a thousand years, in a world that's rotting away. That's the era of Game 6. Apparently, you couldn't romance Evare in 5 because he becomes the hero in 6."

However, if what Evare said in the chapel is true, due to the fiend dragon's absence, he'd never awakened that first time. He probably woke abruptly in Game 6.

"In 6, to slay the corrupt dragon that's destroyed the world, he meets up with the heroine—the only living person in that world—and they leave on a journey through time in search of the sacred sword, in order to rewrite the past."

"And that girl awakens as the Maid of the Sacred Sword?"

"Right. There were two of them, actually. It was probably a double-heroine game. Maybe the one the player chose became the heroine, and the other one became the villainess? There may have been a route where they both became Maids of the Sacred Sword, too."

The sacred swords weren't there to serve as their souls, though. The two candidates Amelia had provided were nothing more than vessels of flesh, and only Machina was actually around. As a result, Evare suspected Lucia, the other one, might be the Maid of the Sacred Sword and came to the past in search of her.

Honestly! That's far too complicated.

Since it wasn't possible to match the elements of the game—the fiend dragon's existence, Estella's position—to the world's present state, the events of Game 5 haven't begun. However, according to Amelia's prediction, that doesn't hold true for Game 6, a thousand years in the future. At some point in time, the corrupt dragon must have appeared and rotted the world.

However, reality was still warped, and the game began with pieces missing—apparently.

"Then the final boss of Game 6 is the corrupt dragon the hero Evare is trying to slay?"

"That's right… I doubt I need to explain who that corrupt dragon is." Dusting herself off, Lilia gets to her feet and looks up at the sky. "What are you going to do, Lady Aileen?"

Aileen sighs. *If that's Charles, then no wonder Master Claude left that curse alone… Honestly, Master Claude. He neglected to tell me.*

Should she turn a blind eye to the fact that they kept her in the dark and consider it a secret only a father and son could share, or is that the last thing she should do? Aileen hasn't become a mother yet, and she doesn't know. It's a tricky question.

"…I'd prefer not to be a mother who meddles excessively in her children's lives." Aileen looks at the wall of magic that's trying to join the floating palace together. Perhaps because the impacts have died down, its momentum seems to have slowed a bit. "I do think giving a bit of a push in certain directions is forgivable, though."

"Heh-heh. That's the spirit. I'll cheer you on, Lady Aileen."

"There isn't much point in you cheering me on. I don't even have a sacred sword."

"And you don't need one, do you? You're my protagonist."

So she fancies herself the player again, does she?

Aileen feels tired to her bones, but just as she's about to retort, the ground begins to pitch again. Then the floating palace fires a blast at Ellmeyer.

She crosses her arms to shield her eyes, but through the gaps between them, she sees the blast collide with the multilayered barriers Claude and Baal have cast. Lilia is watching it, too. "That's no good," she murmurs. "They won't last long."

"Wait—Lady Lilia?!"

Holy sword gleaming, Lilia leaps off the floating palace. Then impossibly, she lands on the ray of light, which Aileen assumes is composed of nothing more substantial than sacred power and magic. "What?! You can stand on that?! Is that even okay?!"

"Heroine bonuses are terrific, aren't they?! I'll buy you time. Give it your best, Lady Aileen!"

While Aileen stands there aghast, Lilia rapidly recedes in the direction of Ellmeyer. Since she is riding a ray of light, naturally, she moves extremely fast. Aileen hears something along the lines of "Eeeeee, this is fun!" but decides to pretend it was her imagination.

"It isn't as if she's surfing. The idea of being able to do a thing like that without the sacred sword… I swear, there's something wrong with that woman."

Partway through, she shakes her head. That isn't what matters now.

Lilia is headed toward Ellmeyer, which has lost Charles's barrier. If a single shot from the floating palace's cannon so much as skims the capital, it will probably vaporize the whole place.

That is why she's gone there.

She really isn't the player anymore. An impressed sigh escapes her, and that alone is enough to let her switch gears. Aileen turns back, leveling the holy sword. *You can do it, can't you, Aileen? Even if this isn't the sacred sword. The sacred sword is—*

With a smile on her lips, she swings the holy sword at the wall of magic that bisects the palace.

The magic wall that separates her from Claude splits cleanly down the middle. It may be just a holy sword, but it's only natural that it could do this much.

The ground lurches, and then the magic that's holding the floating palace together shoots up like a wall, hiding Aileen and Lilia from view.

Lady Aileen, Lady Lilia...!

Charles is probably worried, too; Estella hears him shout a short distance away. "Father! Are you sure it's okay to leave Mother like that?!"

"No, it's not, but she's never once listened to me. You're very similar."

Claude is calm. That's a relief, but for some reason, he glances at her. Scowling openly, Charles yells at her, "Why did you come here, woman?! I told you not to follow me!"

Inside Estella, something snaps. She steps in front of Charles. "Never mind that! The important thing is the floating palace! Father, I'll stop the next attack, so don't concern yourself with the rear."

"Huh?! There's no way you can stop that!"

"You're all talk, Master Charles, so stay out of it!" She glares straight at him.

Charles's lips flap soundlessly, and then he screams, "Oh, for the love of— Once this thing is down, go back to the future like you're supposed to!"

That's all he ever says to her. Accepting the fight he's picked, Estella screams back, "Wait until you've downed the palace to say such things!"

"Ha-ha! A young lovers' spat. This is kinda heartwarmin'."

"Estella!"

By the time Baal shouts, Evare's hands have already closed around her neck.

No—!

Turn back. Fight… But it's the first time anyone has ever tried to kill her, and her reaction is slow.

"Sorry. I'm a coward. I'm takin' you as insurance."

His red eye flashes—and then Estella is in Baal's arms.

Baal looks surprised as well. He gazes back at her.

"F-Father. Thank you for rescuing—"

"No, it wasn't us."

"Don't make me angry, Evare," Charles says in a low voice.

Startled, she looks back.

Evare is where Estella was a moment earlier, his chest impaled by a huge blade of magic. From the sheer intensity of the magical energy rising off it, no one besides Charles could be responsible.

H-he saved…me…?

In that brief moment, he moved faster than anyone else.

Estella gulps. On the ground, run through by that sword, Evare gives a sly grin. Apparently, the wound isn't a fatal one. "Ha-ha! Insta-kill, huh? Talk about merciless. I guess I've incurred your wrath, huh. That's real touchin'. It's not like doin' this is gonna change *how you end*."

"I'm not here to change my fate."

The way Charles puts that seems significant, and Estella frowns.

"You're a real fine prince. Hard to believe you were s'posed to become the brutal emperor who destroyed Ellmeyer 'cause he was the reincarnation of the demon king and wanted sacrifices. Just bein' born in a different age changes quite a lot, don't it?"

What is he talking about? Estella doesn't know. She knows nothing about Charles.

That realization makes unease and anxiety steal into her heart.

"You're all fine folks, so how come my future turned out like that?"

"...Because the Maid of the Sacred Sword wasn't there, right?"

"Yeah, that's right. Because the Maid of the Sacred Sword, the one who was gonna end you before you turned into the corrupt dragon, wasn't there."

Evare touches the magic sword that's piercing him, and it begins to crumble. As everyone watches him warily, he gives a dauntless smile. "You don't care if you die. You wanna die protectin' your family? That's a nice, convenient, spoiled li'l wish. If your wish is that cheap, then lemme have everythin', Prince!"

"You're going to hand over the floating palace and disappear from this era first!"

"Lucia! This prince is the corrupt dragon that's gonna rot the world, the one the Maid of the Sacred Sword needs to slay!"

Lucia darts out from behind the crumbling magic blade, a smile on her doll-like face. She swings the sacred sword down. The floating palace launches an attack, and both Baal and Claude *tsk* in irritation.

"Kill him! He's the world's enemy!"

"Master Charles!" Without thinking, Estella tries to reach for him, but Baal grabs her arm, pulling her away. Estella struggles as she is dragged into the air. "Father, please wait, Master Charles is—"

"Calm down. Neither you nor we can block an attack from the sacred sword."

He's right, but that isn't what she wants to hear.

"Master Charles is the—the corrupt dragon who's going to rot the world? What does that mean?!" Even as she asks the question, her mind keeps racing. Charles is the son of the demon king. The demon king's true form is said to be a dragon. That means it wouldn't be impossible for him to transform into one. Estella has actually seen Claude turn into a young dragon as a result of the curse *he took over* from Charles.

In other words, Master Charles is also cursed to become a dragon.

It can't be. It can't be—

"—the one the Maid of the Sacred Sword has to kill?!"

"We didn't want you to know about it."

That brief remark is enough to make the pieces fall into place for Estella. "...You knew about this. Both you and Emperor Claude."

"He told us himself. Then he told us to stay out of his way."

"And you believed a preposterous story like that?!"

Even if the demon king's true form is a dragon, the idea of Charles becoming a dragon that rots the world is ridiculous. It can't be true. Estella screams the words at him, and Baal gives a little sigh.

"...He showed us what's beneath that eye patch. His skin's turned to tiny black scales. It doesn't happen fast, but if something is pressed against those scales, it rots. The skin on the back of his hands is beginning to turn black as well. He says that in the future, we made that eye patch and those gloves to suppress his symptoms."

Estella knows nothing about this. "They're like Claude's earring," her father's voice says, but it sounds hollow.

"Apparently, he developed this illness a month ago, quite abruptly. He said it was like a curse. That's why, when Evare said he would become the corrupt dragon, he believed him. The discoloration's already spreading to his arms. No doubt it's only a matter of time before it covers him entirely. Even we could do nothing about it."

In that case, Charles has no choice but to be slain. By the Maid of the Sacred Sword.

Below her, Luciel is screaming something, trying to stop Lucia. Claude and Charles are fighting back, but the floating palace's attacks are keeping them busy, and they're forced to stay on the defensive. In any case, the sacred sword is the power of justice that judges both magic and sacred power, so the demon king is no match for it.

Estella bites her lip hard. She tries to shake off Baal's hands, but he won't release her.

"Where are you going?"

"To tell Lady Aileen! Perhaps she can do something about it. She said she's used the sacred sword to restore Emperor Claude's humanity before."

"Don't be a fool. Aileen has no sacred sword now."

"Then am I simply supposed to stand here and do nothing?! That's—"

Abruptly, Machina appears right in front of Estella. Before the shock wears off, the girl pulls her arm. "Huh?! What—?"

"Hey, wait! Where do you intend to take Estella?!"

She doesn't even have to hear the answer to know: right to the center of the battlefield.

Dragging Estella along, Machina flies straight into the thick of a fight exploding with dust and magic and sacred power, where the visibility is so bad, it's hard to tell what's going on.

"—Machina?!"

Charles has noticed them right away, but Lucia's sacred sword is bearing down on him from the side. Machina's great sickle knocks it away.

"Why are you here?! Estella, all you can do is provide backup!"

Why has she come? Biting her lip, Estella grabs Charles's glove. Startled, he pulls away, and the glove slips far enough for her to catch a glimpse of dark, discolored skin.

Charles instantly fixes the glove, hiding his skin.

Estella has already seen it, though.

"When did that begin?"

"...N-now's not the time for that."

She knows. She knows, but... "Why didn't you tell me?"

Is it anger, frustration, or sorrow? Even she doesn't know, but something is building at the corners of her eyes. Charles stares, shocked, then starts talking anxiously. "I—I mean, if I'd said, you would have..."

"Am I that unreliable? Did you hate me that much?"

"No—"

"It's true that I can't become the holy king, and I'm not the Maid of the Sacred Sword! But—"

There might have been something she could have done. Even if it was just one little thing.

"You ain't got time for chitchat!"

Arrows of Evare's magic rain down over them, and she isn't able to finish her sentence. On reflex, Estella covers her head, and Charles pulls her into his arms.

If she's being honest, she's noticed that Charles always protects her first. She realized it when she came to the past. She doesn't know what it means, though.

So why won't he tell me anything?! Why?!

Irritated, Estella looks up. She just can't seem to get used to combat, and the mood tends to overwhelm her, slowing her reactions.

"I can fight, too!"

Violet eyes shining, she destroys all the magic with her sacred power. Claude kicks the airborne Evare out of the way, then comes down to join them. Baal follows a moment later.

"Estella, how reckless can you—?"

"Father, be quiet, please! Look up!"

From the air, Lucia raises the sacred sword high and smiles. Luciel darts in front of her. "Grace, don't! Remember me, please!"

Without a thought for his heartrending plea, Lucia brings the sword down with both hands.

A tremendously heavy attack falls toward them. Luciel manages to block it for a few moments, but he's pushed back and knocked all the way to the ground in no time. Claude catches him, and Baal resists with sacred power, but that only buys them seconds. She quickly breaks through, as if it's thin ice. Finally,

Charles casts a barrier by filling his right hand with sacred power and his left with magic, then combining them together. That holds, but it promptly begins to crack.

"Run now, while there's—!"

Even as Charles screams, another attack arrives, and the second swing of the sacred sword breaks even his barrier.

Estella casts a barrier, pouring all the power she has into it.

"Estella, you idiot! You know you're no match for the sacred sword!"

She does know that, but she keeps her eyes fixed ahead, digging her fingernails into the earth. As feared, her barrier begins to melt away. Still, she keeps facing forward, and she doesn't look away.

Why can't I do anything? Why don't I know anything?

Tears of frustration well up, but they evaporate. Her barrier's being broken down. She's going to lose.

She doesn't even know what it is she doesn't want to lose at. What exactly did she want to become, and how?

With an audible noise, the barrier vanishes. Steeling herself, she closes her eyes.

"Keep your eyes open, Estella!"

Startled, she looks up. With a thundering crash, something has punched through the wall of magic and knocked the sacred sword's attack flying.

"A woman may only close her eyes in front of the man she loves."

Estella blinks at the figure who's standing firm against the wind that tears at her skirts.

The woman is holding a holy sword, not the sacred sword. The history books call her the Maid of the Cursed Sword.

However, she is always as beautiful as the Maid of the Sacred Sword.

"Lady…Aileen. You saved me…"

"It wasn't me who saved you. It was Machina."

Startled, Estella finally notices that Machina is supporting her. When their eyes meet, the other girl pats her on the head again.

"Um…?"

What is that about? Is it sympathy or something? she thinks and is immediately ashamed of her own pettiness. However, although Machina's eyes still look as if they're made of glass, she says, "Watch."

She means the same thing as Aileen: She wants her to keep her eyes open.

Leaving Estella, who's gone limp, Machina faces forward again. Her eyes are fixed on Lucia.

"That isn't…the Maid of…the Sacred Sword."

That isn't the Maid of the Sacred Sword.

Machina's voice is quiet, but it carries a long way. It travels far enough for Evare to hear it, even though he's standing at a distance.

"She ain't the Maid of the Sacred Sword? Quit talkin' crazy, wouldja?" Evare gives an irritated scowl. Taking Lucia's hand, he smiles. "She's obviously holdin' the damn thing. That's the genuine article right there."

Machina doesn't answer; instead, Aileen responds, "No, that isn't the sacred sword. Not a real one, at least… Or rather, I should say it's no longer a real one."

"But that's Grace's sacred sword, so..." Awkwardly, even Luciel is arguing her point.

Claude slips his arms around Aileen's waist and whispers, "I understand, in a vague way."

"Goodness. I'd expect no less of my Master Claude."

"What're you makin' out over there for? Tryin' to bamboozle me with baseless theories ain't gonna work."

"Baseless? The holy sword couldn't possibly send an attack from the sacred sword flying."

Aileen's answer makes Evare's eyebrows come down for a moment, but that's all. "You used the sacred sword for a while yourself. You and the former Maid of the Sacred Sword are even there. It ain't real strange that you'd be able to fight it a li'l bit. It looks like you took out Lilia Reinoise, too."

"Lady Lilia is just fine. She's well enough to go surfing for a bit."

"The heck's that? ...Still, if she ain't defeated, the suggestion got busted. That means she didn't have enough regrets to do things over, no matter what she said. See, the stronger the desire, the easier it is for a suggestion to stick."

No wonder Lilia said such uncharacteristic things.

However, she must have meant at least some of it. What would have changed if she'd been a suitable Maid of the Sacred Sword from the beginning? That was the sort of thing she could think because she'd begun to really live in this world.

In other words, even in Lucia, Lady Grace must be...

What Grace, with all her strength, regretted. What she wished she could do over again.

"That ain't all Lucia's got."

Still smiling, Lucia raises the sacred sword. Everyone braces. Evare eyes them as if he's licking his lips. "All right, who should we go for? Lesse. Let's take out the one who's the most trouble first. —You got stabbed with the sacred sword, and you're still alive, so we're goin' with you, Luciel!"

Lucia thrusts out her sacred sword. Aileen levels her holy sword, ready to fight back, but Machina darts in first. For just a moment, Evare scowls, but then he smiles. "It ain't gonna work, Machina! Yeah, you shoulda been a Maid of the Sacred Sword! You didn't get there, though. You and me know that better than anyone!"

"Machina, no! You can't win against the sacred sword—Mother?!"

Charles tries to go to Machina's aid, but Aileen holds him back.

Evare laughs again. "What, you ain't savin' her? The holy sword should be able to hold out for a bit, y'know!"

"I won't save her because there's no need to."

"Huh?"

"A-Amelia…! Never mind me, go to Grace!"

Machina's great sickle is shielding Luciel completely, but it's begun to melt. She's clearly being overwhelmed. *Tsk*ing, Charles tries to fly to her, but this time, Claude grabs him.

"What, Father, you too?! If we don't do something, Machina's going to— Estella won't be able to return to the future!"

For just a moment, Estella looks at Charles, startled. However, the increasing intensity of the sacred sword's attack and Evare's loud laughter promptly reclaim her attention.

"What did I tell you?! You're no match for the Maid of the Sacred Sword!"

"All right, Amelia."

At the sound of that name, everyone gasps.

Still holding the melting sickle, without flinching from the incoming attack, Machina closes her eyes. "I'll switch…with you."

A raging torrent of light surges up from beneath Machina's feet. The great sickle slowly dissolves, changing shape—becoming a shining, sacred sword.

Eyes wide, Evare screams, "No! That ain't possible!"

Machina's hands close around the hilt, and she sweeps the blade in a horizontal arc. Lucia's attack is split in two, and Machina rushes in the opening. Grimacing slightly, Lucia catches the charge on her sacred sword.

White light envelops their surroundings.

The fragmented attacks fly off in all directions, punching through the remaining buildings and demolishing them. Rubble rains down, and Claude's magic shields them.

Machina stands in the billowing dust, eyes still closed.

In her right hand, she holds the sacred sword.

"Wh-why…?"

Luciel has fallen on his rump behind Machina, and he's gazing at her back in disbelief.

Picking up his unfinished sentence, Evare shouts, "Why?! Why does Machina have the sacred sword?!"

"—Found…you."

Machina speaks in a stilted, awkward voice.

Slowly opening her eyes, she gives a bewitching smile.

"Found you… I've finally found you, my sister. Poor Maid of the Cursed Sword. Heh-heh. You call that the sacred sword?"

It's the voice of the Maid who once saved the world. A proclamation from the queen who led that world.

"I am the real Maid of the Sacred Sword."

The genuine Maid of the Sacred Sword opens her violet eyes wide and flashes a sly smile.

Evare has probably fired on reflex. Machina evaporates his attack with a single slash, but he still doesn't seem able to believe it. He groans. "Wh-what…?"

"Found you— I've found you, I've found you, I won't let you get away again, Sister, this time, I'll kill you for sure!"

Without so much as a glance at Evare, Machina lunges. The sacred sword closes in on Lucia at tremendous speed, and she knocks it away—but Machina's already circled around behind her.

"Too slow."

The attack strikes Lucia's back, sending her tumbling out of the air.

Luciel shouts, "Wait— Amelia, go easy—"

But instead of crashing into the ground, Lucia lands neatly. Machina pursues her, and they both gouge scars into the earth, swords clashing, punching through broken buildings and making the sky explode.

Left in the dust by their momentum, the group on the ground can only gaze up at the ferocious battle unfolding in the air.

"……"

"…………"

"…They're redoing their sibling rivalry!"

"Is that okay?! It's not really what I was imagining!"

Aileen sums the situation up in a forcibly cheerful way, provoking a pathetic response from Luciel. That seems to snap Evare out of it; he pulls on a tense smile. "Th-that's right— Yeah,

Machina was originally qualified to be the Maid of the Sacred Sword, too. Those qualifications woke up, so she's got the same sacred sword. They should be equal, but..."

"If that's all you've got, don't you dare call yourself the Maid!"

Streaking down behind Evare's back, Lucia crashes into the ground. Up in the air, Machina laughs triumphantly, brandishing her sacred sword with a patently villainous look on her face. "Come on, don't die that easily! Not if you're the real Maid of the Sacred Sword!"

"L-let's stop her, okay, Aileen?!" Luciel shrieks timidly.

Aileen shakes her head gravely. "We can't. That's quite clearly Lady Amelia in her prime. I really don't think we could win."

"No...!"

The sacred sword's attack rains down as arrows of light, drowning out Luciel's scream. There's a tremendous explosion, and a cloud of dust rises.

"More importantly, let us drop the floating palace while we have the opportunity, Master Claude."

"Good point; let's do that. If we get in between them, we'll definitely die."

"Even you say to leave them alone, Claude? Why—?!"

Evare's attack comes flying at them from a different direction, but Baal's barrier deflects it before they can turn around.

"Don't get careless, you fools."

"—Explain. What the hell's goin' on?" Evare has turned their way, his palms crackling with magic. "It ain't impossible for Machina to have a sacred sword. Why now? —No, forget that, why is Lucia losin'?! Her sacred sword was the real deal."

His composure seems to have deserted him. There's no trace of his smug smile now.

"Did you do somethin', Luciel?!"

"M-me? No, nothing…"

"You must have known as soon as you stabbed Master Luciel. That sacred sword isn't the real one," Aileen tells him.

Evare's eyebrows come down. "What's that s'posed to mean?"

"What you thought was the real thing was a sacred sword made from the soul of Lady Grace, who loves Master Luciel. It's proof of her love for him."

"Huh? What's this 'love' business…?"

"There are set conditions that trigger the sacred sword's appearance, and separate conditions that make it real. To Lucia, taking in Lady Grace's sacred sword must have been the trigger condition. However, without love, a sacred sword can never be real."

Lucia doesn't love anyone, and so her sacred sword can't perform the way a real one would.

"That makes no sense. Then what? You're sayin' Machina's got this 'love'?!"

"I know nothing about Machina's feelings. Her trigger must have been taking in Lady Amelia's sacred sword, though. In that case, I know where that condition was met— She gained her sacred sword from Lady Grace's when it stabbed Luciel."

Evare looks as if he's tried to smile and missed, but he's listening to Aileen without interrupting.

"Lady Grace's soul was sealed in Lady Amelia's body, which lay on the altar, in the form of the sacred sword. However, body and soul can't be separated so easily. Through the sacred sword, their two souls must have mingled. No doubt it was only slightly, the faintest of traces, and yet…"

It's like an impossible lingering attachment.

"When Master Lucius was stabbed with Lady Grace's sacred sword, the Saint of Salvation recovered him. In the process, Lady Amelia's soul must have regained its power as well. Through Master Luciel, Machina connected with Lady Amelia's soul. That amounts to taking in her sacred sword. That's how she got one, just like Lucia."

Luciel puts a hand to his stomach. "Then…what protected me was what was left of Amelia inside Grace's sacred sword?"

Evare's voice is trembling. "Are you sayin' Amelia Dark is really there, in Machina?"

"That's right… Although, it does genuinely feel as if she's crawled back up from the depths of hell."

An explosion echoes behind them, and the raucous laughter that accompanies it is saturated with malice. She really doesn't want to turn around.

"Still, she is a real Maid of the Sacred Sword."

She didn't return to reclaim her crazed sister.

She came in order to prove she was the one and only Maid of the Sacred Sword. Surely, that was more like her.

"You've gotta be kiddin' me." Evare bursts out laughing, although his eyes are still wide. "I'm not buyin' that… There's no way I could! What's this 'proof of love' business?! That's just—!" He spreads his arms, and a shining conical stone rises over his right palm. "You won't be able to talk such a big game when Ellmeyer's destroyed!"

As Claude and the rest turn pale, the floating palace's cannon spits fire.

The attack flies straight toward Ellmeyer, and the recoil rocks the floating palace.

Aileen doesn't turn around. "It's no use."

"Huh?! What're you talkin' about? Ellmeyer's got no barrier now. It's done for!" Partway through, Evare's face and voice twist up.

Aileen is wearing a wry smile.

"There's one more Maid of the Sacred Sword in this world. And she'll never lose."

Behind her, a tremendous *boom* echoes, and the cannon is blown to bits.

She doesn't even have to look to make sure.

After all, Prince Cedric is there.

Lilia has blocked the attack with her holy sword.

"N-no… There's just…no way that could…"

Light flares overhead, then showers down. Everyone looks up at the sky as if they've been stung.

Turning dead white, Luciel screams, "Amelia… Grace!"

"This is the end, foolish sister."

Grabbing Lucia's head, Machina thrusts a hand into her chest. As she drags the sacred sword out of Lucia, Evare gasps. "Wait. Please wait. If the Maid of the Sacred Sword is gone, I'll—"

For just a moment, Machina glances at Evare.

However, her eyes promptly return to Lucia—*and Amelia smiles at Grace.*

"Sympathy makes me ill."

"A…me…" Grace is trying to call her name.

Amelia puts her face so close that their noses nearly touch. "You're much more inconsiderate than that, you know. Both my sister and my brother-in-law."

The sacred sword slips out of Lucia's body. Instantly, her eyes turn dull, and her body goes limp. Leaving Machina's hand, the sword changes shape—transforming into Grace.

"Grace!" Luciel shouts, catching her. However, although she promptly opens her eyes, she isn't looking at him.

"Amelia."

She calls her sister's name. Her gaze wanders through space, as if she's searching for something. Machina has alighted on the ground, and Grace reaches toward the empty air above her head; she seems to be pleading with it. *"Wait. Don't go. I still haven't… told you…anything… Amelia."*

Aileen can't see anything but the sparkling remnants of what had been the sacred sword. However, Grace is clinging to that spot, as if there really is someone there.

"Wait. Don't disappear without a word. Amelia, I… I'm…"

Grace's words fail her, and her face crumples. Slowly, Luciel embraces her transparent body from behind. Looking up at the same thing Grace is seeing, he smiles. "Thank you, Amelia. It's all right. Someday, I'll return your sister to you properly." Grace turns to look at him, startled; Luciel looks as if he's about to burst into tears. "This time, I really will grant your wish, and Grace's. Just wait."

At the very end, Aileen gets the feeling that someone laughed, just a little.

Then only Machina is there, holding Lucia's body. The sacred sword has vanished from her hands.

"…No…"

"You lose, Evare." Slipping out of Claude's arms, Aileen holds the dazed man at swordpoint.

Evare shakes his head, backing away. "This has to be a joke. If nothin' changes here, *nothin's gonna change there.*"

"Evare, I—" Charles starts forward.

Evare screams, "You! You ruined the world!" Machina, whose face is blank again, turns their way as if drawn by the bitter scream. "I'll be all on my own, for years and years, never talkin' or laughin', in a world where everythin's rotted and dead, an empty world, a world with nothin' in it, all alone— Why?! Why is it just me?!"

Aileen has the feeling that Machina's lips have moved, and she averts her eyes. She can't help it.

In that moment, Evare takes action. He's still wearing that drawn, tearstained smile. "If that's how it's gonna be, I'd rather take you all to hell with me!"

He clenches his right hand again. The floating palace lurches, slowing, and another attack flies toward Ellmeyer.

Even Lilia won't be able to endure shot after shot like that.

*Tsk*ing, Aileen lunges at Evare, trying to wrest the device from his hand, but Evare crushes it and tosses it aside.

Wha—?!

Passing Aileen, Evare grabs Charles by the neck and whispers, "C'mon. Let's destroy the world instead, Prince."

Charles's eye patch comes flying off. Unbelievable clouds of miasma billow from the ground.

Claude flies straight into it.

"Master Claude—Charles!"

Even as she screams, the ground crumbles beneath her. Or rather, it rots.

Trees, rocks, soil, the very earth itself. Thick ooze bubbles to the surface, carrying a fetid stench as everything rots and falls away. At the heart of the sinking mud, there's a black sphere.

Now airborne, Evare laughs. "Plannin' to take on your son's

destiny with him, Demon King?! Your boy's gonna be the corrupt dragon, though. There's no point in holdin' him in with that barrier."

"Evare! What have you done?!"

"Just sped up time a bit."

The black sphere rises into the air. There's something inside it, and every time that something writhes, miasma seeps out. The miasma gradually spreads, melting the buildings, rotting everything around them with astonishing speed.

The pitch-black sphere is a barrier, meant to keep the miasma from escaping. Claude must have cast it.

It's clear at a glance that it won't last long, though. The thick, sludgy substance inside it is already threatening to spill over. An arm densely covered with scales is trying to break out.

Behind Aileen, as if synchronizing with the broken device, the floating palace begins a bombardment.

"This is the destiny I just lost! The destiny you people won!"

The loser defeated by destiny howls with laughter, and it echoes through the sky over the floating, rotting palace. Getting a firmer grip on her holy sword, Aileen bites her lip.

✦ Fifth Act ✦
If You're the Villainess, Tame the Final Boss

"Lady Aileen, you're taking too long up there!!" Lilia shouts, blocking the third attack. Her arms already feel tired and heavy.

I hope I last until the evacuation's completed, at least.

The citizens of Imperial Ellmeyer's capital city have just awakened from their slumber, but they quickly figure out this is an emergency. Soldiers and sundry other people are running around below her. The floating palace is back in the sky and firing at them. Nobody is dumb enough to just stand there spacing out.

The force behind the attacks is gradually weakening, but fielding several shots in a row is just…!

Even as she's thinking this, a fresh attack comes. Gritting her teeth, she fixes her eyes on it from the imperial castle's highest clock tower.

Holding her holy sword horizontally, she sketches a semicircular barrier. A light ray that evaporates everything in its path hits the barrier squarely. The impact hits Lilia just as hard.

"…………!"

The force pushes her backward, grinding down the soles of her shoes. Cracks begin to develop in the holy sword. She's smiling dauntlessly, but her face is dripping with cold sweat.

Please hold up.

This holy sword is the reason she can still wield power similar to the sacred sword. Once it's gone—

"Lilia! Are you okay...? Serenaaaaa!"

She hears an oddly dim-witted voice, and then wings flutter around the clock tower once, and a figure alights near her. "What are you even doing? You're the Maid of the Sacred Sword, remember?! Get it together!"

"Serena."

The other girl has grabbed her shoulders, startling her, and the sacred sword swells with power at tremendous speed. She sweeps it through the incoming attack, and it bursts with a *bang.*

"Oh—"

Unable to stand its Serena-amplified power, the holy sword has turned to dust.

Staring at her empty hands, Lilia mutters, "It can't be. Checkmate? ...Reality is incredible, isn't it?!"

"Have you lost your mind? You don't have to worry—"

"Noooo, eeeeeeek! Don't drop me, please don't drop meeeeeee, Lady ManaaaaAAaaaaaaah!"

With a pathetic cry, something else is falling toward them. Actually, *was thrown* seems more accurate.

"Uuuuuuuh... I know she hates me, but that was mean..."

Having been flung into the clock tower, Sahra gets to her feet, sniffling. She's holding several holy swords. Not having any of it, Serena promptly helps her up. "And you! What are you doing? Come on, shape up."

"I mean, she swung me around and arou— Oh, Lilia! Thank goodness, you're okay! Um, I brought all the ones Ashmael had. Here!"

"O-okay? Um, you're not telling me not to collapse until I've gone through all those, are you?"

"No matter how often they break, I'll work really hard and fix them, okay?!"

"Lady...Lilia... Lady Sahra, Lady Serena!" This time, they hear a voice from below. Rachel, the villainess of Game 2, has just run up the stairs.

"What, you're awake?"

"I am now... I don't know...what's going on, but...! Lady Lilia was...doing something...so Isaac told me to go take a look... Also, I brought you this!"

Getting her rough breathing under control, Rachel holds out a basket. The next thing Lilia knows, she has a bottle of water shoved into her mouth. "There! Drink up, please. You're the linchpin right now, Lady Lilia! I imagine Lady Aileen is up with the floating palace, isn't she?! Keep your strength up, so she can focus on that."

"Amh? Fuu ay ere?"

"Leave it to us: We'll support you with everything we've got! Prince Cedric is moving as well."

Lilia's eyes widen slightly, and Rachel laughs.

"Both Master Claude and Lady Aileen are absent, so Prince Cedric is mobilizing things in his own name. He says, if it comes down to it, he doesn't mind if Master Claude beheads him; he'll take responsibility. Prime Minister Cyril advised him. That's why the army's on the move. We've requested help from Grand Duke Levi as well."

"...I see." Lilia drains the rest of her drink and pushes the empty bottle onto Rachel. Taking a holy sword from the bunch in Sahra's arms, she looks outside. She can see the water dragon heading back toward Ashmael. Did she actually fly Serena and

Sahra here? Even though it can't have been on the demon king or holy king's orders?

Even if the principal consort asked her to, to think she'd carry Sahra…

Upon closer inspection, the men issuing orders to the soldiers turn out to be Lester and Marcus. The demon king's forest seems rather noisy as well; Aileen's lackeys must be running around over there.

The floating palace attacks again. The sight may have drifted off its target, or perhaps something's broken. Instead of a straight line, the attack is wavy. Figures fly in from below and intercept it—the cambion and the holy knight. Or, no, she should probably say Duke Mirchetta and the next captain of the Holy Knights.

"Sorry, Elefas, we left you half! James, help, I'm falling!"

"At least handle the landing yourself, you thoughtless—"

As the two of them fall, a voice speaks from below, "Say, Isaac, isn't this really mean?!"

"Nah, it's not mean at all; he's the most powerful thing we've got right now. Oh, aim this way, Denis."

"An eye for an eye, and an attack for an attack! Give it your best!"

"I have fortifying substances here, so try your hardest."

"…It won't help physically, but if you sniff this herb, you may feel calmer…"

"Elefas! Hang-in-there Dance!"

For some reason, the demons in the demon king's forest all began dancing at once. Apparently, they're trying to provide encouragement.

"Okay, here we go. Give it your best shot, Elefas Gun. Time to die, newlywed."

"Since you've borrowed magic from Master Claude, you can do this. I'm sorry we can't do anything…!"

"First, you summon me, then you tie me to this thing without warning and tell me to power it! It isn't fair!" The attack that's launched from the demon king's palace—along with that tear-filled scream—blows away the floating palace's incoming attack.

"...Lady Aileen's lackeys are as incredible as ever. So is your husband, Serena; I wonder how he got over here."

"From the looks of it, the cambion carried him and flew."

Lilia is about to laugh when, in a corner of the imperial castle, she spies a figure in conversation with the prime minister. Noticing her as well, he hastily opens a window, leaning out. For one miraculous moment, their eyes meet.

"Lilia! You're all right?!"

Yes, she is. Of course she is.

Before she can answer, the floating palace's gun opens fire again. She hears several things: the shrieks of several men and cries of "Elefas isn't recharged yet!" However...

She levels the holy sword again. Serena grabs her shoulder. Taking a step forward, she slashes horizontally, blasting the attack away without a trace.

"Gracious. Who does Cedric think I am anyway?"

Shining sparks similar to the ones that fall from the sacred sword sift down from the holy sword. As one would imagine, a holy sword repaired by the Daughter of God is powerful.

Tucking her chin, she fixes her eyes on the floating palace.

Send anything you've got. There's no way I'll lose. I gave up being the player to get this heroine bonus, and I'd appreciate it if you didn't underestimate it too much.

Well, on the other hand...

"If I had the sacred sword, I could have downed that floating palace with one attack."

"Eeeeeeek! Again, here it comes again, it's coming, Liliaaaaaa!"

"You too, Lady Serena! Stay beside Lady Lilia! Take your place!"

"My 'place'?! Excuse me?! And what, you're just here to cheerlead?!"

Smiling wryly, Lilia levels the holy sword to meet the incoming attack. Tremendous pressure shoves her backward, but Serena, Sahra, and even Rachel all set their hands on her back, supporting her.

An attack of bright white light. As they clench their teeth, bearing up under it, Serena spots a shadow that nearly blots out that whiteness.

"...Look. What's that?"

A black sphere is rising from the floating palace, scattering miasma. It looks patently sinister, but Lilia gives a dauntless smile.

Oh, that must be the current final boss.

All right, villainess, give it your best. The heroine can't save the final boss.

Cedric won't be able to finish drawing his picture of the imperial couple, either.

You don't mind, do you, Cedric? It's all right if it isn't a picture of you as the emperor and me as your consort.

Opening her violet eyes wide, she knocks the attack away. The recoil throws her and the others back. The holy sword shatters, its shards grazing her cheeks, but she stays on her feet.

After all, as long as Lilia doesn't fall to her knees, she's sure Aileen won't, either.

If Evare is the hero of Game 6, the corrupt dragon he's trying to slay must be its final boss. And the Maid of the Sacred Sword he sought must be its heroine.

In other words, either Machina or Lucia is the heroine of Game 6. One is the Maid of the Sacred Sword, and the other the villainess.

However, Machina has returned to her former expressionless state, and Lucia lies as limp and motionless as a doll now that Grace, her soul, has been extracted.

Growing desperate, without the sacred sword that would save the world, the hero has transformed Charles into the corrupt dragon. With the Maid of the Sacred Sword still absent, the final boss has appeared.

No... Aileen glances at Grace. Evare has realized the same thing.

"Yeah, there's still a way. We've still got a sacred sword. Just use that to end the corrupt dragon," Evare says.

Grace can become the sacred sword, then let Aileen take her in so she can use it.

However, that sword is bound to kill Charles.

"...That boy is Aileen's son. He's basically my grandchild. You're telling Aileen and me to slay him?"

"Well, if you don't, he's gonna rot the world."

With a thick *blup*, black sludge seeps out of the floating sphere. It hits the ground with a *hiss*, and the earth begins to rot away.

Stern-faced, Grace rises to her feet. Evare laughs. "That's right. There's nothin' else you can do. It's the only way to save the world!"

"W-wait, please wait! Master Charles hasn't—"

"Hey, don't stress about it too much. It's what the prince wants, too."

Estella, the only one who's tried to protest, stares at him wide-eyed. With the look of someone who's found his prey, Evare goes on. "After all, everyone'll be saved this way. It's a fine decision, real fittin' for the crown prince of Ellmeyer. Don'cha think? As his fiancée, I bet you're proud of him."

"I… That's…"

"And that way, he won't have to crush your dream of becomin' the holy king, either."

Estella looks stunned.

"You shoulda been the holy king, but they made you get engaged to this prince so he could become emperor, right? That worried him a whole lot. He figured it was his fault. Like he'd become shackles for the girl he loved."

Estella's breathing is rapid and shallow; she clutches at her chest, and Baal hastily keeps her from falling over.

There's no telling whether he's frustrated or finds the situation funny, but Evare tips his head back, shouting into the sky, "So you don't need to hesitate. This is what he wanted. He's protectin' his family! Protectin' the dream of the girl he loves! He said he'll die for that! Well, he might drag his dad down with him, but somethin' on that level's just charmin', really. Magnificent, ain't it? That's the crown prince of Ellmeyer for—"

Aileen launches herself off the ground.

She raises the holy sword, swinging it at the black sphere, but magic rushes out like an electrical current and knocks her back. She flips in midair and lands on her feet, gouging the ground with her heels as she skids to a stop.

"Wh…what, huh?" Evare has stopped laughing for a moment, but he tries to keep up appearances by smiling. "Nothin' can slay those two except the sacred sword. Not your husband or your son."

"I am Master Claude's wife. Why must I slay my husband?" Aileen retorts without turning a hair. Catching her balance, she straightens up. "Master Claude is in pain. No doubt he's struggling, trying to save Charles. No, even if he was attempting to take it all on himself and fulfill his duty as an emperor… If I don't save him, who will?!"

"…What are ya goin' on about? Don'cha care what happens to the world?"

"When I acquired the sacred sword, it was in order to protect Master Claude!"

There is no other reason.

As Aileen looks up at the sphere, the corners of her lips curve. "Saving the world is a mere afterthought."

She gets a better grip on the holy sword. She can tell it's shining. Evare's eyes widen.

She plants her feet firmly on the ground, then leaps into the air again. Seeing the black sphere below her, she swings the sword down on it as hard as she can.

The miasma is swept away, and the tip of her sword connects with the sphere. A tremendous blast wind rises from its surface.

"Whoa, wait, if you break that, the corrupt dragon really will resurrect—"

Cracks run through both the holy sword and the black sphere.

People will probably say it's the sound of the world being destroyed. However, Aileen isn't the only one who lunges in without hesitating, and that makes her smile.

With neither holy sword nor sacred sword, arms spread wide, in order to save the final boss—

"Master Charles!"

Come. Our beloved demon kings are waiting for us.

Don't fear the sound of the world breaking. That's just the signal for the start of your dear one's rescue.

She'd always been earnest. She was bold and stubborn, yet also a daddy's girl. She was very proud, yet naive to the ways of the world, and sometimes, she seemed a little foolish. That was the sort of girl she was. She'd always stood as tall as she could and kept her mind keenly alert, insisting she'd become the holy king.

Estella Shah Ashmael, Ashmael's first princess, was a paragon of a royal young lady. A sacred princess with the dignity of a single flower blooming in the desert, one who shone as brilliantly as a star.

Their parents were friends, so Charles had known her since they were small. However, as the youngest child and the easygoing second prince, he just didn't see eye to eye with her. She'd probably be sort of cute if she smiled, but the only looks untidy Charles got from her were glares. Those eyes seemed to ask him, *What are you anyway?*, and he didn't like them much. When had his older twin pointed out that it was rare for him not to like somebody?

"You never fight anybody straight on; you just let everything slide. I hope she does smile for you."

His brother was always causing chaos with the tactless things he said, but he was actually very perceptive.

In her attempts to be outstanding, Estella lived in a way that was the polar opposite of everything Charles did. As the only one of his siblings who'd been born with magic and sacred power, Charles couldn't afford to be outstanding. Although both his brother and sister had mildly concerning character flaws, they both had the capacity to become splendid emperors. Both humans and demons loved them, so there wouldn't be a problem. In an emergency, and only then, he could handle it for them. It would be too dangerous to have the demon king be emperor two generations in a row. If he slacked off and let them underestimate him, he could prevent any needless fighting.

His father wouldn't allow that, though. "You can overpower your sister and brother, so you mustn't be their retainer," he said, and although everyone was hoping for his older brother to be the next emperor, he arbitrarily appointed Charles as crown prince...complete with the bombshell that Estella would be his fiancée.

Charles assumed Estella would refuse. The holy king doted on her, and if she did refuse, he'd make sure it came to nothing. However, she came to Ellmeyer, hair chopped short, and gave her consent. He couldn't believe it. It made him just a little happy. Then when she raised her head and he saw the resignation in her eyes, it was more than he could bear.

He'd crushed her dream of becoming the holy king.

All her effort had gone to waste, and it was his fault.

Black hair and red and violet eyes. It seemed old-fashioned in this day and age, when the demon king reigned as emperor, but a lot of people disapproved of the boy who was destined to become the demon king assuming the throne again. His father had his mother, who'd possessed the sacred sword. She'd apparently done phenomenal things and had silenced any objections. As a result, his parents probably thought he'd need someone comparable if he was going to be the next emperor.

The holy king's beloved daughter. A girl with enough sacred power that she was considered his successor. If they needed a Maid of the Sacred Sword now, nearly twenty years after the dissolution of the Holy Queendom of Hausel, no one was more appropriate than this girl. Both his older sister and his female cousins were famous, but probably not in a way that would qualify them to be a Maid of the Sacred Sword.

However, because of him, everything she'd built had collapsed.

Feeling wretched and frustrated, he shut himself up in the old castle. He couldn't face her. He had to find a way to outwit his father… That was when it happened.

His body had begun to change. His skin had blackened and grown scales, and everything that touched them rotted.

It was like a divine punishment.

His father—who had experience with becoming a dragon—consulted with the holy king, and the holy king made Charles gloves and an eye patch with sacred power worked into them. He was told that Estella could make the same things. *What a joke*, he thought. He didn't want to be any more of a burden to her.

Then Evare appeared. He claimed to come from the future, and that Charles shouldn't actually have been born in this era. Maybe because Charles wanted to atone somehow, he believed that preposterous story.

He would become a dragon and rot the world. In that case, he had to get himself killed by the Maid of the Sacred Sword before that happened. That was why he helped Evare in his search for her. He'd considered interfering with the past and preventing his own birth, but when he thought about his older sister, and particularly his twin brother, he wasn't able to do it.

He didn't go to his family for advice. He wasn't confident that he could explain it properly.

He wrote up a document dissolving his engagement, though. In the end, he'd never seen her smile. *Still*, he thought as he wrote, *that's probably all for the best.*

If I'd seen her smile, I might have fought this.

The ferocious pain that runs through his chest brings him back to his senses.

"Are you awake?"

"...F-Father...?"

He blinks, then realizes something with a jolt. Black miasma is flooding from his chest, like blood. A rounded, egg-shaped barrier is catching it. The miasma is settling in the bottom, and black, turbid water is building up below them.

His father is holding him in his arms, keeping his head above the surface. He also noticed that one of his father's arms has turned into something grotesque from the shoulder down. He's being drawn into Charles's transformation. The parts of him that are soaking in the black water probably are as well.

"What—?"

"Hold still. Your body is smaller, so the progression is faster. I'm taking as much of it as I can and spreading it out, but..."

"Why are you here?! This is— You know it's a bad idea to be in here!"

His father is the one who conjured this smooth, round barrier. He probably meant for it to act like the shell of an egg, and he's trying to slow the progression. By getting inside, he's taken Charles's transformation into himself.

"Hurry, put me down and get out!"

"If I leave, you'll turn into the corrupt dragon all by yourself."

"There's no way to stop that! I told you ending up like this was my destiny, remember?!"

"You've got plenty of energy, don't you? My body is creaking here and there, and I'm feeling a bit worn down."

No, Charles hurts, too. His back spasms as thick scales gradually cover it, and he can feel his cells splitting again and again, as if he's being torn to bits. It's the pain of being reborn as a different creature.

Still, this pain should be all his. He only shared the curse with his father to buy time.

"The sacred sword is still— That's right, we've got Grandmother's. That means it's fine; hurry—"

"You're a strong boy."

Just as Charles is about to scream *Leave me and go* again, his father smiles at him, and he freezes up.

"Frankly, the idea that you're my son doesn't feel real to me yet, so I'm going to say this… I wasn't sure if I'd be able to raise a child properly."

What is he bringing up at a time like this?

Still, even though he's dragged his father into this, the man's red eyes are kind, and he finds himself listening closely.

"I'm not worried anymore. You're a splendid son. You seem to be going through a bit of a rebellious phase, but that's probably proof that you're growing up properly. I did manage to have a family, didn't I?"

"What…are…?"

"Maybe that's why. I jumped in because I couldn't just leave you like this. I think you could rely on me a little—or no, I suppose you can't, can you? No, you can't. When I was your age, I didn't think there was any human who could save me, either. However—"

Wham. A sudden impact runs through them. It came from outside.

"Ah." His father smiles, his eyes softening amid the scales that have begun to grow around them. "There she is… It's all right; I'm sure yours will come for you, too. It's just instinct talking, but even so."

"Come for… What will?"

"Isn't it obvious? The Maid of the Sacred… No, I suppose it's the Maid of the Cursed Sword. The demon king's wife."

This time, the impact comes from over their heads. Something is trying to break through the barrier.

But when this barrier breaks…when this egg hatches, he's going to—

A crack runs through the top of the shell. It's breaking. That noise is the sound of the world collapsing.

"Master Claude!"

It's his mother's voice. She must have come for his father. That's fine.

Light lances in. His mother grabs his father's hand and begins to pull him out. Thank goodness. The relief makes the tension drain out of him. They're apparently very high up. He can feel himself falling backward.

He's been worried about Evare's rampage, but if his mother and father are there, they can stop it. If Machina's safe, Estella should be able to return to her era.

All that's left is—

If he's slain, that will be the end of it. Even Evare will get his wish.

"Master Charles!"

He opens his eyes, which may not even be human eyes anymore—and sees Estella.

"Wh-what…?!"

He's falling through the sky, and she desperately reaches out for him.

Charles can't believe what he's seeing, and he screams, "What are you doing, you idiot?! Run!"

"Is it true that you like me?!"

"Huh?!"

Even at a time like this, it feels as if all the blood in his body is trying to flow backward. Charles is speechless, and Estella glares at him. "No, that can wait! I'll listen to you later. Your hand, Master Charles."

"Wh-what the…? I…"

Estella's fingertips skim his cheek, and he hears a hiss, as if something is scorching. Turning pale, he tries to yell, but then his back spasms. He grits his teeth, bracing against the intense pain as wings sprout from his shoulders.

The wings seem to have slowed his fall. Estella has caught up to him, and she cups his cheeks with her hands. At the same time, sacred power courses through him, with her at its center. She's trying to hold back his transformation.

There's no way she can stop it, though.

"Get away…from me…"

As Charles tries to shake her off, what he sees in that pair of incredibly close violet eyes makes him catch his breath. *Why is she crying…?*

He can see himself in those lovely eyes. His festering skin, his eerie, odd-colored eyes. A half-formed thing, neither holy nor demonic.

Still, without hesitating, she wraps her arms around his neck. "I came to take you back."

She smiles at him. That smile. It's the one he's always wanted to see, even if it was only a glimpse.

He thinks his heart might stop.

Pain rips through him, as if his body is being torn to pieces. Estella's power tries to curb it, and an explosion and lightning lash out in reaction. Seeing Estella's cheek hiss as it touches him, Charles gulps.

No, no, I can't do this. Estella's going to get dragged into it.

He knows that, but his arms have wrapped around her, pulling her close. There's nothing else for him to cling to. He's struggling pathetically.

Gods. Gods, you don't have to save me, so please—

—save the girl I love.

He looks up, as if he's praying, and he sees Machina. She's holding a sacred sword. The one weapon that can kill him.

At that point, he doesn't care why.

"Kill me! Hurry!"

"I won't let that happen!"

Estella hugs Charles tighter, as if she's determined not to let him go. Machina raises her blade, preparing to strike Estella right along with him.

"Machina, stop! Just me—don't drag Estella into this!"

Even as Charles screams, Machina pierces Estella's chest with the sacred sword.

It's like watching a butterfly emerge from its chrysalis. Aileen gazes at the sight, feeling vaguely nostalgic.

"Did you know, Aileen?" Claude is looking up at the same thing, although he's leaning on her shoulder for support. "Having that happen right in front of you is pretty hard on the heart. It's like being petrified with fear."

"My, is that right?"

"Even if it was the only way, I feel bad for poor Charles."

"What do you mean, poor *Charles*?!" Baal screams, almost in tears. "You should feel much worse for us! We told her not to go, but she shook off our hands. We feel as if we've sent her off to marry, and she hasn't even been born yet…! Couldn't you have dealt with this yourself somehow, Aileen?!"

"No, I could not. If I'd loaned my body to Lady Grace, or if I'd used Machina's sacred sword, I could probably have slain Charles, but I couldn't have restored his humanity. After all, I am his mother."

Romantic love is something she can't give him.

Those words are swallowed up in the brilliant light that shines from the sword buried in Estella's chest.

The corrupt dragon's scales fall off, as if it's molting. Evare looks up at the sight in disbelief.

What is it? What's happenin'? Why…?

Aileen broke through the black sphere and rescued the demon

king. Even so, he saw Charles fall, and he thought his victory was assured. At the very least, he wouldn't be alone anymore.

However, the holy king's daughter went after Charles, and Machina went after her.

So even a soulless shell with no sacred sword responds to the corrupt dragon it must slay? He'd been watching with a half smile on his face when Machina manifested the sacred sword. He was startled, but out of the corner of his eye, he saw Grace watching Machina and the others, her fists clenched. She seemed prepared to leap in there herself if this failed.

Since that was so, he assumed that Machina's sacred sword was like a lingering fragment of Amelia— No, whether Charles was slain or not, victory was his, he thought. But then…

…Machina ignored Charles.

The sacred sword sank into Estella; her body was absorbing it. Evare knew what this was.

The Maid of the Cursed Sword.

When all but the hilt had vanished, the girl's body began to glow from within.

It wasn't the sort of light he'd seen before, the sort that simply repelled. It was a gentle light that seemed to wash everything away. That light enveloped Charles's body even as it radiated thick, black miasma.

Those black scales, that ugly, misshapen form…transformed into petals of light and scattered in the wind.

The corrupt dragon was turning back into an ordinary boy.

"But that's… That can't be… Only the real sacred sword could…"

The sacred sword is the proof of love.

In the midst of those fluttering petals of light, the boy and girl look shocked, and then they embrace. Even their tears turn into twinkling particles of light.

No. No, this is no good. If this keeps up—

That pure-white world. Nausea wells up inside him. A world of nothing, buried in pure-white ash.

When he'd awakened, he'd been a boy. The floating palace held only what he needed to ward off starvation. There wasn't a single soul there. He waited several years for someone. Then growing tired of waiting, he ventured outside. He found a map, but there were no longer any destinations to travel to, nor any roads to travel on. Since that was so, he headed for the country where he should have awakened as the evil god.

The desert kingdom had become a land of ashes.

When he reached it, there was nothing. An empty stone monument. The last will of a mother who'd been defeated by destiny. The ruin seemed ready to crumble at any moment, and inside it, he found nothing but a girl who neither spoke nor smiled.

He'd been happy at first. Just having someone else around was enough. She said nothing, though. She didn't smile. She didn't even eat. She just followed him. Gradually, he began to feel even more alone than he had when he was by himself.

After all, she wasn't alive. She simply moved.

It felt as if he was being forced to admit that he was the only living thing.

No one lived here. He couldn't save anything. Nothing could save him.

He spent years and years in a world like that, all by himself.

Rage that felt a lot like fear had welled up inside him, and he'd almost fallen to his knees, but he forced himself to stay on his feet. He couldn't let himself acknowledge the existence of love.

After all, in a world where no one else was alive, there was no way for love to be born.

"There's no way I'm gonna let it end all happily ever after like this!"

In his fury, he takes aim at the defenseless falling pair. The corrupt dragon is being purified; it can't strike back right now, and Charles shouldn't have that sort of strength left. He's just taking his anger out on them. He knows that.

Still, why is he always the only one with no sacred sword, no future, no love?

I wish I'd never been born.

Registering Evare's hostility, Charles holds Estella close. He's planning to protect her. What a beautiful sight. It's so beautiful that his lips twist.

That's a beauty that's never had, and never will have, anything to do with him.

Not him, who lives all by himself—

Break already. This must be what the evil god who should have awakened inside him would have felt like. Or was he only ever the evil god all along? He doesn't know. The urge to kill and destroy simply well up inside him, and he hits them with all the magic he's got.

A little late, the demon king and the others register it and turn his way, but they'll never make it in time.

"Die! Go on and die, everyone, everythin'—!"

The magic, a mass of malice and envy, disperses right before his eyes.

A brilliant flash has cut through it, and Evare stares, dazed.

The sacred…sword.

The thing he's spent so long yearning for has slashed through his attack and is headed straight for him.

Machina is the one wielding it.

Why? He doesn't know if his gasping murmur made it out as speech or not.

Still, he knows he's the only one who mustn't live in this world any longer. Thinking Machina will swing that sword at his neck, he closes his eyes.

In the end, I guess I couldn't beat destiny, huh?

Now, he thinks, he'll finally be able to rest.

His mother must have felt this way when she lost, too.

—And yet with an eye-opening noise, something slaps him across the face.

When Machina slaps Evare's cheek, the sound carries shockingly well. It's almost like an alarm clock.

The dizzying events that have taken place in the span of a few minutes seem like a dream. Aileen blinks, as if she's just awakened.

It isn't a dream, though.

Perhaps the sacred sword has purified it; there's an area where the grass has grown back, and in it, Estella is clinging to Charles. She's probably crying. The arm Charles has hesitantly put around her is the color of rather pale flesh. The wings that sprouted from his back are gone. Baal is gazing at the pair rather bitterly, his arms folded.

Softly, she touches her husband's chest. There's no hardness there, either. The clothes that covered the right side of his upper body are ripped, but there are no scales on his arm or shoulder. Claude is properly human again.

Luciel is holding Lucia's body. Beside him, Grace exhales dramatically. The sternness in her expression has dissolved.

It's over—or so she thinks, but…

"Wha—? Huh?! What the heck is this?! Just a— Why do you keep whackin' me like—? Ow, that hurts!"

Machina is smacking Evare repeatedly with the sacred sword. She's silent and expressionless, but the way she's hitting him puts a distant look in Aileen's eyes. "I've seen something similar very recently…"

"Yes, so have I."

"Me too… Actually, not 'seen' so much as 'experienced'…"

"Where was this?"

Luciel averts his eyes. Grace cocks her head, looking perplexed, even though she's the one who did it.

While this is happening, Machina keeps beating Evare mercilessly with the sacred sword, until finally, a kick sends him flying. He doesn't seem to have the magic to block it, and the way he rolls like a ball is identical to Luciel as well.

The evil god must be something like Father's colleague.

In that case, this development may be almost a cliché.

"Why?! What for?! If you were killin' me, I'd get that, but punchin' and kickin'—what's goin' on here? It makes no sense!"

"…I think Machina may be angry."

"Huh?!" Evare turns to look at Aileen, and Machina slaps him across the head again. "I said that *hurts*! C'mon, what?! If you've got somethin' you wanna say, spit it out!"

"……s…go."

Blank-faced, still holding the sacred sword, Machina speaks awkwardly.

"Let's go…home."

Those words make Evare freeze up. His eyes open so wide, they seem in danger of falling out of his skull. Then he tries to smile again. "Go home?" He hasn't actually managed that smile, and it's painful to look at. Laying the sacred sword across her palms, Machina holds it out to him.

It's what Evare wanted, and yet he shakes his head as if he's afraid, backing away. "That's… No, that ain't it. That ain't…the real thing…"

"Just a moment." Grace has drifted lightly down to the ground, and she gently cups Machina's face in her hands. *"Yes, I see. Amelia really isn't there anymore. Did she say something to you?"*

"…Hap…py…" In Machina's expressionless face, her lips move. "She said…be…happy."

Evare's eyes are on the ground, and he squeezes his hands into fists.

Grace smiles, although she looks as if she might burst into tears. *"I see. Then that is your sacred sword now. The next sacred sword, which Amelia is sending to the future."*

"That's just… Hearin' that now ain't gonna…!"

"It's all…right. Let—" Machina's tongue seems stiff and awkward; she stammers, then says it again. "Let's go home, Evare."

"I mean, you can say that, but— You saw it, too, right? That prince won't become the corrupt dragon now. She saved him… I'd noticed it, on some level. In the future, the corrupt dragon I needed to slay wasn't around anymore. There's nothin'…nothin' I can change…"

"There is."

"What? Huh?!"

"I'm sure Lucia…will wake up. That's what…Amelia wants." Machina gives her answer haltingly, one word at a time.

They look at Luciel, who's still holding Lucia's body in his arms, and he smiles. "That's right. Grace and I need to grant that wish this time."

"Luciel…"

Shaking off Grace's worried gaze, Luciel raises his head. "Don't worry, Evare. Someday, I'll become the corrupt dragon."

"Huh?"

"I know a little about how this world is put together. There's no guarantee that Charles won't become the corrupt dragon later on. Even if he got through this, something's bound to happen down the road. And so when things are really hopeless, I'll take it on. To keep the world from breaking any more than it has to, I'll cover it with white ash, hiding it from its destiny of destruction until the Maid of the Sacred Sword appears."

Evare looks startled. Voice trembling, he murmurs, "A world… of white ash…"

"I can't even imagine what the future you were born into a thousand years from now is like…but you have the sacred sword now, don't you?"

Once again, Evare looks at the sacred sword in Machina's hands.

He probably still hasn't realized that it's *his* sacred sword. However, that sword will definitely become the real thing.

"Why don't we trust the humans of the past to handle the rest?"

"Let's go…home. To…our world," Machina repeats.

Evare hangs his head, looking as if he's about to burst into tears. However, he promptly looks up and gives a genuine smile. "Yeah, well, I did lose, huh! Before I get myself killed, I'd better… Well, actually gettin' killed would probably be easier, but…"

Holding the sacred sword against her side, Machina extends a hand to him. Evare looks at that hand just a little reluctantly, but he doesn't refuse it.

In that moment, centered on their joined hands, a circle of light appears.

Startled, Aileen backs away. Evare gives her a sardonic smile, as if to say the joke's on her. "'Kay then, I'm off."

"R-right now?! What about, you know, basking in the after-glow for a moment?!"

"Nah, no need. I've gotta clear out quick, before I get myself killed."

"Wait a minute, Evare!" Charles is still holding Estella, but he shouts to them. "If Machina goes, what are Estella and I supposed to do?"

"Not my circus, not my monkeys. Fix it with the power of love or somethin'."

"L-love?! Can love do stuff like that?!"

"Get the floatin' palace workin' again. Seriously, it'll be fine somehow."

How careless can you get…? Aileen thinks. Evare grins and waves; his other hand is still holding Machina's. "I won't get my hopes up, but I'll be waitin'. A thousand years from now."

A pillar of light rises from the ground to the sky. Evare and Machina's figures begin to dissolve into particles of light.

Then Machina turns back.

Thank you.

Her voice doesn't reach them, but her lips form the words.

She smiles, and although her gaze looks like Amelia's, her face is nothing like hers.

The pillar of light swirls slowly, then unravels and vanishes. Only particles of light flit through that space; all the figures are gone.

Softly, Claude puts an arm around Aileen's shoulders, pulling her to him. "...It's over."

"No, it hasn't even begun yet. We must save the future."

Claude's eyes widen, and then he smiles wryly. "You're as valiant as ever. Still, I see what you mean. Yes, you're right. We're just getting started."

"Exactly! It's not over yet!" Baal has been silent all this time, but now he starts shouting, as if he can't take it anymore. "Look, boy, how long do you intend to embrace Estella?!"

"I—I wasn't— This isn't a hug, it's—!"

"You are clearly holding her close! Don't toy with us! That's our daughter, and she hasn't even been born yet!"

"She's fainted!" Charles shouts, and everyone else looks stunned. With all eyes abruptly on him, he blushes bright red in a boyish way and goes on, mumbling, "She, um...noticed how I looked..."

Silence falls.

Oh, of course. It all makes sense to Aileen. Claude sighs, slips off his ragged cloak, and takes it to Charles.

Belatedly, the sound of Baal bursting a blood vessel rings out. "Like father, like son, hmm?!"

His son's surroundings are as lively as ever. As Luciel gazes at them with a smile, Grace surprisingly decides to lean against his chest. *"The issue got resolved before I could discuss it with Aileen. Thanks, Luciel."*

He's scared of the day when he'll lose this voice, this shape. It terrifies him so much that he'd curse the world.

As a matter of fact, Luciel had cursed everything once and was slain by Amelia's sacred sword.

"Yes, leave it to me. It'll be fine."

At this point, though, he believes that.

"Really? When I'm reborn, I might not remember you."

"Even so, I won't lose. I love you, and I like Amelia a whole lot, too."

He's sure that will still be true a thousand years from now.

✦ Final Act ✦
Premonition of a Conquered *Otome* Game

Only a handful of people see Charles and Estella off the next day.

All they've told Ellmeyer is that they are staying in Ashmael. No doubt the abrupt state of war has thrown the empire into confusion, but their dependable companions will handle things somehow. The one thing that scares Aileen is her older brother's response: "I'll be looking forward to hearing you attempt to explain this."

However, there are a variety of people that Charles and Estella shouldn't see. More than anything, the floating palace—although it's still floating—is half destroyed, and there's no telling when it will stop working. In the end, Aileen, Claude, and Baal give them a hasty send-off on their own.

"We actually will be able to get back, right?" Even after they've gone down beneath the palace's ruined throne, Charles is dubious.

"It should be all right. Now that I think about it, I believe the floating palace was what sent me back to this age."

"Yeah, but there's no proof, is there? Besides, I'd never heard that they stored the floating palace in the demon realm."

"The floating palace is repairing itself at this very moment. Maybe it was stored in the demon realm so humans couldn't interfere with it? As a matter of fact, I'm considering doing that very thing. I've already decided to let my father take care of Lucia's body, and that would be the most convenient approach. What do you think, Baal?"

The floating palace is technically under the joint administration of Ashmael and Ellmeyer. Baal, who's walking beside Estella, answers Claude's question as if it bores him. "The floating palace isn't something current technology can cope with. Ultimately, we also feel that's the only thing to do with it. That Evare fellow may be slumbering somewhere in the palace at this very moment, but we haven't managed to find him, even though we've checked practically everywhere."

"No matter how hard we look, I bet we'll never find him," Claude says, and Baal shrugs in agreement.

"It may be best to build a dummy of the underground ruin as well. At any rate, the body of the Daughter of God actually isn't there."

"What about asking the Holy Dragon Consort to help? She'll use water and hide it perfectly."

"Maybe we'll do that..."

Aileen, who's walking at the front of the group, senses an invisible wall in the darkness and stops.

The altar really should be beyond this point, but...

After giving it a little thought, she turns back. "Estella, if you would."

"What? Me?"

"I think you'll be better able to reach the place that should be here."

Estella looks bewildered, but she nods. "All right. If you'll allow me, then."

Stepping forward, Estella sets her hand against the doors in the unseen wall—although no doubt it's visible to her—and murmurs, "Hear, O past. Open, O future. I am the maiden who inherits the regalia of saints and demons."

A line of light runs through the doors, and they swing open as if they're being cut out of the darkness.

What lies beyond them isn't the altar.

"This is it. The place I saw for a moment when I was flung into the past."

It's an odd space, entirely white, surrounded on all sides by seamless walls of pure-white stone.

Both the sight and its coloring are the polar opposite of the underground ruin.

In the very center of the spacious room, a pillar of blue light reaches from floor to ceiling. Inside it, a diamond-shaped stone spins slowly. It must be a divine stone. It's quite large—nearly as tall as Aileen.

However, that's all there is. The room holds nothing else.

"—And? What do we do?" Baal asks.

Claude tilts his head, puzzled. "Good question."

"I told you. I said we couldn't let Evare go back. We needed Machina."

"You really rely on Lady Machina, don't you, Master Charles?"

Charles is about to complain, but Estella's cold eyes make him freeze up. His gaze wanders uneasily, and for some reason, he slinks up beside Aileen as if he's running away. "Well, she's gone now, and there's no point in relying on somebody who's not here…"

"Charles… Shape up a little."

"Seriously. How did you grow up this spineless?"

"You're the one who raised me, Father!"

"Did you call me?"

A voice abruptly echoes in the room, and everyone flinches.

"Is there a problem with how I raised my children?"

The low voice echoes, but it carries well. Although there's a little static mixed into it, it's unmistakable.

"Master Claude?"

"Oh, my sweet Aileen. The idea that you're both here and there is rather entertaining."

"Honestly..."

Turning back, Claude hugs Aileen to him and glares at the pillar of light. They can see the dim figure of a man in it, seated in a chair, his long legs crossed.

Charles tucks his chin a little and murmurs, "Father." She can tell from his tone that he's talking to his real father, not to the version of Claude who's here.

"Now then, Charles."

At the sound of his name, Charles stiffens. He acted rather carelessly with the Claude in this era, but he's fully on his guard now.

"Where are you, and what are you doing?"

"...It's really nothing to do with you—"

"Don't you realize how worried your mother and I have been?"

Charles shuts up. Aileen is impressed. He's definitely used to being scolded.

"For the past week, you're all your mother's thought about, and it's all your fault."

"No, see, that's it! That's what you're actually mad about, Father!"

"What are you saying? I'm angry because I've been worried. So worried that it was decided to host a great Demon King Love-Love Dance party for the first time in ten-odd years, with your teacher at the center."

Claude claps a hand over his mouth; he's nearly burst out laughing. Aileen is already dead tired.

"Don't you feel bad? He's nearly forty, and he'll end up dancing like a fiend in front of his wife and children in order to cover for you. I'm really looking forward to it. I want to hold it right this minute."

"See?! You're enjoying yourself! Seriously, what's wrong with you?! You make no sense—"

"So you should hurry home, too."

Those words seem to take the wind out of Charles's sails.

Glancing over at Charles, Estella speaks up. "Your Majesty, it's Estella. I'm very sorry for the trouble."

"I'm glad you're safe, Princess Estella. My son's the one who's caused trouble for you."

"No, I pursued Master Charles of my own will. However, um…we don't know how to get back home."

"Don't worry about that. I'll—we'll open the path. Your sacred sword will point the way."

"…So you know about all this."

"I only remembered the details a little while after you two disappeared."

Charles sulks like a child. "If you knew, you didn't have to ask me what I was doing."

"It's been over a decade. I don't remember all the details… Although, that doesn't seem to be true for Baal. He's very *worried."*

"Father…"

"Baal is waiting for you, Charles."

There's a brief pause. Estella blinks, and Charles looks perplexed. "Why me?"

"Actually, he's waiting right behind me now. It's rather scary."

"Huh?"

"It may be my imagination, but I get the feeling he has about eight

arms, and I think he's grown horns. Frankly, that doesn't look like a human face. It's one of those, what do you call them, Asura demons? He's like that. He has a holy sword, and he's lying in wait for you. For the past few days, every time he opens his mouth, he says 'Kill, kill, kill, kill' constantly, like it's some sort of chant. He must have been carrying this grudge for sixteen years."

Charles turns pale. In contrast, Estella looks thoroughly exasperated. "Father is there with you? I'm impressed Mother allowed that."

"She asked us to take him off her hands because he wasn't getting any work done. However, frankly, I'd like her to take him back soon. I'll give him my son's life if that's what it takes."

"Just a— Why would that even happen?!"

"Don't you know?" The current Baal glares at Charles, who backs away at the sight of his face. "Do you really not know, boy?"

"Um, I, uh..."

"Let us explain it to you, on behalf of our future self. You arbitrarily confronted our daughter with a dissolution of your engagement, then not only took her into the past but also dragged her into something extremely dangerous! Do you think we'll forgive you for that?!"

"Well, that's where things stand. The Baal over here has started silently taking practice swings. It's rather scary."

"D-demon kings shouldn't say they're scared! It makes things even scarier!"

"Even for demon kings, scary things are scary. Oh, that reminds me: Since Baal is scary, I've dissolved your engagement to Estella."

"Huh?!" This time, Charles stares. He sounds anxious. "Wh-why?! I—I mean, Estella said she wasn't going to do that—"

"Yes, you were the one who said you'd dissolve it. That's my son, all right. That document was perfect. All it needed was the holy king's signature. Not only that, but you'd laid all the groundwork already. Such brilliance. I was moved."

"...Come to think of it, I did leave that in my room," Estella murmurs.

Charles totters.

Baal's mood seems to have improved substantially. "Haaaaa-ha-ha! Is that how it was?! That's fine, then. We'll save this grudge of ours and hit you with all of it sixteen years from now!"

"...Well, I suppose he brought that on himself."

"He really did." Aileen can only put a hand to her cheek and agree.

Charles despairs, planting both hands on the pure-white wall. Estella goes over to him. "What's the matter, Master Charles?"

"What... What's... What...?"

"I'll be the one to fight my father, if you like. I do have the sacred sword."

Charles's head snaps up. Estella is gazing at him steadily, and he blushes bright red, but then he averts his eyes— Her son's mind must be a very complicated place at the moment.

Still, in the end, as if he's come to a decision, he looks the girl he loves in the eye. "No need. I'll deal with the lousy holy king by myself somehow."

A smile blooms on Estella's face. "Is that right?"

"What was that 'lousy' for, hmm? Starting now, we don't like this side of you. You're still unborn, and we don't like you!"

"'If that's settled, can we wrap this up? This Baal seems liable to breathe fire soon."

"Both of my fathers, be quiet, please. Um, specifically, what do I need to do?"

Simply being cautioned by Estella makes Baal look dejected. Life is already hard, and he doesn't even have a daughter yet.

"Just produce the sacred sword. It's all right; the former Maid of the Sacred Sword over here says she'll bring you back. She's been eagerly making all sorts of preparations."

Apparently, Lilia hasn't changed one bit.

"I'm afraid we've caused all sorts of trouble for you. Especially you, my dear wife."

At the note of sweetness in his voice, Claude's eyes sharpen, and it makes Aileen laugh. "No, not at all. I only did what was natural for the demon king's wife, Master Claude."

"She's right. It's nothing to do with you."

"You are *me, you know."*

"Even so. You shouldn't meddle with the past. You have your own Aileen—"

"Dear. Quit teasing your past self. It's quite childish."

The cool, chiding voice that breaks in unexpectedly makes this Claude freeze up, and it seems to make the other Claude smile wryly.

Aileen looks up at the figures from the future. The only one she can see clearly is Claude. However, the woman's hand on his shoulder must belong to…

"You're right. I can't have my younger self stealing you away. I'll behave and wait for our son's return."

Realizing that it's time to say goodbye, Aileen retreats. Claude thumps Baal on the back, and Baal reluctantly puts distance between himself and Estella.

Charles and Estella stand in front of the pillar of blue light, side by side. Estella bows to them. "Thank you for all your help. Please give my regards to Mother as well."

"...We'd really appreciate it if you'd avoid making our future self sad."

Baal bids her farewell with words that are pretty close to a complaint, and Estella giggles. "Please don't worry. You're my favorite, Father."

Baal blinks, then clears his throat awkwardly and nods. "A-are we, then...? We suppose that's all right."

"Now then, Master Charles. Are you ready?"

Charles gives them a glance. Then without saying a word to them, he turns his back. "Yes, let's go home. The future will be here really soon anyway."

Estella seems to hesitate a little, but when Aileen nods and smiles at her, she nods back. The sacred sword appears above her palm.

Aileen is sure this isn't the last time that power will save her son.

Resonating with the sacred sword, the divine stone begins to turn. The pillar of light churns as if it's being mixed, and its light grows whiter and whiter. It's as if it's pointing the way to a blank, untrodden future.

"—Listen!" As he becomes a silhouette against the light, Charles speaks abruptly. "Make sure you do have me, too, all right? I've never once felt unlucky for being born."

Without thinking, Aileen almost takes a step forward, and Claude pulls her to him. "Just wait."

He's right. There's no need to be impatient. This future is bound to come in due time.

She thinks Charles just smiled. His shadow links hands with

Estella's, and although she can't hear what he says, she's sure it isn't "goodbye."

The light grows so bright that she can't keep her eyes open, and then a flash sweeps everything before it like a raging torrent, sending Aileen and the rest back where they belong.

When she slowly opens her eyes, she's at the border. It's an area where desert and greenery mingle; they're near a canal.

Right in front of her, as if its role is finished, the floating palace is quietly being swallowed by the sands.

See you soon.

When she looks up, there's just one long, thin cloud sailing across the blue sky. It looks like a road that's pointing the way to the future.

"'When I got back, the world had been saved'... I guess it was never gonna be that easy, huh."

Surveying a world covered in white ash, Evare sighs. Both the sky and the ground are bright white.

The landscape looks like a blank, pale sea, and it's so familiar, he feels like crying. There's nothing here. Hope, the future, and salvation, all buried in ash—this is his future.

However, feeling the unmistakable warmth of a hand resting in his own, he squeezes it. "I guess it's *our* future, huh?"

Machina nods silently. As responses go, it's a little unsatisfying, but that's rather refreshing in and of itself.

"Still... There's really nothin' to do here. Oh, wait—that ain't true. We've gotta find a place to sleep first. Maybe livin's all about stuff like that… Ain't that right, Machina?"

Machina's gazing at him steadily. Since that's so, even though he's asked this question many times before and never gotten a response, he works up the courage to try again.

"Is there anythin' you want to do?"

Machina doesn't answer. She simply points. Evare turns to look in that direction, and his eyes widen.

She's pointing at a human figure. A figure that's waving its arms.

"Oh, there you are, found you! That's Machina, isn't it?! And Evare! Yes, I vaguely remember you people!"

"Huh… Uh, what, huh…? Lucia?!"

It's the girl he just saw in the past. Now, though, as she strides toward them, planting her feet firmly on the blank white earth, she's wearing a vivacious smile. "I finally found you. That Luciel sealed my body so tightly, you wouldn't even believe it."

"Wh… Where have you been…?"

"Dunno. Well, I'm late because I slept in! Sorry!"

The extremely concise answer makes his jaw threaten to come unhinged.

"I'm awake now, though. As promised. Amelia—no, I should call you Machina, shouldn't I? I'm Lucia; I've got Grace's soul and her memories, but that's it. So let's go!"

"G-g-go? What? Where to?" The situation is developing much too rapidly, and Evare can't keep up.

Lucia laughs at him. "To the demon realm, obviously!"

"The demon realm?!"

"Well, I mean, if the demon king's around, where else would

he be?! Let's move!" Lucia brandishes her sacred sword. It's sure to be a sacred sword that will save the demon king.

Lucia forges ahead, but he can't bring himself to follow her. As he's hesitating, bewildered, Machina gently tugs on his sleeve. He has a feeling that the sacred sword in her hand is the one that will save him.

"...The hell? This is ridiculous."

Laughing, he covers his face with a hand. That way, nobody will see the tears that have slipped out.

Lucia turns back, vigorously waving the sacred sword. "Hey, what are you doing? Hurry up! There are a ton of things we need to do: Wake up that idiot Luciel, rid the world of all this ash... No, maybe food comes first? We'll need a house, too. If we're building a house, then I'd like a bath as well, and I want to wake the demons..." Lucia folds down her fingers one by one, absorbed in counting the future.

As if to hurry him along, Machina pulls at Evare's hand.

"So savin' the world's sort of an afterthought, huh?" he murmurs, then takes a step forward.

He sets off, walking over the white ash.

"And? Is this story over now?"

"No, it's not over."

In the afternoon, at one of the tea parties Aileen is still holding in an attempt to drum proper etiquette into her sister-in-law,

Lilia tilts her head. Aileen has just given her a general explanation of the affair.

"We must ensure that this future comes."

"But we're going to gradually forget this incident, aren't we? Because the hero and final boss of Game…um, Master Luciel cast that spell."

The fact that she bothered to rephrase it at all is commendable. Elegantly, Aileen drains her teacup, setting an example for her to follow. "That was done in order to prevent our memories from influencing the future. What else could we do?"

Since forgetting everything at once would have caused trouble for them, the memories are supposed to gently melt into their daily routines, in the same way they'll forget what they had for dinner the day before yesterday. That was Luciel's proposal, and everyone agreed.

"Aww! That's boring, though. I want to remember through sheer willpower. Then I'll just teach the next generation cryptic, significant things. Like the spell to open doors, say. Oh, and that they need to greet me at least briefly."

"Don't. You seem as if you'd genuinely remember, and you actually would say nothing but cryptic things."

"But, Lady Aileen, doesn't it make you sad? Forgetting that you're going to have an extremely handsome son, I mean."

Aileen lowers her eyes slightly.

If she said it didn't make her sad, she'd be lying. The fact that she can't remember Charles's face clearly is already making her chest feel tight. Before long, no doubt she'll have forgotten his name.

However.

"It's all right. I'm sure that future will come soon—"

She's about to bite into a cookie that smells of butter when she claps a hand over her mouth instead. Sudden nausea sweeps over her, and with no time to bother about appearances, she retches.

Rachel, who's been serving them, hurries over to offer her water. Lilia is also startled; she gets up and begins rubbing her back. "Take it easy. Are you all right, Lady Aileen? Perhaps you've been working too—"

Stopping abruptly in midsentence, Lilia blinks.

Dabbing at her lips with the napkin Rachel has given her, Aileen looks at her. "What?"

"...Lady Aileen. I forgot to mention it, but I finally vanquished that 'All Ages' rating."

What is the woman saying out of nowhere? She's already feeling unwell; the last thing she wants to hear about is her brother and sister-in-law's bedroom activities—or so she thought, but Lilia looks unexpectedly serious.

"This is just instinct, but I think it's going to be a girl."

Aileen blinks at her, then exchanges a look with Rachel.

In the historical texts, it is recorded that during the harvest season, a proclamation was made throughout the land that Empress Aileen had fallen pregnant.

✦ Encore ✦
The Final Boss Becomes a Father

Aileen thinks a husband's reaction on hearing of his wife's pregnancy is something to look forward to.

She issues a strict gag order until everything's certain. Once the doctor tells her it's a sure thing, she lays the groundwork, making time for the two of them to have a leisurely chat on their own. At that point, her preparations are complete. It's a time she's eagerly anticipating.

One afternoon, when the demanding work of cleaning up after the floating palace's attack has finally settled down and they're able to take breaks again. When her husband appears at teatime as promised, Aileen tells him the news briefly. "There is a child on the way."

"Whose?"

Apparently, she's been too brief. He doesn't understand. Maintaining her composure, Aileen continues, "I am carrying our child, Master Claude."

In the act of seating himself in the armchair across from her, Claude freezes.

For a little while, he doesn't move or speak. Unusually, the weather carries on unchanged as well.

As Rachel looks on, holding her breath, Keith offers tea from the side in a natural gesture. "Congratulations, Lady Aileen."

"...You aren't startled, Sir Keith?"

"I'd vaguely suspected from the way everyone else has been acting. All right, milord, don't freeze up. Sit down."

His adviser puts his hands on his shoulders and pushes, and Claude falls into the armchair with a soft *thump*. She's never seen him like this before. She assumed he'd be surprised, but she also thought he'd promptly start rejoicing, shower her with ten times as many endearments as usual, and show her the sort of smile she almost never got to see.

And yet no lightning has struck, no flowers have burst into bloom, and there's no rainbow in the sky.

"L-Lady Aileen. Please don't get the wrong idea about this. He's just failing to process the news," Keith reassures her, before she can grow uneasy. "Milord. Milord, are you alive? Come on, breathe. Blink, too. Now, do you remember what she's told you?"

"...A child...is on the...way. Mine and Aileen's..."

"Yes, that's correct. Congratulations."

Once Keith has gotten Claude going again, he smiles and steps back. Then Claude whips around toward her.

He looks at Aileen's startled face, then down—probably at her stomach—then back to her face again, and then he screams out of nowhere, "Is—is it okay for you to be out of bed?!"

"Pardon?"

"Isn't it dangerous for you to be up?! Shouldn't we wrap you in something soft?"

What would be the point of that? she wonders, but Claude is more frantic than he's ever been before. "This is my child. Unless we throw a grand celebration and show our intent to welcome it starting now, maybe it won't be born!"

That's an oddly persuasive theory, and Aileen doesn't know

how to respond to it. Keith, the only one who's kept his cool, does. "It's Lady Aileen's child, so there's no need to worry."

"Oh, I… I see… No, but it is my child…"

"But it's also Lady Aileen's child, so there's no need to worry."

On hearing that response twice, Claude finally falls silent. Then abruptly, he rises from his chair.

"M-Master Claude?"

"I'll go ask them," he says and winks out of sight before Aileen can stop him.

This is completely different from anything she anticipated. As she's sitting there blinking, Keith turns back. "Please don't take offense. He's so startled that his mind's gone completely blank, that's all."

"Y-yes… I'm startled, too. I've never seen Master Claude so shaken…"

"No doubt he thought of his mother. I'm told childbirth wasn't the direct cause, but her recovery was poor. Between that and her worry over the rumors that Master Claude might be the demon king, she weakened and died. Logically, he understands that this is different, but now that it's happening, I think the unease won out."

Oh. Finally, the tension drains out of Aileen, and she exhales slowly. "…He does still have some problematic aspects, doesn't he?"

"If you're able to see it that way, I can rest easy and let you handle this. If you wait a little, he'll come back feeling awkward. Even if he doesn't—"

"Aileen! Are we going to have a prince?! A princess would be good, too!"

"Aileen! Aileen! Show me! I can babysit!"

Beelzebuth and Almond barge in through the open terrace doors.

If Claude weren't happy, the demons' eyes wouldn't be shining like this.

Smiling wryly, Aileen tells the frolicking demons to settle down and gently strokes her belly, which isn't showing yet.

✦

✦

Luciel is with his wife in the old castle, enjoying a cup of tea, when he receives the news that a child is on the way. His eyes light up. "Congratulations, Grace, we're having a grandchild!"

"I'm not the one to congratulate, Luciel. Tell it to Claude and Aileen first."

"All of you come first. I see, a grandchild…! I can't wait. When will it be born?"

Claude freezes up.

"I—I haven't…heard…"

"……Are you all right, Claude?"

"……"

Claude is silent, and Luciel and Grace exchange looks. Then for the first time, the question occurs to him: Why has he come here? He doesn't even know that.

It's no good; he's confused.

"Claude, sit here." Luciel points to a chair, sounding uncharacteristically serious. Claude doesn't feel like defying him; he sits down.

Luciel pats his head. "It's all right. Your child will be born properly. I didn't really know whether I was a god or the demon king, but Grace managed to give birth. Besides, you're fully human. There's no need to worry."

"……"

"My children were born and grew up safely. That's why you, their descendants, are here. Pull yourself together. Aileen's the one who's going to have the roughest time, so you mustn't wear that pathetic face."

"Luciel… Listen, when you heard I was pregnant, you were more shaken than Claude is. I remember you getting so worried and anxious that you wailed, until I finally sent you flying with a good kick."

Grace's explanation shocks Claude, and he feels some of his tension drain away. Luciel sulks awkwardly. "I worked hard after that, though. You'd only eat boar meat, so all I did every day was hunt boars!"

"That's right, you did bring me lots of meat. Even though you were the emperor."

Grace giggles, and Luciel pouts. They share a bond that Claude and Aileen don't have yet. Claude finds himself feeling oddly resentful of that. "You can say that, but you both died and left two small children behind. Even if Mother didn't have a choice, Father rampaged and nearly destroyed the world, neglecting his family…"

Luciel freezes up, making Grace sigh. Claude's shoulders slump. "If these are the examples I have to work from, why wouldn't I be uneasy?"

"I can't argue with that, but stop, okay?! Our oldest was about four at the time!"

"Well, you've got a point, Claude. Frankly, though, I bet Amelia raised them to be a better prince and princess than I would have, so it all worked out!"

"Grace…!"

"In other words, don't worry too much!"

As a matter of fact, Imperial Ellmeyer has lasted all the way to Claude's generation, so there's the proof. Ignoring Luciel, who's dropped his head into his hands in grief, Grace gallantly wrapped up the conversation.

It was a truly pointless argument. However, he does feel as if the weight on his shoulders has grown a little lighter. He starts to get to his feet, but just then—

"Claude! We heard you've sired a child; is it true?! Don't tell us it's that— Huh, we've forgotten his name already. Anyway, it's not that blasted impudent brat, is it?!" Baal shouts as he appears out of nowhere, hauling Claude up by the shirtfront and shaking him wildly. "Well, Claude?! Answer us!"

"W-we—couldn't—possibly—know the gender—at this point… E-even yours—hasn't been—born yet."

When he manages to get a well-shaken answer out, Baal looks miffed and stops. "Well, now that you mention it, that's true… We suppose there's no point in beginning to worry this early. If he's not born properly, we won't be able to kill him."

"Don't kill off my son before he's even born."

After he's said it, he feels a little startled. He'd only known the boy for a few days, and he's already having a hard time recalling his face, but apparently, he'd been unexpectedly precious to him.

"You'll understand once you have a daughter. We're already looking forward to it tremendously, and we're already worried!"

Baal has become a doting parent before his child is even born, and it couldn't possibly be more aggravating than it already is.

"Aren't you looking forward to it a little too much? What would you do if it was a son?"

"If we had a son, we'd teach him naughty ways to have fun without telling Roxane, obviously. You'd do the same, wouldn't you?"

The question makes him blink. It's the first time he's thought about what he'll do if the child is a girl or a boy.

"That's...a good question. I've only just found out, and it doesn't feel real yet."

"Ah... True, we were giddy as well, but it's hard to claim it felt real at first."

"Is that right?"

Baal blinks at him. "Of course. It's not as if our bellies get round. Imagining is all we can do. It's probably different for women, but... When they tell us that Roxane's not feeling well, merely hearing the report makes our blood run cold..."

Still, Baal has the Daughter of God. The idea makes Claude just a little jealous. Would he loan her to them? Granted, he suspects Luc and Quartz would enthusiastically care for Aileen.

If it's a magic-based problem, Elefas will probably look after her... Perhaps we don't have it all that bad here.

He glances up at Baal. As fathers go, he technically has seniority. He's heard that Baal's child could be born any day now. "Is there anything you try to keep in mind?"

"Let's see. We try hard not to cause our wife any extra worry... Setting aside that attack from the floating palace the other day." Baal coughs awkwardly, then claps his hands in realization. "We've also been thinking of names. That's a good way to pass the time; it's fun. We came up with various candidates with Roxane, and we've finally narrowed them down."

"Names… Names, hmm? That's true. We'll need one of those."

"Oh, I thought of names, too. The ones Grace came up with were awful— Ow!"

Luciel sulks; Grace has poked him under the table.

I see. Gender, names… What should I choose? I wonder what else I'll need.

He feels as if his blank, frozen mind has finally begun to move again.

"Hey, I hear the demon king ran away. Don't tell me he's in here."

The door opens. At that point, finally, he realizes where he is. It's the conference room in the old castle, the one the Oberon Trading Firm calls their demon branch office.

Isaac walks in, sees the group, and grimaces. "Why is the holy king here, even? Listen, we rent this conference room. Geez, the nonhuman contingent is here, too."

"Almond appointed Grace and me honorary chairmen of the Oberon Trading Firm's demon branch office the other day."

"I didn't sign off on that. Anyway, we're gonna have a meeting, so scram. Also, Holy King. Somebody just contacted us on the sacred stone and said your wife's water broke."

"Huh?!" Baal turns pale.

From behind Isaac, Luc pokes his head in and gives a significant smile. "It's her first birth, so she's bound to have a rough time. You should probably hurry back— Oh."

Baal has vanished without so much as a goodbye.

Quartz sighs. "…Don't threaten him. Although…it probably will be rough."

"It will. All of which is to say, Demon King, pull yourself together and don't run."

Claude, who involuntarily froze at hearing the phrase "water broke," feels Luc's eyes on him. Timidly, he raises his head. Denis runs up and gives him a smile. "I just heard the news; congratulations. I'll be making a cradle with the demons!"

"Congrats. It does freak you out, doesn't it? I get it."

"Well, well. So there's something that scares even Isaac, the one who used me to power a weapon."

Elefas has entered the conference room, wearing a splendid smile. He's probably been summoned to a meeting regarding the battle the other day. The same must go for Auguste and James, who follow him in.

"Aww, why? Kids are cute. I want to have my own soon. But Serena and I aren't living together, and she has her job… I bet it won't happen for at least three years."

"It's better that way. The idea of you having children makes me shudder. Can you raise them?"

"Huh? I'm really good at playing with kids."

"Playing with them and raising them aren't the same thing."

"Then you help out, James. Both Serena and I will work."

"Why?! I'm a noble!!"

James gets mad, but he does seem as if he'd be very good at raising children.

Grimacing, Isaac turns back. "Making them and raising them is fine. But what am I supposed to do if they take after me?"

"Isaac." Claude sets his hands on his shoulders, gazing straight into Isaac's suspicious eyes. "I get it. Just now, for the first time, I felt glad I let you live."

"So you're not going to quit pointing out whether you're letting me live or killing me first thing. Okay, fine."

"I see. I guess I was worried. I wasn't sure whether Aileen would be all right, whether the child would be born safely, or whether I'd be able to raise it properly."

Those aren't the sort of things Claude can take sole responsibility for or do anything about.

As the others exchange looks, Elefas speaks up. "I don't think you need to hold it all in like that. If it were me, I think I'd just do as my wife said. After all, she's practical. Of course, if I did anything else, I suspect I'd get yelled at..."

"Aileen is practical, too."

"Then don't just stand there competing—get back to her already."

His wife's right-hand man is always unerringly correct. Hastily, Claude vanishes.

Aileen lifted the gag order as soon as she told Claude, and news of her pregnancy quickly spread through the palace in the blink of an eye. An official announcement will be made to the citizens tomorrow. The thought that this commotion will last for a few days makes Aileen feel a bit limp and tired, and she's lain down on a couch. The floor is already covered with presents.

Her brother, Cyril, says that this is part of an empress's duty. She mustn't get discouraged. The hardest part hasn't even begun. Give birth to the child, then raise it—but it does feel as if a shadow has fallen over her feelings.

"Aileen."

However, a husband never lets the fact that his wife is feeling uneasy escape him. He calls it part of his masculine wiles.

Smiling wryly, Aileen sits up from the couch. "Are you all right now?"

"Yes. —Er, I lost my head earlier. I'm sorry." Claude's gaze wanders awkwardly, and his cheeks are a little flushed. It's sweet, and the complaints and sarcasm she considered pelting him with on his return evaporate.

In any case, they are about to undertake the monumental task of having and raising a child together. This is no time for sarcasm.

"We have to think of a name. I'd assumed children were something far in our future, so I hadn't given it any thought."

"Oh, really? But we won't know whether they're a boy or a girl until they're born. Did that child say he was the youngest?"

"That's right. I've been curious about which it will be for a little while now, and it's making me restless."

"Goodness, you won't be able to laugh at Master Baal any longer. Has the reality begun to set in?"

He nods soberly, and the gesture charms her. "I didn't think I would be this—happy. I'm so fortunate."

Those bashful words are praise enough for her.

"I wonder what sort of child they'll be. What do you think they'll be like? There are lots of books I want to read to them."

"I'd like to teach them swordsmanship. That way, they'll be able to live with strength, whether they're a girl or a boy."

"That sounds like you. Do you think they'll be able to get along well with the demons? I'm a little worried."

"Let's raise them to be so energetic that they keep the demons on their toes. This is going to be very difficult, Master Claude."

"Yes, it will… Do you think they'll call me Father?"

"Have confidence. I'm sure you'll be the most splendid father in the world. I'll need to give it my best as well."

"It's going to be fine. You'll be the world's most splendid mother."

Leaning in so that their foreheads touch, they smile.

Beyond the present they're currently building, there lies a happy future.

Afterword

Hello, this is Sarasa Nagase.

Thank you very much for picking up the last volume of *I'm the Villainess, So I'm Taming the Final Boss*. The tale of Aileen, the demon king, and their merry friends is finally at an end. This isn't exactly the conclusion of the main story, though. I wrote this volume specifically for print publication, with the intent of creating a movie version that takes place after the main story has ended.

It's a summation of the story thus far, and a tale that exists because of its predecessors. I tried to write a story that would leave you feeling glad you'd followed the series once you read it.

I hope everyone who's supported me this far will enjoy it all the way to the end.

Once again, Mai Murasaki drew gorgeous illustrations for this volume. Thank you very much. Charles in particular was very cute; I thought it was a shame that this would be his only appearance. I'd also like to thank Anko Yuzu for drawing the splendid comic version; my past and present editors, who've guided me; and the designer, the proofreader, and all the other people who've helped me. This work was fortunate to be surrounded with wonderful people, including the readers who've been supporting it since its days as an online serial. Allow me take this opportunity to thank everyone who was involved with the series from the bottom of my heart. Thank you very much.

Most of all, I'm grateful to everyone who picked up this book. You are the reason the series came this far. Really, I can't thank you enough. That said, there are side stories online, so if you ever have the opportunity and would like to revisit this world, I'd be thrilled if you'd continue to support Aileen and her friends.

Finally, an announcement: I'm releasing a work through Kadokawa Beans Bunko called *The Second-Chance Young Noblewoman Is Romancing His Majesty the Dragon Emperor.* It's about a young soldier girl who's reverted to the age of ten and is struggling to reform—mainly through brute force—an emperor who's destined to join the forces of evil. It's being serialized online, and it's also going to have a manga adaptation, so I hope you'll enjoy that series as well.

Now then, I hope we'll meet again somewhere, along with Aileen and company.

Sarasa Nagase

HAVE YOU BEEN TURNED ON TO LIGHT NOVELS YET?

86—EIGHTY-SIX, VOL. 1–12

In truth, there is no such thing as a bloodless war. Beyond the fortified walls protecting the eighty-five Republic Sectors lies the "nonexistent" Eighty-Sixth Sector. The young men and women of this forsaken land are branded the Eighty-Six and, stripped of their humanity, pilot "unmanned" weapons into battle...

Manga adaptation available now!

WOLF & PARCHMENT, VOL. 1–7

The young man Col dreams of one day joining the holy clergy and departs on a journey from the bathhouse, Spice and Wolf. Winfiel Kingdom's prince has invited him to help correct the sins of the Church. But as his travels begin, Col discovers in his luggage a young girl with a wolf's ears and tail named Myuri, who stowed away for the ride!

Manga adaptation available now!

SOLO LEVELING, VOL. 1–8

E-rank hunter Jinwoo Sung has no money, no talent, and no prospects to speak of—and apparently, no luck, either! When he enters a hidden double dungeon one fateful day, he's abandoned by his party and left to die at the hands of some of the most horrific monsters he's ever encountered.

Comic adaptation available now!